The Secrets We Whisper to the Bees

A NOVEL BY

SAM E. KRAEMER

SUMMARY

What would you do to protect someone you love?

Would you give your life to save theirs?

Would you kill to protect them?

Whom would you trust with your secrets?

※※※

Hilda Wickersham was the proprietress of the Wickersham Inn, a seasonal bed and breakfast located on the Delaware shore, and she needed assistance for the upcoming summer season. When a young man began squatting on her beach, she remembered her biggest regret in life. That memory stopped her from reporting him to the local chief of police to have him removed. As she observed the young man, Hilda could see the redhead was troubled, and her motherly instincts, which she thought buried long ago, nudged her to extend a helping hand.

Jex Ivers was running for his life. He'd managed to escape from a madman and found himself working for a kind old woman who owned an inn on the coast of Delaware. He could tell the widow was suffering from a broken heart, just like Jex, and she needed his help as much as he needed hers. The two of them found a natural kinship with each other, and Jex believed his life might just turn around if he could stay under the radar for a little while longer. When he met Elijah Moore, Jex hoped it was a sign that his bad luck was changing.

Elijah Moore, the chief of police of Haven's Point, lived a quiet life. He had a job he loved, good friends, and a cottage on the beach. And...he was lonely. When a stranger showed up and caught Eli's attention, something about the redhead triggered Eli's protective nature. When he learned more about Jex's situation, the chief determined he'd do whatever it took to keep the young man from harm.

An old woman looking for redemption. A young man looking for a new life. A lonely man looking for happiness. What would each of them do to protect the ones they loved? When everything was said and done, what secrets would be whispered to the bees?

※※※

TABLE OF CONTENTS

I

II

III

IV

V

VI

VII

VIII

IX

X

XI

XII

XIII

XIV

XV

XVI

XVII

XVIII

XIX

XX

XXI

EPILOGUE

A NOTE TO MY READERS

ABOUT THE AUTHOR

ALSO BY SAM E. KRAEMER

I

Hilda Wickersham lived in a comfortable old house on a quiet street in Haven's Point. She enjoyed the fresh sea air that wafted freely through the large windows of her three-season porch when they were open, and her favorite time of day was twilight.

Hilda loved sitting on the porch to watch the returning seagulls soaring over the beach as the sun made its retreat for the day. She enjoyed a glass of sherry...only one...and she remembered so many days spent with her son, Michael, playing on the beach with his father, Neil, when he was young.

Oh, they were thick as thieves back then, Michael and Neil. If Mrs. Wickersham closed her eyes, she could still see them and hear their laughter as they tossed a Frisbee or a football between them while the family dog, Landry, barked and chased after them on the wet sand.

Those summers were so magical, and in her golden years, they brought her immense comfort, which was why she'd never sold the grand old house, regardless of how many times she'd been approached. Hardin Leland, a real estate developer in Haven's Point, had been quite aggressive with trying to strong-arm her into selling the six-bedroom Victorian that had been Neil's parents' home, but she'd never wavered.

Mrs. Wickersham ran a quaint inn from May to August. During the summer, beachfront rooms were at a premium in Haven's Point because its pristine beaches had become a dune sanctuary and were protected by the State of Delaware. The dunes were necessary for holding back the sea from flooding the towns along the coastline, so the state legislature had enacted strict guidelines regarding construction on properties abutting the seashore.

There was no new construction allowed on the coastline, but it was possible to use an existing structure and make modifications or additions on the property as long as the historical integrity of the original structure was maintained. Any additions made to the parcel had to adhere to the stringent guidelines as prescribed by the building codes before a permit was issued.

Hardin Leland had been salivating to do just that on Mrs. Wickersham's double lot for years, but she'd staunchly refused to sell, regardless of the bully tactics the man had attempted. She loved her home, and she wasn't about to allow the charlatan to defile her precious memories with his greed.

During the summers, Hilda rented four of the bedrooms on the upper floors, keeping the two, first-floor rooms for herself as her sanctuary from her guests. When she and Neil had first wed, Mother Wickersham had the very top floor of the homemade into a large studio apartment for the couple, complete with its own kitchenette.

All of the family relics had been removed from the attic space, small things in the basement while the larger items were stored in a shed next to the house. It was also quite handy for maintenance tools and the old box freezer that was still being used.

The shed also contained fertilizers, weed killers, and lime dust for use in the gardens Mrs. Wickersham tried to maintain on the adjoining lot, which was on the other side of the building. In the summer, her sprawling gardens were a haven for butterflies, and several beehives could be found among the flowering plants and bushes.

Hilda missed the days when she could freely move around the gardens, pruning her roses and weeding the beds. In the summer, she offered high tea at four o'clock, complete with tea cakes and finger sandwiches. She gave tours of the flowering bushes and plants, delighted with the praise she received from the guests at the beauty and the sweet scents that flourished in her garden.

The house was always filled with lush bouquets of beautiful flowers, and every other day, Hilda changed out the small vases in the guest rooms with fresh blossoms. Her guests always remarked about the bouquets on the comment cards she had at the front desk.

Hilda feared she would no longer have the luxury of offering fresh flowers because she was unable to maneuver the uneven ground of the gardens as she had before her surgery. The thought of losing the beautiful gardens she had loved to maintain, brought tears to her eyes.

Mrs. Wickersham had always prepared all of the food and maintained the inside of the home herself, but she'd had a spill the previous fall which led to a new hip socket after shattering the old one. She was thankful for the mail carrier, Mr. Kirby, who had a package to deliver that day, or she would have died there at the bottom of the stairs. Her hatred for a curtain or shade on the front door, windowpane had saved her life, she was sure.

When Hilda was released from the hospital to return to her home in October, she'd been diligent with her physical therapy. The male physical therapist had come to the Victorian three days a week to assist with her exercises, and he would always stay after they finished to share a pot of tea while he listened to the old woman tell him about her family.

He was a nice young man, and he even stopped by at Christmas with a lovely fruit basket for her. She'd knitted a scarf she was planning to donate to charity, so she had a gift for him. His name was Ian, and he resided in Dover. He worked at the rehab facility where Hilda had been admitted for eight weeks after her surgery, and she thought a lot of him before he was assigned to another patient.

While Hilda was rehabilitating at home, there was a nurse, Mary Ellen Charles, who came to her house to check on her two mornings a week until she was ultimately back on her feet. It was unfortunate Mrs. Wickersham discovered the woman pawing through her jewelry box. The confrontation had prompted the young woman to suddenly decide to move to Boston without a word of warning to her family at all.

It was appropriate that Hilda was able to explain the circumstances of the young woman's departure to the kind police chief, Elijah Moore, who had stopped by to ask after the Charles woman. Mrs. Wickersham decided not to share the girl's lack of honesty and decency, choosing to say instead she'd been a good nurse before she just took off to reunite with her former boyfriend, choosing not to notify her own family. The police chief thanked her for her time, the tea, and the lovely cookies she'd served.

The hip still pained her if she was on her feet for too long, but Mrs. Wickersham wasn't one to complain. She so wanted to open the inn on the first of May, but she was yet to find someone she believed she could trust to help with the requirements of running the house and caring for the gardens.

Hilda's best friend, Trudy Somerset, had suggested she place an ad in the local paper for an employee who could help around the inn. Mrs. Wickersham, however, was hesitant to call attention to the fact she was a helpless, old woman who now required assistance to operate her business.

She was sure if Hardin Leland caught wind of the fact she'd had surgery and needed help to care for the house, he'd comprise a scheme to oust her from her home and shove her into an assisted living facility. That wasn't anything Mrs. Wickersham was interested in chancing, so advertising for an employee was out of the question.

Hardin's kind...the tall, handsome, ruthless, and cunning men of the world, always found an angle to get what they wanted, that much Hilda knew for a fact. She'd seen it happen more than once over her lifetime, even in her own family. She'd handled that problem, and she would deal with Hardin Leland if he became an issue as well.

As Mrs. Wickersham sipped her evening aperitif, she saw a young man walking on the beach with a large pack strapped to his back. He appeared to be in his late teens, but her eyesight wasn't what it had been during her younger years.

It also didn't help she was behind schedule for getting her eye exam because she didn't trust herself to drive the hour to Dover where her eye doctor had his office. She'd already inconvenienced her friends for rides to her orthopedic surgeon over the fall and winter, so she dare not ask for another favor.

The neighbors and her friends in town had been quite kind to her, with the exception of Brandon Powers, Lottie Powers' grandson. Lottie had volunteered Brandon to shovel the snow from her walks and driveway, but the young man only cleared a path to the street and left her car buried in eight inches of wet snow.

Aside from not performing the chore that Lottie asked of her grandson, Mrs. Wickersham noticed Brandon had taken several of her deceased husband's power tools from her two-car garage where Neil had a workshop. Brandon had put them in the back of his truck without asking to borrow them, and it upset Hilda.

Still trying to give him the benefit of the doubt out of respect for his grandmother, Mrs. Wickersham would have gladly loaned the tools to the young man, who worked construction as his trade. Sadly, stealing from her was something Hilda couldn't abide.

Another thing that displeased Hilda was the fact the young man hadn't even thanked her for the special hot chocolate she'd prepared for him after he gave up shoveling the narrow path to the street. He didn't seem to care the woman was clutching a walker as she stood at the stove to make the drink. Brandon continued rudely ranting on his phone to one of his hoodlum friends about having to *'shovel snow from some old bat's sidewalk to keep my Grandma happy, so I don't get cut out of the Will.'*

When poor Brandon wrecked his truck on the way home later that evening after he lost control on an unplowed road, Mrs. Wickersham bit her tongue to keep from mentioning to Lottie about Brandon stealing Neil's tools from her garage that day on top of being rude to her. Lottie wasn't in any shape to hear the truth of it at the moment, so instead, the old woman offered tea and sympathy as any good friend would want to do under the circumstances.

It was enough for Hilda to know the young man had met his end due to his own disreputable actions. It wasn't pleasant being right all the time.

As the stranger on the beach walked closer to her home, Mrs. Wickersham eyed him carefully. "Please don't be a troublemaker, young man," she said quietly to herself. She watched as he stopped a hundred feet beyond her house and worked to put up a small tent on the beach just inside her property line, using the dunes for cover against the wind.

The local authorities weren't keen on vagrants sleeping on the beach, so the old woman made herself a promise. If the young man didn't cause any problems, she wouldn't report him to the police. Since she had no idea what his plight in life might be, she would observe his actions and decide what to do at another time.

As she watched him, Hilda decided there had to be a good reason the seemingly able-bodied man would sleep on the cold, windy beach in early-March. Unexpected storms popped up all the time, and the gales blowing off the ocean could be quite treacherous, even as nestled into the dunes as the young man seemed to be.

Mrs. Wickersham amended her vow not to call the police, deciding if she didn't see him in the morning, she would report him to the police out of concern that he was suffering from hypothermia. She also considered the possibility that if he was still alive when the sun came up, she could invite him in for a hot meal. Maybe he could help with some chores around the house to return her kindness?

The old woman wrapped the thick quilt around her shoulders and watched the young man come out of the tent and build a small fire. He seemed to know what he was doing by making a pit in the sand and putting the fire several feet away from his tent and the dunes, so Hilda stood from her chair and grabbed the fashionable cane Trudy had given her for Christmas. She decided it was time for dinner, but she pledged she'd keep an eye on the young man. Someone needed to, after all.

The last Saturday of March, Mrs. Wickersham woke at her usual time and took a shower, using the bench she'd been forced to rely on since her hip surgery, yet again feeling grateful she had the two rooms on the first floor. She'd resented the social worker's insistence she had to have modifications made to the bathroom to accommodate her needs or she wouldn't be allowed to stay in her home.

As much as the old woman hated to admit it, the bench and extra handles around the bathroom made her feel much more secure navigating through her morning ablutions on her own.

The remainder of the house had been saved from mandatory modifications due to its historical significance. She wasn't required to meet the standards mandated by the *Americans with Disabilities Act* in order to rent the three bedrooms on the second floor and the studio apartment on the third floor.

Unfortunately, Mrs. Wickersham had only been able to make the trip upstairs a few times since she'd returned home after surgery.

She knew if she wanted to rent the rooms for the summer, the time was approaching when she would need to make the decision, one way or another. It would also be necessary for her to hire an employee to do the things she was unable to accomplish on her own.

After Mrs. Wickersham started her morning coffee, she walked out onto the glass-enclosed porch and saw a scene that had become quite typical over the last few weeks since the young man started camping on the beach. He was taking down the tent to stow it in the dunes for the day. He covered the firepit with wet sand because it had rained the previous night, and he took off toward town with a small bag filled with the trash he'd produced the prior evening.

Mrs. Wickersham turned on the radio to hear the news and the weather for the day before going about making herself her usual breakfast of one-egg, over easy, a slice of toast with orange marmalade, and half of a grapefruit. She was thankful Dowd's Groceries delivered her order to her home, or she'd have been beholden to a friend to pick up her order once a week. As it stood, Marcus dropped off the order himself on Wednesday evenings after closing the store at seven.

Marcus Dowd's father had owned the small grocery store for as long as Mrs. Wickersham could ever remember. The old woman used to ride her bike to town to do errands and shop for groceries while Neil was working in his office. He was the only lawyer in the small village, and Michael was in elementary school.

Back then, rooms weren't rented to guests at the house because Mother Wickersham didn't allow strangers in *her* home. Besides, they didn't need the money since Neil had a lucrative law practice in town.

After his father passed away, Neil's mother was alone in the large house, so she had the attic converted into the studio apartment, just as it still was to that day. Back then, Hilda didn't see the trap Mother Wickersham was setting, but she also didn't expect her husband would fall for his mother's plan to take control of their lives. Hilda would quickly learn a harsh lesson...she didn't have as much power in the relationship as she'd thought.

The couple moved from their small house in town at Neil's mother's insistence, and Hilda hoped to fill the other three bedrooms on the second floor with children, despite Mother Wickersham's protestations. She believed it was selfish to bring more than one child into the world because divided affection was akin to child abuse in her opinion.

According to Mother Wickersham, a mother only held enough love inside her for one child. She believed in sacrificing feelings for a spouse to ensure the child knew they were the most important person in a mother's life.

The greatest sadness in Hilda's life occurred when she miscarried their second child. Michael was eighteen months at the time and the light of her life, and when she found herself pregnant with their second child, Hilda was happier than she ever imagined she could be.

She fantasized about Michael and a little sister or brother hunting shells on the beach during the summers. She'd been planning the colors she'd paint the nursery after she gave Michael a big-boy room next door.

Sadly, all of Hilda's dreams were dashed when she began hemorrhaging at twenty-two weeks. By the time Neil got her to the hospital, it was too late to save the baby.

The doctor told her it was nature's way of ridding the body of an unviable fetus and dared to say it was for the best. He didn't even call it a baby, which crushed Hilda's spirit.

From the beginning, Neil had called the pregnancy a mistake because he agreed with his mother. One child was enough for the couple to live in the grand style in which Neil was accustomed. The miscarriage was a blessing in disguise, he'd said. This statement had decimated any respect she had for her husband, the man she'd vowed to love until death separated them.

After Hilda recovered physically, because she knew she'd never recover from the loss emotionally, she moved from the third-floor apartment into the bedroom where Michael slept to watch over him.

She never shared a bed with her husband again, but eventually, she grew fond of Neil such that they could spend time together without the bitterness that Hilda held in her heart, coloring their interactions. She was doing the best she could because Michael deserved a mother and a father, and she was determined to give him both, regardless of the personal sacrifice.

One summer day when Neil and Mother Wickersham were sitting on the beach while Michael and Landry were playing in the surf, Hilda overheard a discussion not meant for her ears. To say she was stunned would have been an understatement.

"Look how happy we all are, Neil. And Michael, our beautiful Michael, is loved unconditionally by all of us. It is how it should be, and it wasn't harmful to Hilda. She bounced right back without so much as a hiccup. You should always listen to Mummy, Neil."

"Yes, Mummy. You dug it up from the garden, didn't you? I wouldn't want anyone to stumble across it on accident. How did you know it would work?"

"My mother used it to rid herself of a vile situation. Black cohosh has been used by Native Americans for years as herbal medicine. That's where my mother first learned to make a tea of black and blue to induce a miscarriage when she found herself with an unwanted pregnancy."

"The herbs are in the back of the garden where they won't harm anyone, but I'd say not to dig them up in the event you need them

again. When women get it in their heads that they want another child, they will do surprising things to accomplish the goal."

Mother Wickersham suffered the same fate as Hilda's lost child a few months later. As the doctor had told Hilda when she lost her baby, so Hilda said the words to Neil. *"It was for the best."* The day after the funeral, Hilda dug up the entire garden and began replanting it to her own specifications, now that the mean old woman no longer had control of the house and yards.

"Let go of the past and focus on the future, Hilda," Mrs. Wickersham told herself as she walked to the front door to find the <u>Dover Democrat</u> on her front porch, the same as always.

She noticed that the recycle bin was nearly full, and she thought of wheeling it out to the curb since the trash would be picked up the next day, but when she reached for the handle, she found one of the casters on the bottom was bent. There was no way the blue container would be moved due to Mrs. Wickersham's lack of strength, so she would need to find another way to transport the bin to the curb.

Mrs. Wickersham brought the newspaper inside with her and went to the stove to finish her breakfast, trying to decide what to do for the day when the phone rang. She let it go to the answering machine but listened carefully to the message. *"Hi, Mrs. Wickersham. I hope you're doing well after your recent fall and surgery. This is Hardin Leland. I'd like to stop by tomorrow to speak with you about the back taxes owed on Wickersham Inn. I was at the courthouse in Georgetown, and the Clerk mentioned they'd sent you a certified letter to that effect. Please call me back so we can discuss this situation."*

"My offer still stands to buy the inn for market price, but if you refuse to consider it, I'm prepared to wait you out and buy it off the Courthouse steps. Think it over, Mrs. Wickersham. If you sell to me,

I'll help you find somewhere nice to live. If I buy it from the County, I won't make that same offer."

"I look forward to hearing from you," the call ended.

"Viperous bastard," the old woman hissed to herself. She had received a letter requiring her signature the previous week. When Mr. Kirby, the mail carrier who saved her life, rang the bell, she almost pretended not to be home, but she'd already done it the previous day.

Mrs. Wickersham had nothing against the mailman, and she was sure if she didn't answer, Mr. Kirby would worry and probably contact the police chief. Then, an officer would be dispatched to check on her, which wasn't anything Hilda desired to happen.

She'd signed for the letter, but she didn't open it, tossing it on the front desk and carrying on with her day. She hadn't given it another thought until the phone call.

That afternoon, Mrs. Wickersham sat on her back porch, happy it had warmed enough for her to open the windows and allow the ocean breezes to waft through the house. She glanced up from her knitting to notice the young man returning from wherever he spent his days. He had two bags with him, which he placed in the sand as he went to work to put up his tent for the night.

It had been nearly three weeks since the young man had arrived on Mrs. Wickersham's beach, and she decided it was time to get to know the new neighbor, especially since he was squatting on her land.

In the event Hardin Leland lived up to his threat, maybe it would be beneficial to have someone nearby. Who knew what lengths Mr. Leland might go to get her land? Who knew the lengths Mrs. Wickersham would go to keep it from happening?

II

Police Chief Elijah Moore stood at the picture window in his office, sipping his coffee on a mild, March morning. He noticed the same kid walking down Hopkins Lane to the diner, swinging around the side of the building to the back entrance. He had no idea where the kid had come from, nor where he went when he finished doing dishes for Lena Becker, the proprietress for *Lena's Home Cooking,* one of two year-round dining establishments in town.

Old Mrs. Becker had been the *first* Lena to run the café years ago, establishing the small diner as a staple in the tiny burg of Haven's Point. After Young Lena graduated high school, Grandma Lena sent her namesake to college in pursuit of a business degree. Everyone in the small town offered their support to the girl since they all felt they had a hand in raising her over the years.

When the younger Lena returned to Haven's Point after graduating near the top of her class at Delaware State, Grandma Lena decided to go into semi-retirement and let her granddaughter take over the best place to eat in town. Lena Junior, who was known simply as Lena around town, stuck to Grandma's recipes, and the business didn't miss a beat.

After the locals concluded she wasn't going to come home with newfangled ideas and change things drastically, they stayed loyal. Slowly, Young Lena was able to put her own spin on the café.

It was covert, the way she added vegetarian dishes to the menu and slowly changed the eating habits of most of Haven's Point. Eli knew the history of the café because he was a hometown boy. The only time he'd been away from Haven's Point was when he went to college, the year it took for training at the Police Academy, and then the six years he worked in Newark as a cop. He returned to town when his mother passed to look after his father, Glenn, who was the former Chief of Police.

Eli worked on the force for his father until the old man decided to retire and pushed his son to throw his hat in the ring to be elected as the next Chief of Police. Elijah was elected by a landslide to take over the office the first time he ran, and he'd been re-elected twice.

It wasn't because the citizens of Haven's Point believed him to be the greatest Chief of Police they'd ever had, though he hoped they thought him competent. The fact of the matter was nobody ever filed to run against him. Eli didn't even have to campaign, and thus far, he'd held the confidence of the people in his hometown.

Eli turned to look at Yolanda West, the station's dispatcher and office manager. She was also the meter maid, the school crossing guard, and one of Eli's best friends. Her husband, Will, called her his Ebony Queen, and he treated her as such, which always made Eli smile.

Elijah and Will had gone to grade school together and had been good friends, and when Yolanda came to work at the Police Station, both men fell for her...Will in love, and Eli in friendship. The three were inseparable around town, such that when the townsfolk saw one of them coming, they looked for the other two.

"Yolanda, you know who that kid is? I've seen him around town for a few weeks, but I've never heard anyone say who he is or where he came from?" Eli asked as he walked over to her desk, behind which was the coffee pot.

"What kid, Eli?" she asked as she reached over to the printer and pulled off several documents sent from the Sussex County Sheriff's Office. She rose from her chair and went to Eli's office, placing a copy of the papers in his inbox before she went to the bulletin board, pulling off old flyers and adding the new ones.

"The one who's washing dishes at *Lena's*. Where'd he come from, and where does he go?" Eli asked.

"You mean that skinny little white boy with the freckles and long, red hair?" Yolanda asked.

Eli laughed. "You knew exactly who I was talking about. Who is he?"

"He's not a kid, Chief. According to Lena, he's twenty-five, and he's a hard worker. That's all she cares about, and he's pretty easy on the eyes," Yolanda offered the latest gossip with a smirk.

"Where's he staying?" Eli asked as he turned to look at Yolanda, who was gathering her things to head over to the school for crossing guard duty.

"Not with Will and me. Why don't you go over to the diner and ask him? You need to meet someone, Elijah. You're getting a little long in the tooth to be the most eligible bachelor in town. I saw Trudy Somerset checking out your backside the other day. If she starts looking good to you, we got a huge problem, Cougar Bait," Yolanda stated before she grabbed her travel mug and nodded to him as she headed out the door.

After she left, Eli went back to his office and sat down in his chair, curiosity about the redhead filling his thoughts. He checked the contents of his inbox but saw nothing of importance, so he picked up his radio from its charging stand and called out for Lowell Bellows, another officer in Haven's Point. "Car two hundred, where are you?" Eli asked.

"Chief, I'm on my way. Tibby's taking his wife to the doctor in Dover, so I'll be covering for both of us until ten," Bellows responded.

Eli remembered Joe Tibby had mentioned he was taking his pregnant wife to the doctor that week, but he didn't remember it was that morning. "Okay. West is at school, and I'm headed to

Lena's. I'm forwarding the phones to my cell. Let me know if you need me, Bellows, over?"

"Roger, Chief."

Eli grabbed the portable and put it on his belt. He walked to the coffee maker and poured the fresh pot into the carafe to keep it warm before he turned off the machine and locked the door.

When he left the building, he looked both ways before he crossed the street and walked up to *Lena's* door, which was still locked.

Eli gently knocked, and when he saw the lights to the dining room turn on, he knew Lena had likely been in the kitchen starting the flat top and the ovens. Eileen Stewart, the morning waitress, wasn't in yet, which was nothing new. The woman was always late because she had a lazy husband and two kids to get ready for school.

When Lena rushed out from the back, Eli noticed the big smile on her face. "Hi, Chief. Eileen's late. Come on in, and will you make the coffee? I'm having trouble with the damn flat top again," Lena complained.

"Sure. You want me to take a look at it?" Eli offered.

Lena laughed. "You know how to fix a flat top grill, Chief?"

"*I got it, Ms. Becker!*" they both heard from the kitchen.

Lena looked at him with a cocked eyebrow that made Eli chuckle. "Maybe I do, or maybe I don't, but it doesn't matter now, does it?" Eli responded as he followed her to the kitchen. It was his chance to meet the young guy he'd seen around town for the last few weeks, and he wasn't going to miss it.

"What was it, Jex?" Lena asked.

It was then Eli got a look at the man, seeing he wasn't as young as Eli first assumed, having only seen the guy from a distance around town. He was a handsome guy with beautiful green eyes, or so the cop decided. There was something in those grass green pools that seemed sad, but of course, Eli knew nothing about his situation to determine if they always looked that way.

As far as Eli knew, the young guy hadn't broken any laws, so he wasn't going to interrogate him. He was new to town, and Haven's Point was known as a friendly, small town. It wasn't Eli's place to give any other impression to a stranger.

"The main breaker tripped, so I reset it, but I suggest you get an electrician to come take a look at it to be sure it was a fluke and not a faulty breaker. You wouldn't want to burn the place down," the young man, Jex, responded.

"I'll call someone about it. That's the third time this month. Anyway, Jex Ivers, this is Chief Elijah Moore. He's the law around these parts," Lena announced with a strange southern drawl that made Eli look at her twice before he rolled his eyes.

The cop studied the young man to see no reaction at all after he was introduced, which brought a feeling of relief because someone guilty of misdeeds usually became jumpy around cops of any kind. "Nice to meet you, Mr. Ivers," Eli greeted, extending his hand. The guy didn't return the gesture.

"How do you know?" the young man replied before he walked over to the wheeled racks where clean dishes from the previous day were stored. He grabbed a cart loaded with bread plates and full-sized banquet plates, wheeling it to the shelves over the stainless counter before retrieving a rack of large plates to fill the warmer.

Once he was finished, he pulled the rack out of the kitchen to the counter in front and began stacking the smaller plates beneath.

Eli turned to look at Lena, who shrugged her shoulders and pulled on her apron. "What do you want for breakfast, Eli?"

Eli gave his order and walked out to the front where Jex Ivers was now putting glasses on the shelves behind the counter. "So, you're new to town? You have family in the area?" Eli asked as he filled the regular coffee maker and went to work on the smaller decaf machine.

The young man looked up and grinned. "So, you make the coffee in addition to keeping the peace? I haven't seen you come into the diner yet, but I've only been working for Ms. Becker for two weeks, so I suppose we could have been operating on different shifts."

Eli considered the guy's comment and realized he'd actually been working the night shift for the last two weeks so Bellows and Yolanda could take their vacations. Tibby was set to be off after his wife had their baby, so it was only fair for Eli to pitch in to cover as well.

"You're right. I've been working the night shift to allow my officers to take vacation time. We get swamped in the spring until late in the summer. With just the few of us, we have to cover for each other," Eli explained.

He had so many questions, one of which was, why did the guy wear all the leather bracelets on his wrists, one of which looked like a Pride bracelet? Eli was dying to ask what they meant to the young man, but he could read Jex Ivers' body language and determined the man was a very private person.

The chief made a mental note to keep an eye out for the redhead around town. *What kind of name is Jex?* Eli asked himself, considering yet another unanswered question.

Eli didn't believe the man to be acting suspiciously, but the things he'd seen when he worked in Newark had taught him that some people were very good at hiding secrets. Before Eli could ask where the young man was staying, the front door opened and Eileen Stewart rushed into the diner.

"I'm so sorry…" she began giving a convoluted explanation that involved someone with a fever and the dog hiding a homework assignment.

Lena came out of the kitchen with her usual smile, Eli noticed. "It's fine, Eileen. Let's just get things ready for the day. I'm already making the Chief's breakfast, and he's started the coffee. Here comes Dewey. Get him settled while I get the order going," Lena pointed out.

Eli knew his window of discussion with Jex Ivers was over, so he took a seat at the counter and watched the young man finish putting away glassware, finding it hard to pay attention to Eileen Stewart's non-stop monologue about having two boys who were less than cooperative in the mornings.

There was mention of a husband who was on disability due to a back injury he'd experienced while working for a delivery company in Philadelphia before they moved to Haven's Point. Eileen's aunt had a home on the outskirts of town and took them in, which Eileen stated was a blessing because her parents had no desire to help her at all.

To Eli, it was all white noise because he had much more exciting things on his mind, most of which involved a man six-inches shorter than him with a gorgeous head of red hair worn in a ponytail. He had a smattering of light freckles and lush, pink lips that were the devil's temptation. The beautiful green eyes…they were hypnotizing.

Eli found himself counting the minutes until two that afternoon when the café closed. He was glad Yolanda was busy around town, so she didn't continue to remind him how much he was fixating on the newcomer because Eli didn't need reminding. He couldn't get the man out of his head.

It wasn't anything Eli had ever experienced in the past, fixating on a stranger. He'd had relationships over the years with men, some who he missed, but most who he didn't. He had no idea if Jex Ivers was gay or straight, and he wasn't planning to find out.

The citizens of Haven's Point knew their chief of police was a gay man because they'd known Elijah as a boy, and he'd never hidden his truth from anyone. His parents had always been supportive, and Eli's orientation was never an issue.

That was something Glenn Moore still tried to ensure Eli knew for a fact. His father was still very much involved in Eli's life, all the way from Charleston, South Carolina.

Eli didn't see himself with a partner nor a family. He was perfectly happy to allow his job to fill the empty parts of his life, and he had good friends who picked up the slack. He wasn't lonely, even if he was alone, and that suited Eli just fine. This new distraction involving Jex Ivers was just that, a distraction. A very gorgeous distraction...

The chief went back to his desk to continue filling out staffing reports for the City Council. He was trying to get a green light to hire another officer because he was tired of having the Sheriff's Deputies fill in when someone took a vacation, especially Deputy Terry Blake who was relentless in his romantic pursuit of Eli.

The chief preferred to work double shifts to avoid asking for the loan of a deputy, but he knew the City Council frowned on overtime pay for the officers, especially as summer approached. Hiring another officer would be the answer to Eli's prayers.

The four officers, including Eli, worked long shifts, dealt with everything in town, including most inclement weather issues during the winter and the tourist trade during the season. While there was barely any crime in Haven's Point, the tourist swell brought its own challenges.

Having his police force working seven days a week was hard on his officers, and it was time the City Council take a realistic look at the statistics. Mayor Hardin Leland was a local real estate developer, and his primary focus was growing the community, but without the infrastructure to support the growth, Haven's Point had the potential to become overrun with less than savory individuals before anyone on the Council noticed.

The current population of three thousand citizens was manageable, but one never knew when something unexpected would show up and overwhelm the citizenry. Eli was determined to be prepared for anything that came his way. It was what his father had done for years with much success when he was in Eli's shoes.

The door to the station opened, and Eli glanced up from his computer to see Jex Ivers enter the building with sunglasses hiding his expressive features from Eli. The guy looked nervous, or maybe scared? Eli wasn't sure.

Eli walked out of his office, offering his best smile. "Mr. Ivers, what can I do for you?"

Jex gave him a nervous smile as he removed his sunglasses and pushed them on top of his head. "I hope I'm not interrupting you, but I have a few questions about things around town, and I've been told the best place to get information is from the top cop. Could we speak in private?" Jex asked.

"Let's step into my office. You want coffee or water?" Eli offered. He tried very hard not to notice the newcomer's full mouth or those stunning green eyes that wouldn't meet his as the two men faced each other.

Jex held up an aluminum bottle and grinned. "I've got water, but thanks. I don't drink coffee. Too bitter for me. I like a cup of tea when I can get it, though. Honey, no lemon," the young man explained as he stared at Eli in a way that had the chief a bit breathless.

Jex Ivers reached into the backpack he was carrying and pulled out a large, manila envelope, the flap of which was already opened. He handed it over to Eli, who extended his hand for the guy to sit down in the chair across from his desk, taking the one next to him.

Eli retrieved the contents of the envelope and began reading, quickly recognizing the usual legal jargon. The Permanent Protection Order was against a man named Bernard Overman. Eli glanced up to see Jex chewing on this thumbnail as he looked out the picture window in Eli's office.

Eli skimmed the Order to see that it was against a man who had been violent with Jex and was currently incarcerated for kidnapping, assault and battery with intent to do bodily harm, and sexual deviance without consent. The words caused Eli's stomach to turn.

He glanced at the man sitting next to him to see he was quite nervous. "Overman is currently in prison, correct?" Eli inquired.

"He was for several years, but he filed for a new trial due to incompetence of counsel. His new lawyer got him released on house arrest until his appeal is decided. He might get a new trial, so Detective Cather suggested I go into Witness Protection, but I don't trust anyone at the Newark Police Department. While he was still in jail, Overman got access to a cell phone and called to threaten me if I testified against him in a second trial."

"I've been on the run since Overman was released to house arrest. I had to get away from Newark, so I've been traveling off the grid to stay under the radar without Overman or his henchmen finding me."

"The detective, Cather, he said you could call him if you had questions...well, he said any police officer I trusted could call him because I didn't say where I was going. Actually, I didn't know where I was going at the time. I like it here, and I'm hoping I can just blend in with the people in town," Jex explained.

"Is Detective Cather by chance Dennis Cather?" Eli asked, remembering someone he knew from his days on the force in Newark. Jex nodded with an inquisitive look on his face that made Eli grin.

"I used to work in Newark after I got out of the Academy. My rookie year, I was fortunate enough to be partnered with Denny Cather. He was a couple years older than me, but he was a good cop, and he taught me the ropes. I'll get in touch with him for the details, Mr. Ivers. Where do you live in town? We'll put you on the schedule for regular checks on the overnight shift," Eli inquired.

He saw the guy's face flush a soft pink at the question, and it touched something inside Eli. Yes, the young man was good looking, and he seemed to need help, which was a hot button for the Police Chief. He was trying to remain objective, but it was becoming harder by the second.

"That, uh, that's a bit of a problem, Chief. See, I'm currently squatting on the beach. I know a little old lady has seen me out there, but she's never confronted me about it. I'm staying near her house, but I'm respectful, or so I assume because you haven't been out there to arrest me."

"I've seen the signs there's no camping on the beach but trying to remain off the grid means I can't stay in a motel or anything since I can't use a credit or debit card because they're traceable," the young man offered.

Eli nodded. "Yeah, uh, we can't have you sleeping on the beach. Isn't it damn cold?" Eli asked.

"It's been chilly a few nights, but I'm fine. I've got a tent and a few of those heat-trapping blankets. I've made a fire out there a few times, and it's plenty warm. I'm hopeful it doesn't snow again," Jex Ivers enlightened.

"Okay, uh, exactly where on the beach are you staying? Maybe we can find you a better arrangement?" Eli suggested.

"I'm just down the beach from The Wickersham Inn," Jex replied.

Mrs. Wickersham was a local character, and she'd lived in Haven's Point for as long as Eli had been alive. He'd learned from Mr. Kirby, the mail carrier in town, that the old woman had taken a fall down the stairs last year after the end of the tourist season, and she'd been airlifted to Dover where she'd undergone hip surgery and had been in a rehab facility for a few months before she returned home.

There had been an inquiry from a home healthcare business in Dover regarding a missing nurse who specialized in in-home rehabilitation. Mary Ellen Charles had been on record as Mrs. Wickersham's nurse for several weeks around the holidays before the young woman disappeared.

Mrs. Wickersham was very cooperative when Eli went to have a conversation with her regarding the nurse. She told him Mary Ellen came to the house for three weeks and then stopped showing up without a word.

Mrs. Wickersham had overheard the young woman on her phone speaking with a male person-of-interest, but the Dover Police Department couldn't find any male other than her father with whom Mary Ellen Charles had spoken or been seen with before she disappeared.

Eli hadn't seen Mrs. Wickersham in town at all since the accident, but Mrs. Somerset had mentioned to Yolanda that the old lady was looking for a cook at the Inn. Since her injury, Mrs. Wickersham was no longer able to be on her feet for the hours it would take to make food for the guests.

Eli decided it was worth the drive out to the beach to see if there was a possibility she might allow Jex Ivers to stay in her basement if he helped her out around the Inn. If she needed assistance, maybe it was worth a shot?

For reasons unknown to Elijah Moore, he wanted to help the handsome, shy stranger. Making sure Jex had a place to sleep indoors was a great place to start.

III

When the SUV turned into the driveway of the Inn, Jex was nervous. He'd seen the woman watching him since he'd found the beach in early March, but they'd never acknowledged each other. Jex tried to be the least intrusive on the woman's space but knew he was squatting on her land without her permission. The fact she hadn't called the cops on him was a surprise, but he had no idea how long his luck would hold out.

His companion, Police Chief Elijah Moore, was determined to make it his mission to butt into Jex's business, but the man didn't seem to mean any harm. Jex had been on his own for so long, he was exhausted from looking over his shoulder. If he could meet someone, a friend, who would help him remain in hiding until it was time for the second trial, it was worth whatever pieces of his privacy he had to surrender. Life as a loner was far too tiring.

Molly Ivers' son had grown up with only his mother as a parent. She was a beautiful woman who made him feel loved, and he missed her more than he could ever articulate. Molly had done everything she could to care for her son, working two jobs to put a roof over their heads and food in their mouths without a second's help from the man who had fathered the boy.

One night when Molly was on her way home from her night job as a waitress at a diner in Newark, she became the victim of a hit-and-run driver as she was crossing the street to their apartment building. There were no witnesses to the accident, and the case remained a cold case as far as anyone knew.

At the time, Molly's son was fifteen, and after no family came forward to claim him, he spent the next three years in foster care. To say it was a living hell was an understatement, but it was worse when they just cut him loose and kicked him out when he turned eighteen.

Once he was out of the foster system, Molly's son had nobody and nowhere to go. His social worker couldn't have cared less if he'd have jumped off a bridge, so he was on his own. Of course, the streets would eat him alive because his mother had been so protective of him while he was growing up, but as the boy quickly learned, the only person looking out for him was himself. That was until Bernie Overman found him sleeping next to a dumpster outside a pizza place in Newark.

The story wasn't pretty, nor was it new, which was absolutely no comfort at all. For five years, Molly's son became Bernie's slave in every sense of the word. His prison was a townhouse on Lincoln Avenue. The slave wasn't the only person held against his will in the home, but he was the only one Bernie kept for himself.

The way Bernie kept the slave in line was too painful to discuss, but the slave stayed with his captor because he honestly had nowhere to go, nor any idea of how he could survive if he managed to escape.

No one had bothered to prepare Molly's son for a future outside of the foster system, so the slave's best idea was to keep his head down and endure whatever Bernie saw fit to do to him. The course of least resistance was his key to survival.

When law enforcement busted through the front door of the townhouse, it wasn't because of anything the slave had or hadn't done, though he worried it would be perceived he'd been involved and would have to bear the wrath of his master. The reason the police had focused on Bernie Overman was due to the man becoming greedy and trying to purchase a boy of thirteen on the internet to sell on the black market in Europe.

The slave didn't even know the other people who lived in the townhouse because he wasn't allowed to leave his room, but when a cop busted open the door and freed him from the chains around his wrists that made cuts into his flesh, he could have kissed

Detective Dennis Cather out of sheer gratitude. Of course, he didn't because the slave knew he wasn't worthy of such contact. He was no longer a person allowed to take such liberties. He was no longer Molly's son. He was now the slave.

The slave knew he was nothing but useless trash as Bernie told him every day while the slave obediently knelt on the floor and allowed the man to abuse him in a multitude of ways. It was taught early on that slaves had no say in their treatment, so keeping his mouth shut kept him out of trouble.

Bernie would beat him with the belt for asking questions about the people milling around the townhouse or why his master was angry at him, but the answer was always the same. "You're my property, and I can do with you any fucking thing I choose, trash. You're not a person, you're a thing, and if I want to ball you up and throw you in a fire like an old newspaper, not a mother fucker will stop me."

After Bernie was found guilty and sentenced to life in prison for his misdeeds, Molly's son, the former slave, adopted a new identity, Jex Ivers. He prayed he had a chance at a new life, and he was willing to fight for it every day.

Jex found a job working at a restaurant in Newark because he wanted to be able to feed himself. Learning to cook seemed like an excellent idea for a career, so he worked his way up from dishwasher to prep line worker. When he was appointed to a spot working on the grill, Jex was excited and looking forward to his future.

Jex had been working at the restaurant for several years and was considering culinary school when he got a call from Dennis Cather telling him Bernie Overman had filed an appeal because there was a problem with the case. Someone had lied or something, but the bottom line was that Bernie was out on bail, and Jex needed to get the fuck out of New Jersey.

Before he left Newark, Jex filed the paperwork for a permanent Order of Protection against Bernard Overman based on the abuse Jex suffered at the man's hands, feet, belt, whip. Thankfully, the Order was granted by a judge, and Dennis Cather helped Jex disappear without a trace.

At the beginning of his new incarnation, Jex Ivers called Cather once a week for a progress report on the case. He hated to admit it, but it felt good to have someone ask how he was and whether he needed anything. Dennis Cather was a decent guy, and Jex grew quite fond of him as an older brother figure over the months they kept in touch.

Since Jex would need to be available to testify against Bernie in any new trial that might be ordered, he stayed in the tri-state area for a while. He had camping equipment and the small amount of cash Cather was able to give him, so he slept outside most nights, only staying in cheap motels when the weather was dangerously cold.

Somehow, Jex became accustomed to the chilly nights he spent outside. He even came to appreciate being able to gaze at the sea of stars he'd missed because the city lights of Newark erased the light from the sky, much like Bernie Overman erased Molly's son all those years. Every night Jex had to sleep outside, he always thought of his mother and prayed she hadn't suffered when she died in that crosswalk years ago.

The last time Jex Ivers spoke with Dennis Cather to ask if there was a new trial date, Cather informed him Overman had put a price on Jex's head to keep the key witness to the human trafficking operation from testifying. The detective didn't mention the amount of money Overman had offered...Jex figured it couldn't be much because the man used to tell him he was a worthless piece of trash on a daily basis.

Cather said he had no idea how many people knew where to find him, so staying off the grid was his only chance of survival until it was decided when Bernie Overman would receive a new trial. Unfortunately, Jex had been told that scheduling the new trial had been stalled due to the disappearance of several other witnesses. The idea of Overman never being held accountable for his actions broke Jex's heart.

Cather told him not to call anymore because he didn't trust anyone, even his fellow police officers. He instructed Jex should have someone call in his place and ask for Cather directly, but Jex hadn't met anyone he trusted enough to ask the favor.

It was all true until he met Chief Elijah Moore. He hadn't dared to ask yet, but if Jex were going to request a favor of anyone and trust he wouldn't be betrayed, it would be the top cop.

The car stopped, and Jex looked up to see they were parked on the circle driveway of Wickersham Inn, the majestic old Victorian near where Jex had been camping. "Come on, let's go talk to Mrs. Wickersham. I think this might be a good fit for you, and the fact she hasn't called to complain about you sleeping on the beach actually goes in your favor. She's a very particular woman, and nobody would say she's shy about speaking up when she's displeased," Chief Moore told him.

Jex touched the man's arm before he got out of the car, noticing a lot of muscles under his fingertips. "I'm not sure she'll want me living with her. Do we have to tell her why I'm sleeping on the beach?"

When the top cop took his hand and held it, Jex felt a charged current ricochet through his body as though he touched a live wire, but he tried to keep himself together. It was unlike anything he'd ever experienced because Bernie Overman has shown him nothing but pain. The feeling Jex felt when Eli Moore touched him was the opposite of anything Jex ever felt with his former master. Jex didn't know how to handle the kindness the man seemed to be offering, so he decided to ignore the emotions coursing through him.

"Mrs. Wickersham hasn't had the easiest life. Her son, Michael, shot himself when he was fifteen, but I don't think anyone ever knew why. Her husband packed up and left town without a word to anyone the week after the boy's funeral. He, at least, signed the deed to the property over to the woman before he took off."

"Hilda didn't have any family of her own after she lost her son, and she kept to herself for the first few years before she decided to open Wickersham Inn to guests for the summers. Anyway, the house is all Mrs. Wickersham has left, but she's getting older and needs help to maintain it."

"She had surgery last fall after she fell down the stairs, and from what I've heard, Hilda needs help with nearly everything because she can't manage the stairs and all of the guest rooms are on the second and third floors of the house. She was always able to manage the house and care for her guests by herself, but not anymore, or so Trudy Somerset told Officer West."

"Wickersham Inn and some money her husband gave her before he left is her only means of support, or so it has been rumored around town. I do know for sure she's in arrears with the taxes, so if she doesn't open for the summer season, she's probably going to lose everything."

"Mrs. Wickersham is pretty stubborn, and she won't accept a handout from anyone, but if she met a handsome young man who needed a place to live and could help her over the summer season so she could pay her back taxes, I bet she'd welcome you with open arms. You don't have to tell anyone your story, and you'll be helping her out as well. What do you say?" the chief asked.

The situation sounded perfect...as long as Mrs. Wickersham didn't freak out because Jex was gay. If she were some sort of religious nut, he'd rather sleep on the beach. It might be chilly some nights, but the weather was warming up, and he wouldn't have to listen to hellfire and damnation like he did in some of the foster homes.

As Jex considered his options, he came to the conclusion he'd already walked through hell at the hands of Bernie Overman and survived a lot worse treatment than he'd find by living with Mrs. Wickersham. He was sure the two of them could reach an understanding.

The old woman opened the door with a warm smile Jex didn't expect, and he immediately believed all his concerns were ill-placed. She invited the two men inside and stood next to Jex. "You're the young man whose been camping on the beach, aren't you?" she asked as she led them into a quaint sitting room.

"Yes, ma'am, and I'm sorry for not asking if you minded, but I did my best not to make a mess," Jex repented.

When Mrs. Wickersham smiled, he felt relieved. "I don't care about that but thank you so much for cleaning up after yourself. Now, Chief Moore, I hope you're not expecting me to press charges against this... Oh, where are my manners? What can I get you to drink? I just put the kettle on for tea, if you'd care to join me," Mrs. Wickersham invited.

Jex was pleased with the fact the little woman seemed happy to have finally met him. "May I help you with tea? I, uh, I used to enjoy tea with my mother when I was a boy," he explained, not willing to tell her he'd learned how to perform a Japanese Geisha tea service because Bernie became obsessed with a book that was popular years before Jex ever came into the picture.

"Used to...where's your mother, dear boy?" Mrs. Wickersham asked.

Thankfully, Chief Moore held up his hand. "Mrs. Wickersham, before we get into Mr. Ivers' personal life, I wanted to ask if you minded him staying on your property? He told me he's been camping on the beach, and you know we don't allow it here because of the dunes preservation ordinances. If you allow him to stay for another few days, I won't interfere, but Mrs. Powers mentioned she might have a room he can rent," the handsome policeman explained, which wasn't anything Jex had heard until now.

Mrs. Wickersham abruptly rose to her feet and pounded her cane on the floor. "That woman has no business...no. He can stay right here with me, inside," she commanded before she looked at Jex.

"Can you cook anything at all, young man? You see, I run a summer inn, and I want to open on the first of May. I can't stand at the stove the way I used to do, but if you can cook at all, I can explain to you how to make my recipes."

"Together, we can open the Inn for the summer, and I can pay my taxes so that jackass...well, never mind. You can live here with me, so you're not living on the beach, and all will be well in Haven's Point," the old woman announced with a quick nod of her head as if she'd settled everything in her mind.

Jex looked at the Chief of Police to see him wink. Apparently, things had gone just as the man intended, though Jex wasn't precisely sure if they'd gone about it the most ethical way since Jex had never met Mrs. Powers as far as he knew. As a newcomer, however, felt as if things might be going in his favor for the first time in a very long time, and he wasn't going to question it.

IV

Jex and Mrs. Wickersham quickly fell into a routine through the first two weeks of April. They cooked together so Jex could practice making the breakfast offerings Mrs. Wickersham served for her guests, and Jex learned how to make pastries and baked goods to serve at teatime.

He showed Mrs. Wickersham how to brew the perfect pot of tea, as he'd learned from his time in hell. Jex grew to love the time the two of them spent together in the kitchen more with every passing day.

Mrs. Wickersham served a full breakfast every morning as she explained to Jex early on. With twenty-four-hours-notice, she would prepare picnic baskets for guests to take to the beach or on a bike ride, and she served high tea and cocktails every afternoon at four o'clock on the dot.

The guests had to be over twenty-one, and Mrs. Wickersham happily welcomed people of color and members of the LGBTQ+ community. It was a huge relief when Jex learned those tidbits of information and was surprised someone her age didn't seem to have a bigoted bone in her little body. "I enjoy meeting new people because it's so exciting to discover new things, don't you think? I love hearing about places people have traveled and their experiences in life. If we put forth the effort, we can all get along. We just have to find things in common and accept we'll have some differences, but they shouldn't divide us."

"The only exception to that rule is unkind people. I won't tolerate people who are mean to others or who try to make their fortunes by taking what isn't theirs. I 'm not a religious woman who runs off to church every time the doors are open. I don't trust most of the clergy are as pious as they'd like their congregations to believe, but I do follow the Golden Rule and try to treat everyone as I like to be treated. When they cross me, however, I show no mercy," Mrs. Wickersham offered, her voice taking on a somber, sinister tone Jex never thought he'd hear from someone as sweet as his new employer. Jex was significantly freaked out by her comment and the delivery of it, but the very next second, she smiled and giggled, which had him laughing along.

They continued working on the recipes, and Jex enjoyed hearing Mrs. Wickersham tell tales about her life and her travels before she married Mr. Wickersham. She'd been to London on a trip with some girlfriends during the nineteen-sixties, one of who was Trudy Somerset.

They'd been school mates growing up, and they'd added Charlotte Powers or Lottie as Mrs. Wickersham called her, as a friend after Lottie and her husband moved to town.

"Lottie is a dear friend, don't get me wrong, but it's obvious she wasn't raised with the caliber of manners as Trudy and me. Our mothers were best friends, you know. We were taught to be gentile young ladies, though I suppose manners aren't as important these days as they were in the past," Mrs. Wickersham explained as she sat on a padded stool Jex had ordered over the internet so she could assist with food preparation when she wanted.

Jex nearly went off on a story about being forced to wear a ball gag for two days because he'd chewed with his mouth open in front of Bernie, but quickly thought better of it when he looked at Mrs. Wickersham to see her gentle smile. It was definitely not appropriate to discuss such things with a refined lady.

Over the next few weeks, Jex learned how to prepare the rooms per Mrs. Wickersham's specifications when one was hosting guests. She taught him how to clean and air the bedding so the sheets were bright and the rooms smelled of fresh sea air. He delighted in listening to stories of her son as a child and even had a few stories to tell from when he was Molly's son.

It was nice to reminisce about the things he had never shared with Bernie. In little ways, it brought back his mother's memory, which he'd missed for too long. When he became the slave, he locked Molly's memory away in his mind so it couldn't be touched by the darkness the slave endured. It was nice to air out her memory as Jex aired out the guest rooms.

One thing Jex noticed was Mrs. Wickersham never actually mentioned Michael's death or the aftermath. She spoke of him as if he was still alive but off somewhere on an adventure and would return for a visit any day. She also never mentioned anything about her husband's disappearance, though, in all honesty, she rarely spoke of him at all.

Jex also noticed she didn't ask about his life aside from his childhood before his mother was killed, not even mentioning anything regarding his time in foster care, which he'd explained one night while telling her a story about living with a foster family where he was learning to play the piano from the mother.

The woman was kind, but her husband was a son-of-a-bitch who got off on intimidating Jex and the other foster kids when the mother wasn't around. It didn't seem as if Mrs. Wickersham was one to pry, and Jex appreciated it very much. They worked well together, and it was a relief not looking over his shoulder for once.

A beautiful April morning found Jex in the kitchen doing an inventory for Mrs. Wickersham to determine what things were necessary from the grocer. She was in her sitting room on the phone while Jex checked expiration dates, finding some things were long past their prime.

He blamed it on the fact Mrs. Wickersham had been away from home for a few months and couldn't get around as easily as before her surgery. Jex worked quickly to dispose of the items before she returned to the kitchen.

Hurriedly collecting the empty jars and cans, Jex carried them out to the recycling can on the porch, seeing it was full and the back wheel was wrecked such that it wouldn't easily roll. Jex picked it up and carried it to the shed in hopes of finding an empty box to dump the recyclables while he repaired the roller on the bin.

Jex was yet to have ventured into the shed because they hadn't begun work in the gardens, but he saw lots of equipment designed to be used around the property. He walked over to a stack of boxes near a freezer that had a latching hasp with a large padlock on it, even though it was plugged into the heavy-duty outlet and the motor was running.

After pulling on the lock to see it was secure, Jex looked around for a key, but he found nothing. "Jex, dear?!" he heard from the back porch, so he quickly hurried out the door of the shed, pulling it closed behind him.

He rushed inside to see Mrs. Wickersham sitting at the counter on the tall stool, perusing the list he'd begun. "Everything okay, dear?"

"Uh, yes, ma'am. The wheel on the recycling can is bent, so I was going to fix it, but I didn't find pliers in the shed. I'm glad to see lots of gardening equipment. I thought we could get out there tomorrow and begin cleaning up if that's okay with you," he offered to the old woman.

"Oh, that sounds grand," Mrs. Wickersham responded as she continued to inspect the list and write down additional staples. "We need honey as well," the old woman announced as she wrote it on the list.

Jex opened the pantry door and held up a large jar of honey. "What about this? Does honey go bad?"

Mrs. Wickersham looked at him with surprise before she tempered her face into a kind smile. "Oh, that's a different kind of honey I save for special occasions. We'll need the clover honey Mr. Dowd has in the organic section of his store."

"Also, I think I'll set up a scheduled delivery every Tuesday on our day off. Oh, I've set aside Mondays and Tuesdays for the Inn to be closed to give us time to clean up after the Sunday departures and prepare for the Wednesday arrivals, along with giving ourselves some time to regroup."

"I think I'm going to host a card party here once a month so I can catch up with my friends in town. When I host the parties, you're welcome to plan your own activities, dear. I'm sure a handsome young man like you would enjoy time away from the hen club. We need some downtime, I believe. You need to get to know young people around town, don't you think?"

Jex was surprised at her decision, but he thought, perhaps, if she took time off to enjoy time with her friends, maybe he could take time off to enjoy seeing someone he wanted to be very friendly with...Chief Elijah Moore. The idea of spending time with the man was divine, and Jex was looking forward to the possibilities...if the man was interested. That was the great unknown.

That weekend, Mrs. Wickersham approached Jex as he was pressing duvet covers and pillow shams. She had a sweet smile on her face, and Jex found he was happier living with the woman than he'd been in a very long time.

"I've been thinking about May 1, and I think it might be best for you to move into the sitting room next to my bedroom. I know you'd planned to sleep in your tent on the beach after our guests began to arrive, but I'll feel better if you're in the house since I'm not as agile as I used to be. With a house full of strangers, I'd feel much safer," Mrs. Wickersham told him, offering a gentle smile.

Jex nodded and continued to press the linens he'd hung outside in the sunshine all afternoon. The towels hung on the line until they were damp, and then they were put into the dryer to soften them. Mrs. Wickersham had explained the softer bath sheets were best during the summer if the guests stayed in the sun too long and their skin was tender. Jex couldn't find fault with her logic.

"Tomorrow, we can go out into the gardens to begin cleaning up the debris. I'll show you where the hives are so you can avoid them. My bees are temperamental and only used to me, so it's best if you avoid them at all costs. I've been out to the garden to see they're becoming more active, so I'll clean the hives to get them ready for the summer," Mrs. Wickersham explained.

"Sure. You mentioned garden furniture and beach loungers. Where are they? I should probably clean them up as well," Jex suggested.

Mrs. Wickersham clapped her hands in glee. "Oh, that's wonderful. I have the most beautiful wicker sets I haven't been able to bring out in a few years because they're heavy, but we can set up the beach like I used to do years ago. Oh, this is going to be lovely."

Unfortunately, the plan to bring all of the summer wicker and the wooden tables, chairs, and loungers outdoors that weekend to clean them and allow all of it to dry in the sun came to an abrupt end when the spring rain took over for three days. All of the furniture was stacked in the large shed where the gardening tools, lawnmowers, and the strange freezer was housed.

The wooden furniture needed a fresh coat of paint, so after consultation with the lady herself the previous evening, Jex made a plan to stop at the small hardware store in town to grab some paint samples for her consideration after he finished his morning shift at the diner.

He was coming out of the back of the kitchen with the dish rack when he saw the Chief of Police knocking on the door early that morning. Lena wasn't there yet, but she'd given Jex his own key to let himself in so he could turn on the flat top and the ovens to have them ready when she arrived at five-thirty.

Jex walked over to the door and opened it, seeing the very handsome man with a bright smile. Elijah Moore was over six-foot-tall with broad shoulders and bright blue eyes. His hair, while quite short, was chestnut brown, and he wore a short beard. The man spent time working out somewhere because his arms were like steel bands, and he had a small waist and a bubble butt, not that Jex noticed or anything.

"Forget giving me a key. Lena should give you the key to come in and turn on everything in the morning. How've you been?" Jex asked as he closed the door of the diner and followed the sexy man to the counter which he went behind and began making coffee.

"I've been well. I understand you've been busy helping Mrs. Wickersham get the Inn ready. I told you she'd love having you around to help," Chief Moore offered with a kind smile.

"I felt bad taking time off because I hate leaving Lena in the lurch, but I've been learning the recipes and how Mrs. Wickersham expects things to be, and let me tell you, she's a perfectionist. You, uh, you should come over for a tasting on Friday," Jex offered, unsure what entity had taken over his mouth because inviting the top cop to his other employer's home was a liberty he shouldn't have taken.

The chief's head snapped up, and a big grin blossomed on his handsome face. "I'd love that. Tell me what time, and what kind of wine to bring, and I'm there," Elijah Moore suggested.

Jax felt bad at backtracking because he should have consulted with Mrs. Wickersham before he extended the invitation. "Let me speak with Mrs. Wickersham, and I'll let you know. I, uh, I should have asked her first about having you out, but if she's not on board, I'll make us a picnic, and we can meet on the beach. She goes to bed at nine after she watches a show about women who kill because they get pushed too far. How's that for an alternative plan?"

Jex heard the man chuckle. "Sounds like a better idea. I'll draw you a map to this great place where we can meet. It's about half-a-mile down the beach," Eli offered.

Eileen Stewart came flying in the front door as Lena came in through the back, both women out of breath. The cop sat down at the counter, and things proceeded as usual. Of course, Jex couldn't wait for Friday night, deciding not to run the first idea by Mrs. Wickersham after all.

V

That Friday afternoon, Eli felt more than a little nervous, which was unlike him. Things didn't rattle Eli Moore. People didn't make him jumpy, or so he believed until he came face-to-face with Jex Ivers. He'd seen the newcomer every morning at the diner, but Lena had only been late on Wednesday, so the two of them had just the one conversation without the woman butting in. Eli was intrigued with the young man, and...dare he should admit it...a little more than just attracted to Jex.

Eli really hadn't had the opportunity to flirt with Jex Ivers as he wanted, and he was dying to ask the man out for a date. It was probably for the best the opportunity hadn't come along because Eli wasn't even sure the man welcomed his advances, especially after Eli reviewed a portion of the case file involving Jex and his time with Bernard Overman.

Of course, as a law enforcement officer, he had access to information others didn't, but Eli vowed to be judicious regarding his searches when it came to Jex. He didn't want to alert anyone who might be trying to find the newcomer's current location.

While the law enforcement community was generally forthright when it came to cases, there were instances when someone took the money offered from a less than honorable source and fucked up the trust of the citizens they'd sworn to uphold. It became all about the cash, and a cop on the take was generally ruthless because they had everything to lose.

It was also the reason Eli didn't call Denny Cather directly, instead, setting up an alarm regarding any news alerts or stories regarding Bernard Overman on the internet instead of using NCIC, the FBI information system. An innocuous search engine on a public platform could provide as much information sometimes and didn't draw nearly as much attention, which wasn't what Jex needed at the moment.

Yolanda West walked into Eli's office before she headed to the grade school for traffic duty. "Did you get the message about Terry Blake's call today? I left a note on your desk," she pointed out.

Eli had seen the note, but he ignored it. "Did he say what he wanted?"

"Not to me. Maybe if you call Blake back, he can tell you? He's sweet on ya, isn't he?" Yolanda teased, laughing at Eli's sour face.

"You know I have no interest in him. He's an asshole, Yolanda. Ask Will. We knew him back in high school, and he's is a total dick. I'm not calling him back, and if he calls again, tell him if it's not business-related, I have no interest in speaking with him," Eli barked out just as Joe Tibby walked into the office for his evening shift.

"Wow, the negative energy in here is suffocating. What's going on?" the young officer asked.

"How's Shannon? Any news on a due date?" Yolanda asked, seeming to ignore Eli's rant.

"Nothing yet. My mother-in-law came to stay, so I'm more than happy to put in overtime until she goes into labor if you need me, Chief," the young cop offered.

Eli laughed and came out of his office, totally bored out of his mind. He waited until Tibby and Yolanda left before he closed up the station and sent out a message he'd forwarded the phone to his cell.

He climbed into his SUV cruiser and drove down the street, making a left to see what he'd hoped he'd find...Jex Ivers walking toward the Wickersham Inn with two bags from Toomey's Hardware. Eli pulled into the curb lane and rolled down the passenger-side window. "Jex, you need a ride?" he asked as he saw the handsome man jump and turn toward the vehicle, breathing a sigh of relief.

Eli hit the locks to open the door and motioned for the young man to join him. Jex opened the passenger door and hopped in, offering a big smile. "What's in the bags?" Eli asked.

Jex smiled. "Mrs. Wickersham has this incredible, antique, beach furniture, but it needs to be painted. She said after we picked the paint color, she'd make cushions, so I brought some paint samples for her to decide. How's your week been going?"

Eli pulled the SUV down Persimmon Drive, which led to the beach, and he stopped at the end of the street. "See that house right there?" Eli asked as he pointed to the small clapboard house at the end of the cul-de-sac.

He watched as Jex looked to the right and smiled at the sunny yellow structure with the windchimes on the side porch facing the beach. "Yeah, it's cute. Those windchimes are pretty cool. Are you friends with the owners, or is it just a must-see tourist stop in town?" Jex joked.

Eli chuckled. "That's my house. My dad lives with me during the summer, but he won't be here until after Memorial Day, so it's just me right now. I've got something to ask, Jex, and if I'm reading things wrong, please tell me, and I'll knock it off."

"I'm perfectly happy with our remaining friends, so don't freak out about this. I thought...I mean, it's probably stupid of me to even ask...never mind," Eli hedged, feeling quite guilty for his thoughts and his desires.

He felt Jex's hand on his forearm and turned to see the handsome, redhead's smile. "Ask, Chief. That business with Bernie is history, and I'm doing my best to get beyond it. I, uh, I think you're beautiful, you know. Am I anyway near what you wanted to discuss?" Jex asked him.

Eli turned to him and picked up his hand, kissing the top of it. "Yes, as a matter of fact. I find you very attractive as well, but we can go slow. I'm in no rush to push you beyond your boundaries, so spending time together sounds like a good first step," Eli offered. He turned the SUV around and pulled back onto Hopkins Lane to The Wickersham Inn.

Five minutes later, Eli pulled into the driveway and turned to look at Jex. "So, how about you come to my place after the old lady goes to bed? I'll leave the lights on for the stairs from the beach. Come in through the back door. I'll be on the lookout for you," Eli offered a wink as Jex hopped out of the large vehicle and grabbed the bags from the hardware store.

"I'll bring dinner," Jex offered before closing the door and returning the wink.

Eli patrolled Haven's Point and circled by the station to finish the end of his shift. He'd love to say he felt guilty for leaving the station so he could take Jex Ivers to Mrs. Wickersham's Inn, but it would be a lie.

He'd watched the handsome redhead walk down Hopkins Lane every day since the man started working for Lena Becker, and everything about him had fueled the dreams Eli had about the man every night. It was time to take the next steps, or the chief would never get a full night's sleep again.

Eli slid into his SUV cruiser and started for home when he saw smoke coming from *Lena's Home Cooking.* He pulled over and ran toward the front door, finding it locked, so he rushed around to the back door and reached for the handle, feeling the burn to his fingers. He kicked the door in and rushed inside, seeing the kitchen filled with smoke and a visible flame coming from under the flat top.

Eli rushed to the pantry where he knew there was a fire extinguisher, reaching for the pin only to find it missing, and when he pressed the lever on the tank, it was flat. He heard coughing coming from the office, so he rushed back to find Lena on the floor with blood on her temple.

"FUCK!" Eli yelled before he reached for his radio, only to find it missing. It was then he remembered he'd left it in the charger on his desk.

Eli picked up Lena and carried her outside before he placed her on the grass next to the diner. He grabbed his phone and called nine-one-one to hear the county dispatch answer. "*Nine-one-one, what's your emergency?*"

"This is Chief Moore. I need fire and ambulance at *Lena's Home Cooking* on Hopkins Lane. I have an occupant on the grass outside. She's suffering from smoke inhalation, I think," Eli yelled into his cell, forgetting all of his training because it was a friend, not a random citizen. It shook him to his core.

He rushed to his SUV and found the oxygen tank and the first aid kit before he rushed over to where Lena was coughing as she tried to sit up. Eli turned on the tank and fastened the mask around her nose and mouth, gently pushing her back onto the grass. "Stay right there. Ambulance and fire are on the way. Can you tell me what happened?" he asked Lena as he checked her for burns, thankful to see there were none.

Within minutes, Eli heard sirens and looked up to see the fire department, an ambulance, and Sussex County Sheriff Cummings along with Deputy Blake. "Eli, are you okay?" Gerry Cummings asked.

"Yeah, I'm fine. Check on Lena. She was in the building, and I think she hit her head. I was on my way home...," Eli began as

Tibby rolled up on the scene. Within an hour, the entire police force and Sheriff's Office were at the diner as the fire department worked to put out the blaze.

The inhabitants of the other shops on Hopkins Lane raced to the scene as well, and everyone had an accounting of what they believed happened, even though none of them had been eyewitnesses to the actual events.

"It had to be that redhead. I saw him leaving the diner today with bags in hand. I bet he took the money from the register before he knocked Lena out and set the place on fire," Eli heard Mrs. Jones, who owned the yarn shop, speculate. No doubt she was referring to Jex.

Unfortunately, Terry Blake was questioning her. If they delved into Jex's history, it wouldn't be pretty for the newcomer because it might tip off someone to his whereabouts. Eli couldn't have it because he'd grown very fond of the man, and he wasn't about to allow rumor and speculation to scar Jex's reputation.

Eli walked over to Terry and tapped him on the shoulder. "Can I speak with you?" Eli asked. Seeing the blonde's eyes light up made him uneasy, but if he could stop the rumor mill from manifesting into a lynch mob, he would do whatever necessary.

The two men walked to the side while the firemen continued to do their jobs. "Are you okay?" Terry asked as he touched Eli's shoulder.

As much as he wanted to shrug off the unwanted attention, Eli considered the greater good. "I'm fine, Terry, but I know for a fact there were issues with the wiring in the diner."

"Lena was intending to get an electrician to come out and check the electrical box because the breaker for the flat top keeps tripping, but I'm sure she got busy and forgot to make the call. The young guy who works for her had nothing to do with this," Eli explained.

He saw Terry puff up his chest and pull out a pad from his uniform shirt. "Who is this guy?" the deputy asked.

Eli wanted to roll his eyes, but he didn't. "He's new to town, and he's been working for Lena a few months. He left at two this afternoon, which was his regular time. The fire was just starting at five when I saw the smoke. The young guy isn't involved," Eli defended.

Unfortunately, Eli's protestations only fueled Terry Blake's curiosity. "How do you know this guy? How long has he been in town, and where is he staying?" Terry asked.

Eli didn't want to appear as if he was obstructing justice, even though he knew Jex had nothing to do with the fire or even with Lena's injury, so he decided to cooperate with the asshole deputy. "He's staying with Mrs. Wickersham. I've gotten to know him since the guy got to town, and I can vouch for him being a decent guy. He's helping Hilda get the Inn ready to go for the summer if you must know, and I actually gave him a ride home because he was carrying paint. He's got nothing to do with the fire, Terry," Eli ordered as they both watched the ambulance quickly leave the scene with Lena in the back.

Terry Blake turned to Eli with a smirk. "I'd suggest you leave the scene, Chief. It sounds as if you're conflicted regarding this incident. You should go home and write a statement regarding the events for the report Sheriff Cummings is going to need to file. I'll come by later to check on you," Blake suggested.

Eli sighed. "Don't bother."

He stomped off to his SUV and drove home. He needed to get to Jex and get him somewhere the Sheriff's Department couldn't get to him, but if Eli stepped in at all, it could become a huge fucking mess. He'd always been an honest man, vowing to uphold the law at all costs, and he would enforce the law as he'd sworn when he took office. He'd be faithful to his vow until the point where upholding the law conflicted with the safety of a handsome, young man who had already been treated like shit enough to last a lifetime.

VI

"So, Mrs. Wickersham, what do you think about these shades of green?" Jex asked as he knelt next to the beautiful beach lounger he'd pulled from the stack of chairs in the large shed. It was raining, but the weather was predicted to clear up on Saturday, and Jex was anxious to paint the frames.

"Okay, number one is fern green. Number two is bamboo green. Number three is..." Jex offered as he pointed to the five shades he'd painted on a board he'd found in the shed. They both heard sirens in the distance, but nothing had come their way, so they went back to the task at hand.

Jex turned to see Mrs. Wickersham leaning on her cane as she studied the colors. "Can you bring that board onto the back porch and give me time to study it? I have some fabric in mind that might work, but I need to give it a little thought. How was work today?" Mrs. Wickersham asked as Jex followed her onto the back porch and placed the board on the table as she set the wet umbrella on the floor of the porch.

"Uh, work was fine. Ms. Becker paid me cash, which I appreciate. She's a nice lady," Jex offered as he followed the old lady into the kitchen.

Jex knew he should have asked Mrs. Wickersham if it was okay for him to schedule a dinner date, but he wasn't sure how to approach the topic with her. He disappeared into the bathroom and grabbed a towel to dry his hair. When he came back to the kitchen, he saw Mrs. Wickersham staring in his direction. "You have something on your mind, don't you?" the kind woman asked.

Jex felt his face flush, which had been his curse since he was a boy, what with his red hair and freckled skin. He was pale, and he burned easily when he spent too much time in the sun. His skin also scarred easily, as evidenced by the marks on his wrists and ankles. Those marks would never go away, but Jex was doing his best to try to move beyond the emotional scars. It would take time, but he had hope. Someday, Jex would have a good life. He just had to work for it.

"I, uh, I kinda have a date tonight. I should have been honest, Mrs. Wickersham. I'm gay. I should have told you the truth before I moved in, and if you feel uncomfortable about it, I'll pack up and leave right now," Jex offered.

The old woman stood next to the table and pulled out a chair. "Have you ever tasted sherry?" she asked as she walked to the cabinet where her fancy crystal was housed. Jex had washed all of it by hand to freshen it, and when she pulled out two of the small, pedestal glasses with a 'W' etched onto them, he smiled.

"I haven't. Let me help you, Mrs. Wickersham," he offered as he stood and walked to the dining room to retrieve the crystal bottle she kept in the breakfront. She took one glass of the liquor every night, but she'd never offered him a drink until that Friday evening.

Jex carried the bottle into the kitchen and handed it to the old woman. She poured the two of them each a glass of the aperitif before she put the stopper in the bottle and gave it to him to return it to its proper place.

When he returned to the kitchen, she had the small glasses on the table with a small cheese plate and a basket of crackers. "When did you do this, Mrs. Wickersham?" Jex asked with a smile for the woman.

"Earlier today, while you were at work. I wanted us to have a discussion, Jex. I've grown quite fond of you, and I wanted to show you I'm happy you're here to help me. It's a blessing, and no, I don't care that you're gay. I had a member of my family who was gay, and I loved him with everything inside me."

"Now you've just shared something important with me, and I thank you for telling me. I don't ask questions of you because I figured you had a reason to sleep on the beach, and I believed when you were ready, you'd tell me what you wanted me to know. I thank you for finally trusting me enough to offer personal information," Mrs. Wickersham explained.

Jex nodded but felt he needed to offer a little more honesty. "I, uh, I have a dark past I'd rather not go into if you don't mind. You gain nothing by knowing such awful things about me, so if we could just skip it, I'd rather. You see, I like being here with you. Your house feels like home to me, and I like being here more than I've ever liked being anywhere else since I lost my mother."

"Do you mind if I go out for the evening?" he asked. It felt better not to lie to the woman, so he'd be honest about what he could, which was the fact he had a date with Eli Moore.

"Of course, dear. Are the two of you planning to eat a late dinner?" Mrs. Wickersham asked.

Jex felt the heat in his face once again. "I was hoping maybe you could talk me through a salad and a main dish for us? I'll gladly give you the money Ms. Becker paid me for work this week to cover the cost of the food. I should definitely pay you for letting me live here," he pushed. When Mrs. Wickersham laughed, he couldn't help but grin. Her face seemed to light up, and it was a relief.

"You owe me nothing, Jex. You help me, and I help you, dear. Now, let's work on something for your dinner with the handsome Chief of Police. What did you have in mind?" Mrs. Wickersham asked as they nibbled on cheese and enjoyed their sherry as the sun sunk lower in the sky.

Jex chuckled. "I never said who I was going out with tonight."

He watched as the woman offered a big smile. "You didn't have to, dear. I can see you're in love, and Elijah Moore is a wonderful man. I think it's wonderful. So, let's think about what you'd like to make. The chief is a rather muscular man, so a substantial meal seems appropriate," Mrs. Wickersham suggested.

The two of them finished their sherry while Jex made a meatloaf, rosemary roasted potatoes, and a fresh salad according to Mrs. Wickersham's detailed instructions. Once the food was in the oven and fridge, Jex began cleaning up the mess. When the phone rang, Mrs. Wickersham went into the entryway to answer it.

Jex went upstairs to shower and change, and when he came out of the bathroom of the studio apartment in the attic, he was surprised to see Mrs. Wickersham sitting on the bed next to a pair of slacks and a shirt that appeared to be vintage.

Jex was only wrapped in a towel, his chest exposed to show the scars he kept hidden under his clothes as much as possible. He never took off the bracelets except when he showered, so Jex wasn't surprised when he heard Mrs. Wickersham gasp. It was a brutal sight to see.

"I'm sorry, Mrs. Wickersham. I, uh, I shouldn't have come to stay in your home. You don't need to see this mess..." Jex began.

The old woman stood and slowly walked over to him, putting her right hand on the mark over his heart. Her skin was paperwhite, in definite contrast to the angry, red scar over his heart. "Why did he do this to you?"

Jex swallowed, realizing how foolish it was to even begin to imagine Elijah Moore could find ugly trash like him interesting, much less attractive. It had become easy for Jex to forget the horrors hidden beneath his garments, but when he was stripped bare, he was a mangled mess. Inside and out.

Jex looked into the old woman's cloudy blue eyes to see nothing but kindness. "He, uh, he branded me. 'S' for *slave*. I was his slave until I was set free by a police detective. The man, Bernard Overman, he put his mark on the things that belonged to him, and I belonged to him," Jex explained, wondering why in the hell he didn't move to get dressed. Standing in that room in a towel in front of Mrs. Wickersham was inappropriate, but he couldn't seem to make his body walk away.

Mrs. Wickersham took a step back and turned toward the bed. "Those were Neil's things. I've had them in storage for years, but they were in a nice cedar closet in our bedroom, so they have no moth holes. I thought they'd look nice for your date, so I pressed them for you. I'd suggest on Sunday, we move your things downstairs so you can ready this room for guests."

"Now, go ahead and get ready, dear. We'll take care of each other, you and me," Mrs. Wickersham told him. She gave him a gentle pat on the forearm and made her way downstairs as Jex watched after her from the top of the landing.

Jex shaved and brushed his teeth, staring at his reflection while he vacillated over the right thing to do when it came to dating the top cop. He knew he was attracted to Eli Moore, but once Jex had his shirt off, would the repulsion he'd see on Eli's handsome face snap the one tether Jex had to thoughts of maybe being loved someday? He wanted to give the man the benefit of the doubt, but as Jex studied himself in the mirror, he knew he was unlovable. It was undeniable.

Knowing he didn't have Eli's phone number to call him to cancel the date, Jex dressed in the clothes Mrs. Wickersham had loaned him, loving the fact the shirt didn't need to be tucked into the trousers. He stepped into the black, high-top sneakers he wore every day and headed downstairs to explain his decision to Mrs. Wickersham to cancel the date.

The old woman had a picnic basket on the table where she was beginning to pack up the food. "Mrs. Wickersham, I'm going to cancel the date and tell Chief Moore I can't see him as anything more than a friend. You saw my chest and arms. It's unfair to him for me to think he could be attracted to me. I'd just become upset when he isn't, and I'd rather skip the whole messy drama."

"I won't disrespect him by standing him up. I owe him more than that because he's been kind. Don't worry about anything. I'll clean up the mess when I get back," Jex suggested, feeling his heart aching as if the whole incident with Bernie Overman was happening all over again.

He tried not to give the monster space in his mind, but when something happened to remind Jex he was worthless, all of those awful memories rushed back like a tsunami. How he ever thought he could outrun them had to say something about how deep in denial he'd sunk.

He saw Mrs. Wickersham shake her head before she braced her hands on the table and looked up at Jex with a sweet smile. "Dear, if that's what you want to do, that's your business. I'd say the neighborly thing to do would be to at least offer the man the meal you prepared. If you don't believe there's a chance for the two of you to have a romantic relationship, a friendship would still be beneficial to the both of you, I'm sure."

"Let's go ahead and pack up the food, shall we? I have a friend drop by in a little while, so why don't you go to Chief Moore's home now and think about this before you make a definite decision you may regret later?" she suggested.

Her gentle advice talked him down from the frenzied mess he'd been when he first got out of the shower. Considering the compassion Chief Moore had already shown Jex, it was only right he stick with the original plan to share a meal, but Jex planned to make it clear being friends was all they could ever be. Mrs. Wickersham was right. It was the neighborly thing to do.

Jex had everything packed up in the picnic basket as he watched Mrs. Wickersham preparing tea and cookies, slicing lemons and putting a small dish filled with sugar cubes on the tray along with cups, saucers, spoons, and a small pitcher of milk. "Shall I carry that into the front parlor for you?" Jex asked.

Mrs. Wickersham smiled. "That would be lovely. That way I only have to bring in the teapot. Now, have a nice time and make sure Chief Moore gets his fill. I'll leave the back door unlocked for you and the porch light on. I know he just lives down the beach, but be careful, Jex. No place is completely crime-free, you know."

Jex laughed and kissed her cheek before he picked up the tray and carried it into the formal sitting area Mrs. Wickersham called a parlor. The room was beautiful with the polished wood trim and antique furniture, including a gorgeous Persian rug that filled the center of the room. He put the tray on the bench under the picture window before going to the breakfront in the dining room to find an embroidered mat to place on a mahogany, tilt-top, tea table he would set up between the two, matching Queen Anne chairs facing the fireplace.

Jex pushed down the tabletop, latching it into place as Mrs. Wickersham had told him every time they used the table. If the latch weren't secured, the top would pop up and spill the china onto the rug. Jex didn't want to be around if it ever happened.

The china had been "Mother Wickersham's pride and joy," as he'd been told when he washed the delicate dishes and serving platters to prepare them for the opening of the Inn on the first of May. The task for Saturday and Sunday was to sand and paint the beach and patio furniture, but things were nearly ready aside from the outdoor decorating.

Jex returned to the kitchen and watched Mrs. Wickersham bustling about. He noticed she had pulled out the honey that was only used for special occasions. Jex watched as she filled a small dish with some honey, humming a tune he'd never heard. "So, Mrs. Wickersham, what makes that honey so special," he asked, trying to shake off his earlier dark mood.

Mrs. Wickersham placed the large jar back in the pantry where it was kept, he'd noticed. "That honey was harvested last summer from bees here at the Inn. I showed you where the hives are located. While you're painting tomorrow, I'll work with the hives. I need to get reacquainted with my bees, you see. The winter was milder than last year, so they should be fine," she explained.

"I'd like to try that honey sometime," Jex offered as he started to walk past her to get the picnic basket.

Mrs. Wickersham grabbed his arm, offering a grip that shocked him for someone who appeared to be so delicate. "Never, ever touch that honey, Jex. I'm protective of my bees and don't want people to find out about the honey because I don't plan to ever sell it. That honey isn't meant for you or me to enjoy. Promise you'll never taste it," Mrs. Wickersham demanded.

Jex was taken aback by her attitude, but he knew elderly people had proclivities he'd never understand, so he nodded. The old woman released his arm, and he glanced down to see the perfect, red imprint of her small hand from her vice-like grip.

"Now, you look very handsome. Off with you and tell Chief Moore I said to be a gentleman," she teased him as she tapped his cheek with affection.

Jex was somewhat shocked by her behavior, but she was right. He needed to go because it was already eight-thirty. He was anxious to clear the air between Chief Moore and himself before he had a panic attack and wound up face-first in the sand.

VII

"I called to tell you I've met someone," Eli Moore told his father, Glenn. He'd grown so nervous since he'd arrived home earlier in the afternoon, even a run on the beach didn't help calm him. He decided to call his father instead of continuing to pace the floor of the small house while he waited for his date.

"That's great, Eli. Is it someone I know?" Glenn asked. Eli could hear the excitement in his father's voice, and it reminded him how much he missed the man. They may have had their differences when Eli was growing up, but that wasn't anything new in the history of fathers and sons.

His father was the Chief of Police when Eli was a teenager, and all of his friends gave him shit about it to the point Eli resented every word his father ever uttered, even if it was supportive. He always felt he owed Glenn Moore an apology for being such an ornery little bastard back then.

"No, Pop. It's a new guy in town. Oh, I almost forgot to tell you, *Lena's* caught fire today. Lena was unconscious in the office when I arrived on the scene. She suffered a blow to the head, so they took her to the hospital. I called to check on her before I called you, and they said she inhaled a little smoke and has a slight concussion, but she'll be home by Monday," Eli explained, remembering that Terry fucking Blake had decided Jex was a person of interest in the fire.

"Hells bells, that electrical system in that place was bad at the time Old Lena bought it, and that was in the seventies when I was first hired for the force. It still has the old knob-and-tube wiring, I'd bet. Hardin Leland's mother, Charlene, talked Lena into counteroffering a lower price instead of pushing the owners to update the wiring in the place, and if it was never done, it's a wonder it didn't burn down years ago," Glenn advised.

"Yeah, well, goddamn Terry Blake told me I needed to leave the scene because I'm conflicted," Eli complained.

"How?" his father asked.

"The guy they're trying to pin this on is the guy I'm seeing. He helps Lena in the mornings with dishes, bussing tables, anything she needs, really. He said the other day she needed to call an electrician because the breaker keeps tripping on the flat top. Anyway, I put in a call to the sheriff, but I haven't heard back from him yet," Eli explained.

"You tell Gerry Cummings he needs to keep that smart-mouthed little asshole on his own side of the city limit sign. You're the Chief of Police in Haven's Point. Don't let them try to push you out of the way. I get the impression Terry Blake would like to have your job, so don't let him get the upper hand," Glenn reminded.

Just then, Eli saw movement off the back porch. "Let me call you on Sunday evening when I have more time, Pop. My date's here. Love you, old man," Eli signed off.

Eli tossed his phone on the counter and walked to the back door, opening it to see Jex standing with a picnic basket in his hands. He appeared to be nervous, which made Eli laugh. "Come on in, Jex. I see you're as nervous as I am."

The guy's nervous laugh made Eli smile. It had been so long since Eli had actually gone out or even looked forward to going out with someone. Sadly, he couldn't remember the name of the last guy he'd dated more than three times.

Eli hadn't really been into casual sex since he'd turned thirty, choosing to take care of things himself instead of putting in the effort with a man who had no desire to have more than casual hookups instead of an actual relationship. His parents had given him the roadmap to a happy life, and Eli wanted it for himself as well.

"Smells good," Eli remarked as he watched Jex put the basket on the kitchen counter.

"Uh, yeah, Mrs. Wickersham talked me through it. I forgot to ask if you're allergic to anything," Jex inquired in a soft voice.

Eli walked over to the cabinet and pulled out some plates, placing them on the counter as he studied Jex. "Lena's going to be okay, you know?"

When Jex's head jerked up, Eli saw the man had no idea to what he was referring. "The diner? Didn't you hear about what happened at the diner?"

"I didn't hear anything," Jex responded, ceasing to unpack the hamper.

"Lena's diner caught fire today. It was the flat top, not surprisingly. Lena was in her office when it happened, and she inhaled a little smoke after she hit her head on something. She'll be okay, but they're keeping her in the hospital in Dover for a few days. She'll be home by Monday," Eli explained. He took hold of Jex's hands and placed them on his chest so he could wrap his arms around the man's waist.

Jex pressed his forehead against Eli's chest, his body trembling at the news. "God, she could have..." Jex whispered just as the front doorbell rang.

Eli gently eased the man into a chair at the table. "I'll get rid of them," the chief whispered before he walked out of the kitchen, closing the door behind him. Eli rushed to the front door and opened it to see none other than Terry Blake. He was holding his go-to meal from the other permanent restaurant in Haven's Point, a bucket of chicken from KFC.

"Don't you look handsome? Are you okay? I see you remembered I was coming by to check on you," Terry reminded before he came into the house without an invitation.

"Look, Terry, this isn't a good time right now," Eli told him. The deputy sheriff put the chicken and beer on the coffee table and wrapped his arms around Eli, shocking the police chief at his boldness.

"Babe, it's okay. I know you were upset today, so I'm not mad you were bitchy about me handling things because you had to recuse yourself. You know I was right, and you're welcome for me taking over, so you didn't get into trouble with the prosecutor's office for showing favors," Terry said.

Eli couldn't get away from the man fast enough. "I know you were right? You're full of shit, Terry. One, I'm Police Chief in Haven's Point, and the fire happened in my jurisdiction. I wasn't about to take that shit up with you in front of the whole fucking town. Two, it's not your investigation, and if I decide I'm conflicted, which I'm not, then I'll discuss it with Sheriff Cummings and the State Police, not you."

"I let it go because I was worried about Lena because she hit her head. She wasn't attacked, and you have no right to take over anything related to this case. Now, if you'll excuse me, I have plans, and none of them include you," Eli snapped as they both heard the backdoor slam shut.

Eli ran into the kitchen to see the food on the counter and the room empty. "Goddammit, Terry. How many times we gotta go over this? I'm sorry, but I'm not interested in you as more than a friend. You need to get it through your head," Eli snapped as he rushed out the door to see nothing. Jex was nowhere to be seen, and Eli was pissed.

Eli walked back into the house to see Terry was gone as well, having left the chicken and beer on the coffee table. "Fucking hell. I have enough food to feed an army and nobody to share it with," Eli complained to himself. It just wasn't his night.

Eli drove by the diner on Saturday morning, seeing it was closed per usual. He was frustrated to hell because he'd called Mrs. Wickersham's house the previous night and earlier that morning to speak with Jex in hopes of explaining things to him, but he only got the answering machine. Eli needed to get the investigation of the diner fire under control, so he called several people and asked to meet everyone at *Lena's* at ten-thirty that morning.

Eli put the meatloaf, potatoes, salad, and the bucket of chicken in the refrigerator and washed up Mrs. Wickersham's fancy containers to return to her that night, hoping Jex would be there and allow Eli to explain himself. He wasn't sure what the young guy thought had happened when Terry showed up unannounced, but Eli swore to himself he'd talk until he was blue in the face to clear it up and assure Jex there was nothing between himself and the deputy sheriff.

Since the diner was closed anyway on Saturday and Sunday, Eli sliced off a piece of meatloaf and made a sandwich to take with him that morning instead of making himself breakfast. He had an appointment with the Sussex County Sheriff, Fire Marshall, Building Inspector, and Haven's Point Mayor, Hardin Leland, that morning to see if they could identify precisely what started the fire at *Lena's Home Cooking*. The sooner they had a substantiated cause for the blaze, the sooner Terry Blake would get it out of his thick head Jex Ivers had anything to do with it.

Eli went to the station and opened the front doors to see it was dark, just as he expected it to be on Saturday. Tibby had the overnight shift, and Yolanda West was taking the swing shift, leaving Eli to take care of things in town until two that afternoon.

While Eli had Mayor Leland with him, he planned to push the man for a date when he could get approval from the City Council to hire another officer. Tibby was scheduled to be out on paternity leave for a month after Shannon had the baby, and it would be a lot of work for the three other cops to carry the load.

In his office, Eli went through his email to find nothing of importance until he scrolled to an alert regarding Bernard Overman. Eli sat closer to the computer, unwilling to admit he needed to get his eyes checked, and spread his fingers on the screen to make the alert larger.

District Attorney Sets New Trial Date for Accused Human Trafficker and Kidnapper

Newark District Attorney, Antonio Sharpe, was granted a Motion for a New Trial in the case of New Jersey vs. Bernard Overman. Overman was tried for attempted human trafficking, kidnapping, sexual assault, and various other charges stemming from his attempt at purchasing a minor child over the internet from an undercover sting operation conducted in Newark in 2016.

Overman, 38, was sentenced to life in prison with no chance for parole, but the conviction was overturned in early 2018 due to allegations of entrapment in the human trafficking charges and suppression of exculpatory evidence to support Mr. Overman's claim he was in a consensual BDSM relationship with one of the key witnesses against him. The unnamed witness claimed he was being held against his will in Overman's residence, an allegation Overman vehemently denies.

The Appellate Court of the Third District overturned the conviction, and the defendant was released on bail. A new trial date has been set to begin on September 3,

2019. Defendant's counsel has not returned our request for comment.

Eli looked at his watch to see it was just after eight, so he took the chance and put in a call to Detective Dennis Cather who was listed on the paperwork associated with Jex's Order of Protection. The phone rang twice before it was answered. "Third Precinct Detectives Division, Ratajkowski speaking."

Eli didn't recognize the name, so he decided to punt. "Hello, this is the Chief of Police of Haven's Point, Delaware. I'm trying to track down a detective named Dennis Cather. Is he, perchance, available?"

"Hang on," Eli heard before the muzak began playing over the line. After thirty-seconds, he heard, "Cather."

Eli smiled at the abrupt tone of the man's voice. It was just as he remembered. "Denny, it's Eli, Eli Moore. We worked together back when we were both unis. You got stuck with me for my rookie year," Eli reminded, sorry he hadn't kept up with the cop. He'd been a good guy.

"I'll be damned, Moore. It's good to hear from ya, man. Where the hell did you land?" Cather asked.

The two men caught up about the missed time, and finally, Eli got to what he wanted to discuss. "You still involved in the Overman case?"

"Hey, I gotta go out on a call, Eli. Here's my cell number, so give me a call you when you've got time. Betsy and the girls are fine, as a matter of fact. They're in high school now, but I'm sure they'd love to get together soon, so gimme a call," Denny stated abruptly. He quickly rattled off a number and hung up the phone. Eli's gut churned as thoughts raced through his head, none of which he liked very much.

The chief sent a text to the number, "Can't wait to hear from you." He rose from his desk, having devoured the delicious sandwich and poured himself a cup of coffee before he decided to get out of the station to check things around town.

He filled a travel mug and went out to his SUV, placing his phone in the holder on the dash before he started the vehicle. He had his portable on the console next to him, and he decided to take a ride out by the beach, specifically by The Wickersham Inn, to check on Hilda and Jex since no one was answering the phone.

When he slowly drove by, Eli could see Jex was in the two-car garage to the left side of the house. There was a large machine shed on the right of the house Eli remembered seeing closed up all of the time. Mrs. Wickersham had been an avid gardener before her fall, so Eli imagined she hadn't sold any of her tools, which was good because now she had Jex to help her.

He checked the clock to see it was only nine-thirty, giving him an hour before he needed to be at the diner, so he pulled up the shaded driveway of the Inn and parked in front of the garage. He felt more nervous than he had the night before their dinner plans were totally spoiled by Terry Blake showing up. That morning, he needed to talk to Jex about the trial date, a much more important topic than whether the two of them should be dating.

He got out of the SUV and straightened his shirt and jeans, trying to look his best. Eli didn't carry a gun usually, but he had one in the Tahoe if he needed it. Haven's Point was hardly the wild west, so he didn't really need to be armed, but he did like to be safe.

Eli walked over and stepped into the garage through the open door, taking in the gorgeous sight of Jex Ivers bent over a lounge chair with a paintbrush. The music in the garage was loud, and Jex was focused on his task such that when Eli touched his shoulder, the man fell on his ass, green paint splattering on his arms and face.

Eli held the laugh, though seeing Jex scrambling like a fawn on ice was pretty cute. The top cop walked over to the radio on a workbench and turned down the volume before he walked back to offer his hand to help Jex to his feet. "Sorry to scare you," Eli offered with a smirk.

Jex stood and reached for a bucket of rags to wipe his hands and arm. "I seriously doubt it, Chief. What can I do for you?"

"I walked back into my kitchen last night after I got rid of my uninvited guest, ready for a delicious dinner with a handsome man. Do you know what I found when I got there?" Eli asked, not holding the sarcasm.

Jex's face blushed a little, which brought Eli's gaze to the green splatters amidst the cute freckles. "Your boyfriend from the living room?" Jex responded, equally sarcastic. *This one's sassy,* Eli thought to himself, loving the idea of sparring with the man every day.

"As a matter of fact, that man isn't, nor has he ever been, my boyfriend, regardless of how many buckets of chicken he shows up with at my front door. He's the Deputy Sheriff for Sussex County, and he believes he and I should be in a relationship. I've told him countless times I'm not interested in him or the damn chicken, but he doesn't get it when I state it outright to him because he thinks himself god's gift to gay men on the shore."

"I happen to believe you hold that title, and I'm wondering why you didn't stay so I could convince you of it?" Eli asked as he picked up a rag and dabbed at the green specks on Jex's cheeks, seeing the flush he was coming to love as it made its ascent from the column of his slender neck to his beautiful face. It was all Eli could do not to kiss him, but he didn't have the all-clear yet. He was a gentleman, after all, and a gentleman waited until he received permission.

Jex stepped away from Eli's reach and walked to a workbench where a bottle of water was dripping on the wooden top, making a mark. "Look, Chief Moore, I think we came to the wrong conclusion when we decided to date. I'm not ready, for obvious reasons, and I don't want to get in the way of someone who might be perfect for you by giving you a false impression."

"Last night when I got to your place, I'd already made up my mind to tell you I thought it was a bad idea for the two of us to pursue anything romantically. Your friend just gave me the perfect reminder that I was right."

"Now, thank you for coming by, and if you let me know when you're finished with Mrs. Wickersham's dishes, I can pick them up from your back porch. If you'll excuse me, I need to get busy painting this furniture, so it's dry enough to put out for guests. Thanks again," Jex stated flatly, a tone Eli hated hearing.

Eli Moore wasn't one to give up easily, not when he found something he wanted, and he wanted Jex Ivers for a hell of a lot more than a friend. "Overman's trial date has been set. September 3. I called Denny Cather this morning, but he told me he'd get back to me."

"That means Overman has a little over three months to kill you before the D.A. has to drop the charges because there's nobody left to testify against him. I'm not going to let him touch a hair on your head, Jex. You were attracted to me, you said so. What changed?" Eli asked.

Much to his surprise, Jex whipped off the t-shirt he was wearing and held out his arms, not covering his body. Eli was shocked momentarily to see the handsome man's pale skin was marked with scars, an especially ugly one over his heart. It was a lowercase 's,' and it made the bile climb from Eli's gut before he got himself together.

"This is why you'll never be attracted to me, Eli. I'm not worthy of someone as beautiful as you. We were both kidding ourselves we could be more, so I'd rather skip the whole thing where you pretend how I look doesn't matter when we both know it really does," Jex whispered as a tear rolled down his cheek.

Eli couldn't stand still any longer. He crossed the space and kissed Jex's cheeks before he held him in his arms. "Sorry. Too late. I'm already in love with you, and I'm not letting you go." Eli felt the tears in his own eyes, but he fought them because Jex needed him to be strong right then. There would be time for his tears later.

After a few minutes of the two of them rocking together, Eli's arms wrapped around his love's back and felt more of the marks on the soft flesh. They seared images into his mind of how they found their way onto Jex's skin, even though Eli hadn't actually seen them. If he ever got near Bernie Overman, there wouldn't be a need to spend more of the State's money to keep the monster locked up. Eli would happily rip the man in half with his bare hands.

The chief reached for a clean rag and pulled a few inches away from Jex, drying his tears in hopes they would stop one day. Eli didn't know when or if it was even possible for the beautiful, young redhead to be whole and happy again, but he was prepared to do whatever it took to make sure the man felt safe with him. "I'm sorry that shit happened to you, Jex. You didn't deserve any of it, and I'll do anything I can to ensure it never happens again."

"Where's Mrs. Wickersham?" Eli asked as he picked up the t-shirt from the floor of the garage and slid it over Jex's head, helping him find the armholes before gently pulling it down his slender body. Once it was settled, Eli reached up and pushed a stray strand of hair behind his ear and leaned forward, kissing Jex's forehead.

"She's out with the bees," Jex offered as he stood in front of Eli, not touching him, but not pulling away from his touch.

"Bees? Oh, shit, I forgot about that. She has bees," Eli recalled from his teen years. The old woman threatened the kids in the neighborhood to stay away from the bees, and she put up a fence to keep them out so they couldn't steal the honey. She made a point of telling Chief Moore, Senior, that if any of the hoodlums broke into her hives, she would prosecute them to the fullest extent of the law. Eli's dad put the fear of god in the town kids that summer to ensure it didn't happen.

Looking back, it seemed silly to Eli that the woman was adamant no one bother the bees, but then again, it was the woman's personal property. He didn't think anyone even knew the bees were still there, so it was for the best not to mention them around town.

Mrs. Wickersham wasn't wholly unknown around town, but she did mostly stay to herself. Eli couldn't call her a recluse, but she was one of the less active members of the community, even before she broke her hip.

Eli guessed everyone had their reasons for isolating themselves...Mrs. Wickersham because of the loss of her son and abandonment by her husband; Jex because of the nightmare he'd endured at the hands of a mad man; Eli's father because he couldn't face the memories in Haven's Point of losing the love of his life. Everybody had a reason, and it was for the best to respect it and move along.

"Yeah, but maybe don't mention I said anything about them. Mrs. Wickersham's very protective of the hives, so I probably shouldn't have brought anything up. So, uh, what now?" Jex asked.

Eli grinned. "You owe me a date. I tasted the meatloaf this morning, and it was damn good. Can we try it again tonight? No interruptions this time. We can heat up leftovers."

Jex chuckled and wrapped his arms around Eli's waist, which felt damn good to the cop. "Okay. What time?"

"Five. I also find myself with a bucket of chicken if you're interested," Eli told him, seeing the big grin on Jex's face.

"Yeah, maybe not the chicken." Both men laughed and embraced before Eli went back to his SUV. He waved to Jex before he pulled around the circle driveway and out to Hopkins Lane to get back to town. Eli was thrilled to have a take-two on a first date. He was going to make damn sure it went a lot better than their *first*, first date.

VIII

Jex finished painting the furniture and placed it behind the house on the patio to dry in the sunshine. He walked back through the gardens to see Mrs. Wickersham was dressed head-to-toe in a beekeeper's costume with the netted hat under her arm and a small jar of honey in one hand with a wooden cane in the other.

Jex walked out to her, taking the hat and jar before offering his arm for support. "How are your bees?" he asked.

"They are very happy for spring, having weathered the winter quite well. The gardens look lovely, Jex. You've done a good job out there. One of these days I'll have to introduce you to the bees. I think they'd quite fancy you. They are very good at keeping secrets, you know."

"Did I see a police car pull up the driveway?" Mrs. Wickersham asked.

Jex chuckled at the idea of her talking to the bees. She was a little on the quirky side, but she was indeed a lovely woman. He cleared his throat and smiled down at her. "It was Eli. We had a misunderstanding last night, and I left his home rather abruptly, I'm afraid. Seems the deputy sheriff has a crush on him and won't take no for an answer. I thought they were a couple, and Eli was trying to cheat on him with me, but I was mistaken."

"I hope I didn't wake you when I came in so late. I sat on the beach for hours trying to figure out what went wrong, but it turns out it was a silly mistake," Jex explained.

Jex had sat on the beach with a blanket until well after midnight, relieved to see Mrs. Wickersham's room was dark when he finally locked up the house. Jex was beyond grateful she wasn't waiting for him when he finally came inside because he didn't want to explain the events of the night to her. Overreaction wasn't attractive on anyone, and it felt particularly ugly on Jex. Jealousy wasn't a flattering color either, as he'd recognized the previous night while he stared out at the silver shimmer of the moon's glow casting over the water.

In his final attempt to push Eli away, he'd shown his scars and waited for the rejection he expected, but it didn't come. Acceptance and empathy...dare he say love?...flowed from Eli's arms into Jex's body, and it was nothing like Jex had ever imagined.

Mrs. Wickersham gave a gentle squeeze to Jex's forearm. "I'm glad to hear it. Are you going out again?" the spry little woman asked.

Jex felt his face flush. "Tonight. We're having leftovers," he explained.

Mrs. Wickersham offered a ringing laugh he didn't expect from someone so reserved as the woman seemed to be. "That's wonderful, Michael," she told him as they went into the house. Jex chose not to correct her. She was in her late sixties, and she was allowed to slip every once in a while.

Jex knocked on the back door of the small beach house, seeing Eli coming toward him with a phone to his ear. Jex had brought a cherry crisp he'd made that afternoon with Mrs. Wickersham's help. She had a jar of cherries she'd purchased from a fruit farmer outside of town the last time Mrs. Wickersham and Mrs. Somerset spent a day together. The woman suggested Jex use the cherries to make a crisp because all men loved a crisp. He hoped she was right.

The chief opened the screen door and took Jex's hand. "You need me to come out, Gerry?" he asked as he led Jex into the house and stood in the kitchen, holding his hand. The gorgeous man was wearing jeans and a short-sleeved, button-up shirt and no shoes. His hair was damp, likely from the shower, and he smelled incredible.

Jex put the crisp down on the counter and stared at Eli as the man continued to stare at him while listening to the conversation on the phone. Finally, Eli exhaled. "Well, it explains why he didn't show up today for our meeting. I'm glad we got the cause of the fire settled. I'll call you in the morning to meet. You say he was alone and on his way home? Do we know from where?" Eli asked the caller.

Jex looked into the man's gorgeous blue eyes and believed he saw his future, but that was ridiculous. He'd read too many stories as a wide-eyed teen about love and romance. Happily-ever-after's were never guaranteed. He knew better than to believe in a fairy tale.

"Thanks, Gerry. Be safe," Eli stated before he ended the call and placed his phone on the counter.

"Sorry about that. Seems the mayor had a car accident last night and passed away. That was the Sussex County Sheriff, Gerry Cummings. His deputies found the car outside town on the way to the mayor's big house off Route Nine."

"It was his parents' place, and he inherited it when his mother passed about ten years ago. He's a real estate developer and a real asshole a lot of the time, but he didn't deserve to die by himself," Eli offered.

"Did the accident kill him?" Jex asked, not a fan of talking about death since he knew there was a price on his head and the fact that Bernie had threatened to kill him many times over the years he was held hostage by the horrible man.

"Gerry said the car went off the road and hit a tree, deploying the airbag, but it didn't seem like it did much damage. The coroner thinks it might have been a heart attack but hell, he was only in his mid-forties. That scares the fuck out of me if I think about it too much because I'm already thirty-eight. Shit, how old are you, Jex?" Eli asked with a look of worry on his face that made Jex want to laugh.

"Twenty," he offered without looking up.

"What?!" Eli gulped.

Jex couldn't hold the laugh any longer. "I'm twenty-five, Eli, and I'll be twenty-six later in the year. You're not robbing the cradle."

Eli grabbed him and hugged him. "I almost am, but I don't give a shit. If a hot young guy like you is interested in an old fart like me, I'll take it," Eli teased. They both laughed and worked together to heat their interrupted dinner from the previous night.

They sat out on the small back deck of Eli's home and ate the meatloaf, potatoes, and even the salad. After they finished the food and washed the dishes, Eli asked, "Wanna take a walk down the beach to settle our dinner before we have dessert? I have many questions for you, Mr. Ivers."

Jex froze and turned to see the handsome policeman smiling at him. "No worries. I'll start. Favorite color?"

"Blue like the ocean," Jex offered, referring to the striking blue color of Eli's eyes. "Yours?"

"Green like the grass," Eli replied with a wink.

"Favorite movie from when you were a kid?" Eli asked as they washed the dishes.

"_Inspector Gadget_. He was an idiot, but Penny and Brain made him look so smart. You?"

"God, that was so long ago. Uh, _The Adventures of Milo and Otis_. Come on, dog and cat getting lost and finding their way home together? It's the ultimate buddy movie," Eli joked as the two argued while walking down the beach, both having left their shoes on the patio.

There were twelve years between them. Jex didn't know what those twelve years meant to Eli, but he knew his time had been filled with ups and downs. The last ten had been the hardest of his life, but he was still alive, so that was something.

Jex had never really had friends since he was young and living in Newark with his mother. Even back then, they sort of stayed to themselves, which was okay with Jex. He and his mother depended on each other, and after he lost her and went into foster care, he never trusted anyone enough to become more than an acquaintance. It was sort of a dog eat dog world back then. As an adult on his own, if he were going to learn to trust someone he believed would have his back, Eli Moore seemed like the perfect candidate.

After their walk on the beach and gorging themselves on the cherry crisp, Eli built a small fire in the firepit on the back deck of his house and grabbed blankets for the two of them to snuggle under while sharing the glider. He filled their wine glasses with the last of the merlot they'd enjoyed with dinner so they could continue with their game of what had to be *fifty* questions by then. Jex noticed the man was careful to avoid any queries concerning his time with Overman, and he appreciated it.

"So, you were a cop in Newark when I was growing up there? Why'd you leave?" Jex asked as he sipped his wine.

"My mom had a brain aneurysm and died while I was working there for the police department, so I came back to Haven's Point to be here for my dad. I knew he'd miss her a lot, and I couldn't imagine him being alone. It wasn't a hard choice, really. I didn't hate living in Newark, but I loved my pop, and I made the decision to move home and work for the force here. Working for Glenn Moore was a trip back then," Eli joked as he placed his empty wine glass on a side table before pulling Jex closer and taking his hand under the blankets. Jex felt the surge of energy all the way up his arm when Eli touched his hand and intertwined their fingers.

"Was he the chief of police when Mrs. Wickersham's son died?" Jex asked, curious about any information regarding the mysterious family.

"Uh...yeah, he was. Hell, Michael was a few years younger than me, I guess when it happened. I was away at college by then, but I remember Pop telling me about it. He was fourteen or fifteen at the time if I remember correctly. He shot himself in the living room of the house. Pop said it was an awful mess."

"The whole town came by with food and flowers, offering condolences and asking when the service would take place because everyone wanted to support the family. They were well-known because Neil grew up here, but I remember Mom saying it was weird that the family decided to have a private ceremony, just the two Wickersham's and the Methodist minister back then. After the service, Neil Wickersham packed up all his stuff and took off, somehow. They only had one car, and he left it with her."

"Talk around town was that he was having an affair with his secretary, and she gave him a ride after Hilda made it known she wanted him out. His secretary, Sue Ann Messner, was also married with a family and lived in town. She swore she had no knowledge of where he went, and nobody's ever heard from him again, as far as I know."

"I forgot to ask, where'd you get those clothes?" Eli asked. He moved his left arm from under the blanket and wrapped it around Jex's shoulders while he grabbed his hand with the right.

Jex chuckled. "They were his, as a matter of fact. Mrs. Wickersham said they were in this cedar-lined closet in her bedroom. I've never seen it because I don't go into her rooms...well, room because I'm going to be moving into her sitting room while we have guests, but I'd love to see the inside of that closet. It sounds like a time capsule," Jex speculated.

He saw Eli's face morph into a question, but when Jex heard a clock chiming inside the house, he knew he needed to go back to the Inn. He had a full day of moving furniture and freshening the studio apartment the next day, along with helping Mrs. Wickersham with the new cushions for the patio and beach furniture.

They only had a few days before the first guests would arrive, and Jex was anxious to see how it would be to act as host, cook, housekeeper, and Mrs. Wickersham's Man Friday. He felt a lot of pressure because he'd never done anything like it before, but the old woman seemed quite confident he could handle it.

"I'm afraid I need to get home. I had a nice time with you tonight," Jex told Eli as he started to rise from the glider.

Eli pulled him down and wrapped both arms around Jex, giving him a kiss on the cheek. "Are you busy tomorrow night? I'm driving up to Dover to see Lena and talk to her about what happened at the diner, and there's this great Chinese place in Georgetown on the way home. If you're free, I can stop and pick up some food for us to share after I get back," Eli requested.

"I'd like that as well. I'm moving from the attic apartment into the sitting room next to Mrs. Wickersham's bedroom tomorrow so I can get the room ready for guests, but I'm free in the evening. Chinese sounds good," Jex replied.

"How about I bring over food for the three of us? After we eat, you and I can take another walk on the beach if you'd be willing. Mrs. Wickersham might get jealous if I monopolize all of your time.

Maybe if we include her, she'll allow me to see you more?" Eli proposed.

Jex laughed. "You're covering all the bases, aren't you? She doesn't really have a say over who I see, but I appreciate it you'd consider her feelings."

Eli gently placed his hands on either side of Jex's face. "When it comes to you, Jex, I want to make sure I've covered all the bases. You're too precious to leave anything to chance," Eli whispered before his lips touched Jex's in a soft kiss.

It wasn't aggressive or sloppy. It was just a brush of Eli's lips before making purchase, not rushing, but seeming to savor the sensation of flesh on flesh. Jex felt his knees grow weak, but before he could slide his tongue over Eli's lips to deepen the kiss, the top cop broke away and offered a crooked grin.

"Come on. Let me walk you home. My mother would be disappointed if I didn't at least pretend to be a gentleman," Eli joked as he picked up the picnic basket filled with clean dishes and Jex's sneakers, taking his love's right hand to guide him down the stairs to the cool sand of the beach. They walked the distance to the Inn, taking turns squeezing each other's hands as if they couldn't believe the night was real.

When they arrived at the stairs to Mrs. Wickersham's back patio, Eli placed the basket and the sneakers on a step and took both of Jex's hands. "Favorite night?" Eli asked as Jex stood on the stairstep above the sand.

Jex felt his face heat, but he couldn't lie. "Tonight."

Eli stepped forward and wrapped Jex's arms around his shoulders. "Mine, too." With that, he gently kissed Jex lips a few times before he pulled away, kissing the tops of Jex's hands, and motioning for his love to climb the stairs.

When Jex got to the top of the landing and turned to see Eli jogging down the beach, he knew beyond a shadow of a doubt, he'd fallen totally and irrevocably in love with the police chief. He wasn't going to stew on it. He was just going to allow the warm feelings to take him away from everything. It was a glorious first.

IX

Eli woke at five-thirty on Monday morning and dressed for a run. It was the middle of May, and Haven's Point was teeming with tourists, so he started his days earlier than usual. The summer season was well underway, and Eli was happy to say he and Jex had been making progress as a couple.

They'd had a few heavy make-out sessions after the two of them made dinner at Eli's house, and saying goodbye at the end of the night was beyond difficult. Things seemed to be settling between them, and the chief had never been happier.

Mrs. Wickersham had invited Eli to join them for evening cocktails a few times over the past few weeks, and before the top cop knew it, he was part of Haven's Point's summer social scene and local welcoming committee. He couldn't lie and say he hated it, especially when he watched Jex in his element.

The man had taken to the work of running the Inn like a duck to water, and Eli could see the guests enjoyed themselves during their stays. Many of the guests had tried to schedule an additional visit for later in the summer, only to be told they were completely booked. Almost all of them asked to be put on a waiting list in the event of a cancellation, and Eli could see Mrs. Wickersham was quite thrilled her back taxes would be covered before the end of the first week of June.

"Well, well. I guess we're ready to go?" Eli heard, looking to his left to see Jex strolling up the stairs to Eli's deck.

Eli stood from the chair where he'd been waiting and hurried down the stairs, kicking off his flip flops because he and Jex usually ran barefoot on the sand. They enjoyed their morning runs, and on Mondays and Tuesdays, Jex stuck around, and the two men shared breakfast.

Those mornings were when Jex and Mrs. Wickersham allowed each other private time because they spent the rest of the week joined at the hip. Eli could tell a little went a long way when one spent time with a very demanding, set-in-her-ways Mrs. Wickersham. Jex seemed to enjoy hanging out with Eli in the early mornings, and heaven knew Eli loved the time as well.

After a moment's thought, Eli had an idea for an alternative to running that morning. "Actually, we're going to change it up this morning. Let's go inside," Eli suggested, hoping and praying they could get over a hurdle he very much wanted to cross.

Jex had finally gotten comfortable with taking off his shirt so they could have physical contact, but those bottoms seemed firmly secured. Eli hoped maybe they could come off that morning, but if the man objected, Eli would back off and just enjoy whatever kind of contact his love preferred.

"Everything okay?" Jex asked as he followed Eli up the stairs. The two men stepped onto Eli's deck and walked over to the faucet to rinse their feet before they went into the kitchen where the chief had two towels waiting for them.

"You want some coffee or orange juice?" Eli asked as he grabbed two mugs from the shelf over the toaster.

"Uh, sure. Orange juice is fine. I, uh, is something wrong? Did I do something wrong?" Jex asked, nerves filling his voice before Eli could assuage them.

Eli poured himself a cup of coffee, filling Jex's mug with orange juice before placing the cups on the kitchen table and pulling out chairs for them to take their seats. "Everything is more than okay, Jex. I was hoping we could discuss your boundaries this morning. I mean, you've got a little time before you need to go back to the Inn, and I don't have to be at the office before seven. I have a meeting with Tom Lahey, the interim mayor, regarding hiring another officer, but that's not until eleven."

"I don't mean to pressure you, Jex, and if you never want to do more than what we've done so far, I'll be fine with it. I'd just like a little guidance regarding where you see us going," Eli broached, hating the fact that he'd been the one to ask that *where are we going* question at the ungodly hour of six o'clock in the morning.

Eli was falling in love with Jex Ivers more every day, and he was worried maybe he was the only one in the relationship. He'd told Jex he was in love with him, but the man never responded one way or the other. Eli would like to say he was a patient man, and if the other man never fell in love with him, it would have to be fine, but how could anyone ever prepare to have their heart crushed?

Eli knew Jex had a lot of issues from his past to overcome. As far as Eli knew, the road to love was never smooth. If only the chief could have some indication of whether he was going to be waiting in the wings for decades until the man loved him back, maybe he could prepare his heart for a long, long journey? It was time to find out before he lost his fucking mind.

Eli saw Jex duck his eyes as the color climbed his throat. It seemed as if the top cop had blown it before they ever started the discussion. "It's okay, and I'm sorry if I pushed you..."

What Eli didn't expect was for the gorgeous man to stand from the table, pull back the chair Eli occupied, and slide onto his lap. Jex pulled off the t-shirt he'd been wearing and removed the elastic from his long hair, fastening the band around his wrist.

Those green eyes captivated Eli as he waited for the man to make the next move. "I can't promise you I'll ever be able to have a normal sexual relationship, Eli. Hell, I don't even know what a normal relationship means, but I want us to have something more than just kissing. I want more," Jex whispered as he kissed Eli's lips with a newly unveiled fervor, wrapping his hands in Eli's short hair and having his way with the cop's mouth.

Eli would have loved to put the man on the kitchen table and rip off his pants to have a taste of the cock he'd felt harden against his own more than once, but Jex deserved more than uncontrollable manhandling.

At that moment, Eli was sure the lovely man in his lap would go along with anything he asked, but that would be treating him the same as Bernie Overman had done in the past. It would be as if Jex did what he believed Eli expected him to do as if he didn't have a choice of whether he wanted to continue or his choice was irrelevant in the first place. That was the last thing on Eli's mind.

As the kiss deepened, Eli knew he had to take a breath, so he pulled away and looked at the gorgeous man in front of him to see if he was panicked yet. "You okay? We can slow things down if you want," Eli whispered as he kissed Jex's neck, inhaling the intoxicating scent that drove Eli nearly insane.

Jex offered a groan as he pushed his hard dick into Eli's. The sensation had the chief about ready to come, and they hadn't ever brought each other to climax, but damn if Eli didn't want it. He placed his hands on Jex's hips to stop him. "I don't want us to do anything you don't want, Jex. I want you to set the pace, so tell me what you want," Eli pleaded.

"I want us to go to your room to see if we can go from just making out to making love. What do you say?" Jex asked as he stood from Eli's lap and took his hand, tugging gently.

"Oh, god, yes," Eli growled as he followed his love down the hallway to his bedroom, which was a spot they'd never tried, always settling on the glider on the back deck or the couch in the small front room.

When Eli had Jex on the bed, facing each other, he took a deep breath to calm himself because if he got too far ahead of things, Eli knew he'd blow prematurely. That was the last thing Eli wanted to do that morning. He pulled the man closer to his body and kissed him again, allowing Jex to take the lead.

Eli's old sleeveless t-shirt came off between the intoxicating kisses before Jex devoured his mouth, and when their bare flesh touched, Eli couldn't help but groan at the delicious feeling of having Jex on top of him. When the gorgeous man sat up, his ass firmly planted atop Eli's erection, the cop nearly creamed his shorts. He placed his hands on Jex's hips to keep him from moving. "Are you okay?"

Jex seemed to study his face before his own flushed. "I'm ready to take off my pants. I mean, if you're ready to take off yours, then, uh..."

Eli gently moved Jex to a kneeling position so he could quickly remove his shorts and boxers. Once he was naked, he latched his hands behind his head and looked up at the stunning beauty above him. "Before you take off your pants, I want you to be certain it's what you want to do, Jex."

"We can do anything or nothing, but I want you to know I'm yours. You are totally in control of this relationship, and I really hope it's a relationship," Eli whispered, trying not to startle the man he loved and wanted to protect more than anything.

Eli felt the tears spring into his eyes, but he wasn't about to stop talking. There was a future there, he was sure, and he wasn't going to back away because it seemed too hard. All the good things were hard; that was what made them worth it.

"I want more, Eli, I seriously do. Thing is, I might not be able to..."

"That's okay, baby. I'm as happy bottoming as I am topping, and if it's just not something you ever want to do, we don't have to even try. You might not believe it, but I'm so fucking happy just holding you. If we get a little skin-to-skin contact, well, I won't hate it."

"There are a lot of things more important in life than sex, and I'm not just spouting clichés to make you believe we're on the same page before I pounce on you. To me, emotional intimacy is more important than the physical sex act, and there are many, many ways to make love, most of which don't involve intercourse."

"I told you I love you, and I mean it, so we go as far as you're comfortable going, okay? I want you to be mine, whatever that means to you. I'm already yours if you want me," Eli explained, hoping he wasn't putting too much pressure on Jex.

When the gorgeous man took off his shorts and briefs, Eli saw, felt, and smelled Jex's desire, which made his heart flutter in his chest unlike he'd ever felt in his life. When Eli pulled Jex down so he could relax on top of the chief, it was like a pressure valve had been released, and they had a new footing in their relationship. It was the best thing that had happened to Eli in quite a long time.

The two men kissed, caressed, and rubbed their bodies together until they found bliss in unison using the other's body for friction. After they both caught their breath, the two of them relaxed on the sticky sheets, Jex's head on Eli's chest with the cop's arms securely wrapped around his body. "You feeling okay? Was it too much?"

"Oh, Chief, I feel far better than okay. I feel like I've had my soul washed, and it's all clean again like it was when I was a little boy if that even makes sense. All these years, I felt like I've been covered with the smell of rotting garbage I couldn't wash away."

"When I first got away from Bernie and was staying in the safe house, I'd use up all of the hot water trying to get the stench off my skin. Sometimes, I'd come out of the shower, having scrubbed my skin so hard I was bleeding. It took a long time for me to realize that smell was my soul rotting from the inside, not anything on the outside."

"Then, you came along, and you took the time to get to know me. You made an effort to ask me about myself, which nobody has done since I lost Molly. You showed me that you actually care what happens to me, and it touched my soul and began to heal it."

"Just now, you showed me there is more to sex than pain. There's love and joy and kindness, and I never imagined I'd feel any of it, but you showed it to me," Jex told Eli before he snuggled closer and settled his head on Eli's chest, his soft breath washing over Eli's skin like a gentle ocean wave.

The tears rolled down his temples as Eli gently brushed the soft red strands that had fanned out over his pecs. He didn't believe he'd ever heard anything so beautiful said to him before in his life. It made him that much more determined to keep the exquisite creature in his arms safe at all costs. The man was perfect for Eli, and he'd work damn hard to be worthy of Jex.

"Chief, what's your location?" Eli heard over the radio as he sat at his desk on the Friday before Memorial Day. Haven's Point township had become a hotbed of activity with the long, holiday weekend. The additional tourists presented a problem since they were shorthanded at the station, but the solution wasn't much to Eli's liking either. Terry Blake was assisting with patrolling the town since Tibby's wife had their baby, and he went on paternity leave.

The good news was the City Council had approved the hiring of another patrol officer. The bad news was that Terry Blake wanted to apply, and Eli was pushing back against it with everything inside him. "I'm at the station. I'm getting ready to drive out to do the beach patrol. Is there a problem?" Eli asked Terry Blake.

"I'm heading out to The Wickersham Inn to talk with your boyfriend about Lena's fire. I talked to the Fire Marshall last week, and he said it was reasonable that the wiring could have been tampered with because it's worked fine all these years without a fire. Lena said that kid had fixed the breaker the last time it tripped, so he was the last person to touch it. I'd say it's worth a conversation, and I'm sure you'd agree if you weren't too close to this situation to be objective. I'll report in when I've finished. Blake out," Deputy Blake reported.

Just as Eli was about to call the asshat back, his cell rang with an unknown number. He tossed the radio on the desk and answered his phone. "Moore."

"Hey, Rookie, it's me, Cather. Sorry for not calling you sooner, but I've been busy. What's your interest in the Overman case? Where'd you even hear about it?" Detective Dennis Cather asked.

Something in Eli's subconscious sounded an alarm in his mind, so he decided to hedge a bit. "Uh, I was doing a search on a case in Sussex County that's gone cold so I hit NCIC to see if there were any related cases in the country that could be similar to my cold case," he lied.

The other end was silent for a moment before Cather cleared his throat. "Oh, I'm sorry to hear that. I've sort of been looking for someone, and I thought maybe she asked you to check in with me."

"She's sort of in the wind right now, and I need her to contact me. The trial date's been set for the end of summer, and I wanted to tell Molly...my witness...to meet me somewhere. She still has a lot of people hunting for her, so I wanted to find a neutral location to meet in secret," Cather explained.

Eli wasn't sure if Denny was honest, and there was something else going on with the Overman case, but he suspected Denny was testing him to see what he knew. What Eli didn't know was if it was a good omen or a red flag.

The two men made small talk for a few minutes as Eli paced the sidewalk in front of the station after locking up because as soon as he finished the call, he was going out to Wickersham Inn to deal with Terry Blake, once and for all.

Just before Eli was about to sign off, Cather said, "I've got some shit going down at the department in Newark, and I can't take one step to jeopardize the victim in my case because I don't know who the fuck to trust anymore. If I tell anyone in the department about it, I worry my witness would have more than just the suspect looking for her."

"I owe this person every protection I can offer because they were willing to do everything they could to put that bastard behind bars, only for some fuckhead to annihilate the prosecutor's case by stupidity...or malicious intent. I wish to fuck you were still on the job, Rookie. This kid deserves a Pitbull like you to watch out for her."

"I was able to call because we've got the girls away for a long weekend. The next time we're going away is the Fourth of July, so I'll call to wish you happy holidays then. Be safe, man," Cather offered before the line went dead.

Eli gleaned that his friend was as sharp as Eli always knew him to be, and it was his way of letting the chief know Jex was still in danger. Eli already had an inkling things were touch and go based on the previous, short conversation he'd had with Cather several weeks ago, so at least he had confirmation.

With Jex's safety on his mind, Eli hopped into his SUV and started for Hopkins Lane to see what the fuck was up with Terry Blake. The man needed to get a hold on himself before Eli had to take the problem to Gerry Cummings.

Eli didn't want to get the sheriff involved in his personal life by telling Cummings that Blake's advances were unwanted and bordering on a harassment lawsuit. However, he'd embarrass himself if it was necessary by filing a harassment case to get Terry to back the fuck off and leave him alone.

Of course, that wasn't the way Eli's day would go, nor would he be happy at the end of it.

X

"How are we doing, Mr. and Mrs. Manning?" Jex asked as he carried a basket on his arm to cater to the guests. He was equipped with frozen hand towels, sunscreen, and small bottles of water to offer to the couples in the four romantic set-ups on the beach, each consisting of two loungers, a side table, a large umbrella for shade, and a bamboo mat for catching some sun.

Jex was wearing a pair of jean shorts that Mrs. Wickersham had tailored for him with a cuff he loved. She'd made them from a pair of Mr. Wickersham's old dungarees. They were vintage, he could tell, and paired with the striped cabana shirt he wore over a tank top, it took him back in time to the old scrapbooks Mrs. Wickersham had from the early years when she'd first opened the Inn for the summers.

"Oh, Jex, we're doing just fine. I wouldn't mind water," Mrs. Manning requested. Jex didn't like to stereotype anyone, but Mrs. Manning reminded him of a real housewife with over-the-top hair, makeup, various surgical enhancements, and long fingernails that made him wonder how certain things were cleaned without pain. She did seem nice, unlike her husband.

Jex offered two of the cold bottles and placed them on the table between the couple, giving them a smile. "I'll bring your picnic basket out at twelve-thirty if that's okay," Jex asked, seeing a sheriff's patrol car pull around the driveway.

"That would be great, Jess. Can we sit over there under the shade to eat?" Mr. Manning asked.

"Of course, Mr. Manning. I'll set you up over there and let you know when it's ready," Jex responded without correcting the rude man addressing him with the wrong name. The guy seemed to be staring at Jex when the two of them were in the same space since the couple had arrived Wednesday morning.

It was unnerving, but they were guests at the Inn, so Jex didn't make a big deal out of it. Maybe he had one of those faces?

Jex walked down the beach to check on his other guests and offer water or a cold towel, unable to keep the smile off his face at how happy he was with his new job. In his mind, the people staying at the Inn were *his* guests, and he treated them like kings and queens.

Mrs. Wickersham seemed perfectly happy having Jex take the proverbial driver's seat when dealing with the guests, and he never wanted to let the old woman down. It gave him a rush he'd never felt in his life at seeing everyone enjoying themselves because of his doting on them.

After he walked their little slice of beach, Jex rinsed his feet under the spigot at the top of the stairs and slid on a pair of cheap Zorba thongs he'd bought at a discount store in town. He'd unearthed a bike from the garage and had the tires replaced at Dewey Zellner's garage on Oak Street, so he had wheels. Jex had never learned to drive a car, but he had learned to ride a bike, and his new mode of transportation gave him a wonderful sense of freedom.

Jex walked in through the back door to see the kitchen empty, so he followed the sounds of chatter into the parlor where Mrs. Wickersham was sitting with a handsome blond Jex recognized from the brief glimpse he'd seen at Eli's house the first time he went for dinner, and everything went to hell.

"Young man, I'm not sure what you're asking me," Jex heard Mrs. Wickersham address the deputy sheriff.

"It's not complicated, ma'am. I want to speak to your employee, Jex Ivers. There are several discrepancies regarding the man's behavior since he showed up in Haven's Point, and I want to get to the bottom of them."

"Will you tell me where I can find him, or whoever he really is. Until two years ago, Jex Ivers didn't exist," Jex heard, feeling his heart begin to pound in his chest.

"Who are you again?" Mrs. Wickersham asked as Jex backed away from the door and went into his bedroom that used to be the sitting room for the old lady.

He wasn't panicked because he was afraid he'd be caught having committed a crime. Jex was worried because the more people who knew he was in hiding and where he was, the more risk his life would be in. As he thought about it, he was sure it wouldn't just be him in danger.

He'd just met Eli Moore, and he had real love in his life for the first time since his mother died. Jex wasn't ready to lose it just yet. If Bernie Overman came around and threatened Jex's life, he'd give it to keep Eli safe, but this man, the deputy, had no business poking into Jex life. *Why does he care?*

There was a soft knock on his door, so Jex opened it to see Mrs. Wickersham with a gentle smile on her face. "I'll deal with the deputy. Help me in the kitchen. He's out on the beach looking for you, so we have some time. Tonight after the guests are settled, we need to talk, Jex. I suppose I need to know a little more information about your predicament before we lose control of the situation," the old woman suggested.

Jex looked at her, seeing a new side of the woman he never anticipated. "How do you know..."

Mrs. Wickersham touched his arm and offered a kind smile. "Dear, I don't know more than you've told me, but I'm a great study of human nature, and Deputy Blake has an ulterior motive for trying to accuse you of a crime to get you to leave town."

"I'm sure it has nothing to do with your past, so please, allow me to handle it. Let's keep this between us for right now." Jex had no argument, so he returned to the kitchen to prepare the picnic baskets while Mrs. Wickersham brought out the makings for tea.

Oh, Jex could have panicked, but he hadn't done anything to prompt a feeling of culpability, so he went about his regular business. He began putting together the beach picnic...barbecue ham with seared pineapple slices and sweet potato chips accompanied by a honey-mustard dip Jex and Mrs. Wickersham had worked out together after he suggested they try something new.

That was what Jex loved the most about living with Mrs. Wickersham. The two of them would sit in the kitchen or in the garden, and Mrs. Wickersham would ask Jex about things he loved to eat. They tried to create unique dishes, sometimes unsuccessfully, and there were nights even Eli laughed about the food. There were lunch meats and vegetables to make salads in the event of a fail, but those evenings were few and some of Jex's most favorite.

Once he had the picnic baskets filled for the day, he loaded the cart to take them to the beach for lunch, and after he passed them out, Jex returned to the house to find Mrs. Wickersham cleaning the dishes. "I'll get that," he offered as he stepped to the sink and pulled out her hands from the hot, soapy water.

He handed the old woman a towel and watched as she put away the honey jar...the one she saved for special guests. It was a little unsettling she brought out the special honey for everyone but him, but then again, she treated him like a member of her family, so how could he ever be ungrateful over something as silly as honey?

Jex was cleaning up the beach that evening before the sun made its exodus to allow the stars to come out and play. He'd stacked the loungers and tables near the house and covered them with a waxed tarp to keep them dry. The umbrellas were secured in a large barrel Jex found in the gardening shed next to the old freezer, which still puzzled him, and the bamboo mats were rolled and wrapped in a wax tarp of their own.

He was emptying the trash for the night when he saw the handsome Chief of Police walking up the beach toward him, still in uniform, which Jex found to be quite sexy. The man didn't carry a gun that Jex had ever seen, and something about the man's confidence sparked the fire inside Jex.

Eli walked up to him and offered a tender kiss. "How was your day?" Eli asked.

"It was great, as a matter of fact. The ham and pineapple sandwiches were a hit. Tomorrow, we have an order of seafood coming in, so I'm going to make fish and chips on the beach. Mrs. Wickersham has a large fryer she hasn't used in a while, so I'm going to get it out and check to see if it's in good shape. How about you? How was your day?" Jex asked as Eli took the trash bag and walked along with him to help clean up.

"I, uh, I spoke with Denny Cather this morning. In fact, I was on my way out here when he called. Did Deputy Blake come by? He was aggravating the piss out of me today, so I was coming out here to send him back to the Sheriff's Office, but I got tied up with an accident off Old Iron Bridge Road."

"Two idiots decided not to take turns on the single-lane bridge and both refused to back up to allow the other to pass. One guy in a big truck decided to push the Honda off the bridge, and they got into a fight. I had to call in Bellows to help me out with them. They're both in lockup for the weekend because they were both DUI. I love summer, but I don't love what it does to some folks."

"Was Blake here today?" Eli asked again as Jex picked up the smaller trash bag from inside the barrel and put it in the large, heavy-duty bag to put out by the curb on Monday morning.

Just as Jex was about to tell Eli that Blake had been by the Inn, Mrs. Wickersham came outside and down the stairs to the beach. "Jex, dear, come inside for dinner and bring the chief with you. I've made smothered pork chops and mashed potatoes. Come eat while it's still hot," the old lady demanded.

"Come on, you know she won't take no for an answer," Jex coaxed as he took Eli's hand and led him up the beach, noticing the man was barefoot, which made Jex smile.

"Where are your shoes and the rest of your cop stuff, Chief?" Jex teased.

Eli laughed at him. "I got my shoes, socks, and my belt off and couldn't wait to see you another minute. Come on, Smartass," the cop chuckled before flipping Eli over his shoulder and leaving the trash in the can at the bottom before carrying him up the stairs.

He put Jex down, both of them laughing as they rinsed their feet off the sand, Eli tickling Jex's foot to make him laugh harder. "Stop it, I'm ticklish," Jex gasped as he jerked away from Eli to reach for one of the towels on the table outside the door to the three-season room.

Once they dried off, they went inside only to find out that Mrs. Wickersham had set the table in the kitchen for the three of them. The other guests had gone out for dinner because the Inn only offered breakfast and a picnic lunch. The guests were on their own for their evening meal, but there were more places open for dinner now that the summer season had started.

Many of the restaurants in neighboring towns rented booths at the large food court near the beach, so there were lots of choices, and there were even three chefs from Dover who opened fancier restaurants for the summer. There was no shortage of food choices in Haven's Point.

The three sat down at the table and were digging into the food when they heard a commotion from the front porch. There was the sound of something being knocked over and breaking pottery, which brought Jex to his feet. They listened to the front door open. "You're an idiot." It sounded like Mrs. Manning.

"Stay here, babe," Eli ordered before he left the kitchen.

Mrs. Wickersham placed her knife and fork on the table and turned to Jex. "Did something happen today with Mr. Manning? He seemed agitated when he came into the house earlier. Did he give you any problems this afternoon? I've been watching him, and he stares at you more than he should. Do you know him?"

Jex thought about it, and it occurred to him the man did seem vaguely familiar, but he couldn't place where he might have met him or under what circumstance they could have crossed paths. Jex got up and went around to the front desk, flipping through the guest cards to see the one with the Manning's address, *13085 South Seventeenth Street, Newark, NJ.* Jex froze at an idea he hadn't considered prior to that moment.

"It can't be possible. My head was shaved. Nobody could recognize me," he whispered before he felt a gentle hand on his arm.

"Come back to the kitchen. I'll go see what happened," Mrs. Wickersham stated as she went around the desk and out onto the front porch.

Jex went to the kitchen and put the three plates on a baking sheet and into the oven to keep warm before he began clearing the table, having lost his appetite. He ran dishwater, reminding himself that he'd look into the cost of a dishwasher to save the two of them a lot of time and effort.

He heard footsteps and turned to see Mrs. Wickersham with a small smile on her face. "Your gentleman is quite something. Seems Mr. Manning had a bit too much whiskey tonight. Chief Moore is sitting with him on the porch because he probably can't maneuver the stairs to the second floor."

"Get into the cupboard and bring out the black enamel tin with the pretty pink oleander flowers painted on the front, will you, dear?" she asked as she put a kettle on the stove and turned on the burner.

Jex did as she requested, and when he returned, he saw her placing ice into two plastic bags. "What's that for?" Jex asked as he opened the lid to the canister and looked inside, seeing some sort of dried petals inside.

"Your Chief Moore just hit Mr. Manning in the mouth with his fist. I'm not sure what the man said to rile the chief's temper, but he's still on his keister on the porch. I'm just going to make Mr. Manning some tea that should sober him up so Mrs. Manning can take him home."

"They've decided not to spend the rest of the week, and I agree wholeheartedly. Will you please write a check to refund the Manning's' stay for tonight and tomorrow night? Go ahead and sign it, will you? I added you to the Inn's accounts at the bank when Trudy and I went to play Bridge last Tuesday."

"That reminds me, Jex, I'm having my friends over on Sunday afternoon for tea. Do you mind making yourself scarce?" Mrs. Wickersham asked.

She took the dried flowers and put them in a tea ball before she grabbed a coffee mug and filled it with hot water, placing the stainless ball inside to steep. "Grab a tray, dear," the old woman instructed.

Jex was still surprised by the news Eli had punched the man. The rest of her words went in one ear and out the other. Mrs.

Wickersham pushed him out of the way, grabbing the tray and the two compresses before she reached for the mug of hot liquid and placing it the dish as well. The old woman removed the tea ball and added a cube of sugar, stirring it around for a few seconds. She then turned to Jex and smiled.

"Put on a pair of shoes before you come out, Jex. Mr. Manning broke a pot when he drunkenly fell up the stairs. Subtract fifteen dollars from their refund to cover the cost of the plant and planter," she ordered before she took the tray and left the kitchen.

Jex ran into his room and slid into his flip flops before he went to the desk and pulled out the large checkbook, seeing new checks clipped into the brown, leather binder. There, under the name of the Inn and Mrs. Wickersham's was his, "Jex Ivers, Co-Proprietor." He was stunned.

He quickly calculated the refund, less the cost of the pot, and wrote the proper amount on the check, blowing on it before he tore it out and headed out to the porch. There, he saw Mr. Manning sitting on the porch swing holding an icepack against his lips between sips of the drink Mrs. Wickersham made for him.

Eli held the other icepack on his hand while he knelt on the porch and picked up the shards of pottery while Mrs. Wickersham swept off the dirt that had spilled when the pot broke. The green ivy that had been in the container was on the fern stand awaiting attention, and when Eli looked up to see Jex, he saw the man was worried.

They heard a sound on the stairs, so Eli looked at Mr. Manning. "Unless you'd like to explain to your wife what you were doing in a BDSM dungeon at the end of another man's leash, I'd suggest you keep your mouth closed and live your life like I just gave you a second chance. Otherwise, I can guarantee you nothing good comes of you telling anyone about The Wickersham Inn, are we clear?"

The man nodded as the door opened, and Mrs. Manning came out with two suitcases. "Mrs. Wickersham, I'm so sorry about this. I have no idea what came over him tonight. He doesn't usually drink like that, and where he came up with that wild tale about Jex and a dungeon master, I have no idea. It has to be more of his drunken ramblings. Harry, get in the goddamn car," the woman demanded.

Jex looked at Eli, who winked before he stood and took the suitcases from Mrs. Manning to hand them to Jex. "Can you get those into her car?" the chief asked him.

"Sure," Jex responded as he handed Mrs. Manning the check and grabbed the bags to carry to the Mercedes on the right side of the circle drive.

"Mrs. Manning, it's unfortunate this happened, and I'm sorry to say I won't be able to accept reservations from you again, but I'll give you some advice. Mr. Manning is probably going to need access to the restroom very soon, so I don't think I'd try to get too far out of town before I found a place to sleep for the night. That much whiskey has a tendency to make an ugly return," Mrs. Wickersham stated before she picked up the ivy plant and went inside the Inn.

Eli half-carried Mr. Manning to the car and helped him inside, buckling the seatbelt around the man before closing the door. Jex settled the bags and closed the trunk before he walked to the side of the car where Mrs. Manning was waiting.

"I'm so sorry about this, Jex. I believe he's jealous of how remarkably beautiful I think you are. I talked about you all through dinner, and he kept drinking instead of eating his food. I feel responsible for this embarrassment. Keep the check, and if you ever decide you'd like to do some modeling, call me at this number," Mrs. Manning told him as she handed him the check and a business card. It read,

Manning's Models, LLC
1415 South Hanover
Newark, New Jersey
(732) 555-9684
Contact: Barbara Clay-Manning

"Thank you, Mrs. Manning," Jex replied, not elaborating on the fact he would never allow another living soul to see him without his shirt...except for Eli. He'd already bared his shame to Eli Moore, and the man simply poured more love into Jex than he ever believed would be possible.

The two men watched until Mrs. Manning made a right out of the driveway onto Hopkins Lane. Jex turned to Eli and gently took his hand, seeing his bloody knuckles. "What did he say about me? Did he recognize me?"

Eli wrapped his arms around Jex's waist and pulled him closer. "They were fighting when they got here, and she decided they were going back to Newark. She went inside to pack up their things because he'd made an ass of himself at dinner."

"After she was out of earshot, he said he saw you at something called a *Munch* in Newark. He said you had no hair, but he was sure it was you. He also said his master knew your master. I got the distinct impression his master wasn't Mrs. Manning, though she gave me every indication she'd be pretty handy with a whip if given a chance," Eli joked before he kissed Jex on the lips, gently at first before they sunk into it together.

Jex wrapped his arms around Eli's neck and brushed their bodies together such that Jex believed he could see sparks between them, or at least behind his eyes. "Michael, you and Eli come to eat, dear. I'm reheating your food," they both heard before a small giggle resounded and the front door closed.

Jex pulled away and looked at Eli, who was staring at the direction Mrs. Wickersham's voice had come from. "Does she call you Michael a lot?" Eli asked.

Jex smiled at his...person? Lover? Boyfriend? Partner? E, all of the above was the only right answer. "Only once before. I think she just misses him. It doesn't bother me, really. If it gives her a little comfort, then I'm fine with it."

The two men walked arm in arm up the steps to the porch and into the house. They went into the kitchen to find Mrs. Wickersham had heated their food and reset the table. "Let's eat. Poor Mr. Manning is in for a very difficult night," she commented.

"What was in the mug, Mrs. Wickersham?" Jex asked.

"A tea to help him expel the vile things inside him. He'll have a long night ahead of him because monkshood is meant to teach a lesson, but he'll be a better person for it," Mrs. Wickersham stated as she pointed to the table.

Jex looked at Eli, who shook his head before digging into his hot food. "Where did you learn to make herbal remedies?" Eli asked the woman between bites.

Mrs. Wickersham smiled. "Mr. Wickersham's grandmother was from southern Louisiana. She was of Creole descent and learned herbal healing from her mother. Those things are passed down in a family. I'd like to teach you some general things over the winter, Jex. It could be helpful to you someday. Actually, Chief Moore, if you'd be so kind as to allow me to make a poultice for your knuckles, Jex could learn and repeat the remedy if you ever need it. It works in just a few days," Mrs. Wickersham explained.

Eli smiled at her and reached for Jex's hand with his left, which was uninjured. "Thank you, Mrs. Wickersham, but I have Arnica gel at home to use for bruises. I do appreciate your thoughtfulness."

She smiled at him and nodded. "I understand. Jex, dear, I'm going to bed. Will you be sure to lock up after all of the guests have come home? I think I'll read for a little while."

"Chief, thank you for diffusing a potentially violent situation. I doubt Mr. Manning will remember too much of his night that doesn't involve vomiting and diarrhea. Goodnight, gentlemen," she offered before she left the kitchen.

"Man, I'd hate to piss her off. She's something else," Eli joked as they began gathering the dishes to wash.

"She's mentioned things when we work in the gardens regarding the plants. I guess I never thought about the correlation between the things she grows and their medicinal uses. Maybe I'll start writing down her home remedies. Could come in handy," Jex thought out loud.

"Hey, couldn't hurt to have some organic options," Eli offered as Jex washed the dishes, and he dried. Jex had more questions he wanted to ask Mrs. Wickersham, but he decided not to ask them in front of Eli. The top cop might not want to hear the answers Jex imagined she might give.

XI

Eli woke up when he heard a knock on his front door. He got up from bed, pulled on a pair of sweats and a t-shirt before he grabbed his firearm. The chief released the safety and held it behind his back while heading to the front door. "Who is it?" he asked, seeing his front porch light must have burned out.

"It's Sheriff Cummings, Chief."

Eli engaged the safety and placed the gun on the table next to the door before opening it. Gerry Cummings was standing there in full uniform looking very upset. "Hey, Sheriff. Come in. What time is it?"

"It's a little after four in the morning. I'm sorry to wake you, but I went by the station, and nobody was there," Cummings explained.

"Uh, Bellows is on patrol, and since we don't house prisoners, there's no need for a uniform to be at the station overnight. Those two idiots from yesterday should be in your jail, Sheriff," Eli reminded.

"Yeah, uh, they are, Eli. Problem is, I'm looking for Deputy Blake. When was the last time he checked in?" Cummings asked.

Eli tried to clear his head because the previous day had been a doozy. He distinctly remembered asking Jex if the deputy had stopped by the Inn on Friday, but he couldn't remember ever getting an answer.

"Uh, I spoke to him yesterday morning. He was headed out to Wickersham Inn to speak to Jex Ivers, who works for Mrs. Wickersham. He worked for Lena before the diner caught fire, and Blake was determined to link the fire to Mr. Ivers, come hell or high water."

"Didn't Blake talk to you about this? I told him to stay out of it because it wasn't the county's jurisdiction. He told me I was too close to the investigation to be objective, and since he was helping us out, he was going to investigate it himself."

"There's this issue between Blake and me, Sheriff. He has a crush on me, and no matter how many times I tell him it's not going to happen, he won't let it go," Eli highlighted before he headed to the kitchen to turn on the coffee pot.

He'd stayed late at the Inn with Jex, the two of them watching a movie until midnight when the last guests came in. Jex locked the front door and walked Eli down to the beach where the two of them kissed and laughed, walking halfway between the Inn and Eli's little beach house. After goodnight kisses, Eli stood on the sand and watched Jex walk backward the whole way so they could wave to each other.

Eli felt like a lovesick teenager, and considering he was middle-aged, he decided the best shot he'd ever had to his ego was meeting Jex Ivers. They'd made a date for Jex to spend the night at Eli's home on Sunday, and the chief was making all sorts of plans in anticipation of the event.

"He said you were too close to the investigation to be objective? Hell, I was there with you and the others the day the Mayor was killed in that accident. Lon Boyer said it was the wiring after he had two of his guys go through there with a fine-tooth comb, and Lena's already getting bids to do the repairs."

"I'm not sure what Terry's getting at, accusing someone of starting the fire, but I'll talk to him when I find him," Gerry answered.

"Let me change clothes and help you look for him. I'll get Bellows to meet us at the station. Blake had one of our radios, so maybe we can track him through the GPS?" Eli suggested.

Eli quickly dressed while he listened as Cummings called the Sheriff's office to get a few more people to help them search. The chief promptly called Bellows cell phone and explained the problem, telling him to meet them at the station.

After he hung up, Eli called the Inn. Jex didn't have a cell phone for obvious reasons, but the top cop needed the answer to his previously asked but unanswered question. "Wickersham Inn," Eli heard whispered after three rings.

"Babe, it's me. I'm sorry to call you so early, but you never answered me last night when I asked, and I forgot about it after that shit with Manning. Did Terry Blake stop by the Inn at any time yesterday?" Eli inquired as he tucked in his uniform shirt and waited for an answer.

He heard hushed whispers before a woman's voice came over the line. "Hello? This is Hilda Wickersham."

"Uh, Mrs. Wickersham, I'm sorry I woke you. I was asking Jex if Deputy Blake came by the Inn yesterday. He hasn't checked in since early in his shift, and he mentioned he wanted to come by to talk to Jex yesterday," Eli explained.

"Oh, uh, that Sheriff's Deputy? The pushy, blond one? Yes, he came by yesterday. Jex was outside attending to our guests, so I don't think he saw the deputy, but I spoke with the man. He was asking very personal questions about the Inn and my life, and I told him it was none of his business and asked him to leave. He finally did," Mrs. Wickersham enlightened.

"What time was that, Mrs. Wickersham?" Eli asked as he walked into his living room.

"Oh, uh, I suppose it was around lunchtime. Yes, that's when it was. The deputy kept me from helping Jex make the picnic baskets, as a matter of fact. Is he out telling my business to the gossips around town?" the old woman reacted, not sounding very happy to have spoken to Terry Blake.

"Not that I'm aware, Mrs. Wickersham. Sorry to have bothered you. Tell Jex I'll see him later this morning, please," Eli signed off.

He looked at Gerry to see the man was ready to go, so Eli grabbed his service revolver, and the two men went out to their respective vehicles. They met five-minutes later at the police station, and Eli was surprised to see Yolanda and Tibby were both there as well.

"Thanks for coming out, you two. I guess Bellows called you?" Eli asked. His officers nodded their heads, and the crew went inside and pulled out a county-wide map, dividing the territory into grids to make the first pass. Gerry said if they didn't find the cruiser, he was going to call in other first responders from Sussex County. One of their own was missing, and they were going to locate him.

At eight that morning, Sheriff's Deputy Terrence Blake was found at the bottom of an embankment in Love Creek. His cruiser had rolled down the hill and landed on the roof where Terry seemingly drowned. Blake was thirty-seven years old, and Eli was left speechless. The chief had wanted Terry to leave him alone, but he didn't want anything to happen to the man. It seemed so damn senseless to Eli, and he prayed the man was at peace.

Sunday afternoon, there was a soft knock on Eli's back door. He'd been lying on the couch in the living room thinking about Terry Blake's last moments. *Did he suffer horribly, or was he killed when the cruiser rolled down the hill? Was he seeing anyone, or had he decided I was the one for him? Did Terry go off that hill on purpose because I told him I was only interested in Jex Ivers?*

Eli opened the door to find Jex looking quite concerned. "Uh, are you okay? The guests are finally gone, and Mrs. Wickersham has friends over. We're not cleaning up until tomorrow, and before this accident with Deputy Blake, we talked about me making a special dinner and me spending the night."

"Since this happened, I get the impression you'd rather be alone. I wanted to drop off this casserole for you, and then I'll leave you alone," Jex clarified.

Eli took his hand and pulled him inside, closing the door. He reached for the casserole to place it in the fridge without saying a word. Once it was secure, he led Jex into the living room where the chief had been reclining on the sofa and pulled his love down with him. "I want you here with me, Jex. I had planned to stop by this afternoon, but then, uh, something bad happened."

Eli pulled Jex closer and kissed his cheek. "What happened yesterday? I mean, do you know what happened to Deputy Blake?" Jex questioned.

Eli exhaled as he threaded his fingers through Jex's soft hair. "Mrs. Wickersham said he stopped by the Inn yesterday and asked invasive questions. She said you were outside with the guests but did you see him at all?"

Jex was quiet for a bit of time before he looked up and propped himself on Eli's chest. "I saw the car pull into the driveway, but I was busy outside and didn't speak to him."

"Mrs. Wickersham said he was rude to her, asking about her private life. Did she say anything to you about that?" Eli asked.

"Not really. Mrs. Wickersham told me to take care of the guests, and she'd deal with Deputy Blake. He was only there for a short time, as far as I know. The two of them..." Jex faded off.

Instead of finishing the sentence, Jex moved up closer to Eli's lips and kissed him passionately, which was precisely what the chief needed. Feeling the heat from Jex's body gave Eli the courage to ask a question he was sure Jex wasn't ready to answer. The chief needed something, and if he couldn't ask Jex for it, who could he ask?

When they broke the kiss, Eli looked into those beautiful green eyes. "I have a question regarding a sexual situation. Are you comfortable talking about it?"

Jex giggled, which surprised Eli because he'd never heard that particular sound out of the man. "What the fuck was that?" Eli asked as he started laughing right along with his love. The two of them continued laughing for a few minutes, which definitely relieved the tension Eli had been feeling before the knock on his door.

"Stop it. I hate when I giggle. It sounds so childish," Jex revealed.

Eli placed his hand on Jex's soft face and guided it up to look into his eyes. "There's absolutely nothing wrong with enjoying life, babe. I feel like my life got richer since I met you. Now, about that sex question?"

Jex blinked, smiled, and nodded, so Eli plowed forward. "I'm making a wild leap by assuming you didn't have a say in some of the sexual acts you were required to perform but have you had the opportunity to experience, uh, to be pleasured orally?"

Eli felt Jex's body tense, so he began backtracking. "No, Jex, I don't mean that you'd do anything to me. I just wondered if you'd let me do something for you?"

"You...no, Eli. You're not the type of man... I'll gladly suck your cock, but you're too good to suck mine," Jex offered as he moved down Eli's body and began reaching for his shorts.

Eli grabbed his hands and pulled him forward again. "No, Jex You're wrong. I'm not too good to...this shit goes back to Bernie Overman, doesn't it?"

Jex's head rested on Eli's chest as he held the man tight. "You don't have to answer me. I feel like I already know the answer, and

I'm sorry for pushing you. I'll be more patient in the future, I promise," Eli told him as the two of them relaxed on the couch again.

Several minutes later, Jex got up and sat on the floor next to the couch. "Is this okay? I feel more comfortable here for this discussion." Eli nodded and turned to his side, reaching for Jex's hand.

Jex kissed the top of his bruised right hand and looked up at the man, offering a small smile. "I was trained to provide pleasure without question, Eli. I know how to drive you out of your mind. I can edge you for hours. I was taught how to pleasure a man, but I was never taught how to receive pleasure myself.

"What we did the other morning was the first time I had a sexual release without being punished. I was supposed to be able to keep myself in check until my master allowed it, which he never did. Half of the marks on my back are from early in my training when I couldn't keep from coming."

"Bernie was a sadist and loved showing others how he would discipline his slave for not following his orders to the letter. His favorite device to use on me was a chastity cage he'd had made just a little too small, so there would be pain if I even started to get an erection."

"He'd leave it on me twenty-three hours a day, and it got to the point I couldn't get hard anymore. At first, he left it on for weeks at a time, but one of the other Doms told him I could get an infection, and it would be a shame if such an adoring slave died from mistreatment. He offered to buy me from Bernie, which pleased him, so he started taking it off an hour a day."

"The fact I could no longer get an erection pissed him off the same as if I did. He'd say, '*You believe you're too good to be fucked by me? Well, I've got half a mind to turn the boys loose on you, so you come back and beg me to fuck you because I'm the best you've ever had.'"*

"I spent hours begging him not to do it until I finally convinced him I could get hard, but I was trying to remember he was my master, and I shouldn't do anything he told me not to do. He couldn't really argue with his own logic."

"It's been a very long time since I've actually enjoyed feeling what I felt with you the other night. I'll do anything you want to show you how much I love you, but there are things I don't think I'm ready to have you do for me," Jex explained before he leaned his head forward and rested it against Eli's hand on the side of the couch.

What Jex had said left a lot to process, but the thing that took away Eli's breath was the three words he hoped to hear eventually. He sat up and slid to the floor next to Jex. "You love me?"

He saw his love tense up before he looked down. "I'm sorry. I realize you deserve so much better than me, Eli. I wish I were worthy of…"

Eli grabbed him and pulled him closer to keep from hearing those ugly words that would break his heart. "No! Don't ever say that, Jex. You are more than worthy of being loved, and if I ever find that motherfucker, I'll make sure he knows how much I love you before I end his life," the chief whispered.

He didn't expect Jex to jump him, but he was happy just the same. "I won't allow you to do anything that would jeopardize your job, your future, or your life, Eli. Yes, I love you more than I ever imagined I could love anyone, and I'll get used to saying it, I promise. Can I stay tonight?" Jex asked.

"Yes, please," Eli responded before he kissed the gorgeous man. They went on to heat the casserole and have dinner, taking their wine outside to sit on the deck of the beach house to relax on the glider, no blanket necessary.

"Mrs. Wickersham put my name on her bank accounts. The checks list me as a Co-Proprietor. What do you think that means?" Jex asked.

The chief wrapped his arm around Jex's shoulder as he took a sip of his wine while they swung in time with the sound of the waves meeting the shore. "I think that means she trusts you to sign for charges. I think she might believe you're her son, but I don't think it's harmful. You're not taking advantage of her, so I'd say it's fine," Eli offered.

The two men sat outside and watched the stars and the moon play in the light. When they finished their wine, they went inside, and Jex spent the first night in Eli's bed. They didn't pursue sexual delights, but they did sleep without the barrier of clothes, and when Eli rolled over and pulled Jex into his arms, the feeling of contentment flooded his soul.

After the tragic death of Deputy Blake, life in Haven's Point picked up where it left off. By the end of June, Lena opened the diner again once the rewiring and repairs were completed, and Eli had a new police officer under his employ.

Her name was Irina Ford, and she had a fifteen-year-old son, Luke, who applied for Jex's job as a busboy and dishwasher at *Lena's Home Cooking.* The kid got rave reviews for being polite and a hard worker. Eli agreed with the general assessment, as well.

Eileen Stewart came back to work at the diner, and things were going well in the sleepy little town. The City Council was hosting a large Fourth of July fireworks display, and the tourists, as well as the residents, were excited to attend.

Eli had been making plans for holiday patrols with his four officers, and they had a schedule in place to everyone's satisfaction. Tibby was back to work full-time, and everyone enjoyed getting to know Irina Ford...especially Lena Becker, who was the topic of the latest gossip circulating the grapevine of Haven's Point.

Terry Blake's body had been sent back to his family in Pennsylvania, but the town had a memorial service for him. There had been an autopsy to establish a cause of death, but the fact Terry's spinal cord was severed after he went through the windshield when the cruiser went over the bank of the creek left only one cause of death for the coroner to conclude. The man had died because he wasn't wearing a seatbelt.

Eli hated to hear it, but thankfully, there was no nefarious tampering with the deputy's car, so the case was closed. Life moved on as it always did, and the top cop was even more in love with Jex Ivers. They were looking forward to celebrating the Fourth of July together, and they'd made plans to spend the night together at the Inn after the fireworks.

Jex had spoken with Mrs. Wickersham about it, and he'd reported that the woman had given her blessing for Eli to spend the night when he wanted. Eli felt as if he'd scored the permission from a parent, but he knew the woman loved Jex, so if she gave her seal of approval? Eli had no complaints.

Eli walked over to the diner for breakfast that morning as he had since the grand reopening in the middle of June. He saw Irina Ford dropping off her son for work, so Eli waved at her before he went inside behind the kid.

"Chief, you want some coffee?" Luke Ford asked.

"I'll make it. You go ahead and start the grill for Lena. You and your mom getting accustomed to small-town life, okay?" Eli asked as the filled the coffee makers and turned them on.

Before the boy could answer, the front door opened and Eileen Stewart rushed inside. "I'm sorry I'm late, but..." she began.

"Whoa, dude! What the fuck?" Luke Ford asked as he drew Eli's attention to Eileen's bruised face.

"Oh, I got hit with a baseball yesterday. Riley and Rooney were playing in the yard, and I made the mistake of stepping into the line of fire when Riley hit the ball to Rooney," Eileen offered. Eli knew it was all bullshit. Eileen showed up with bruises on her face, neck, and arms far too often for it to be a coincidence. Nobody had that many accidents.

"Luke, can you go see where Lena is?" Eli asked.

Once the boy left the front of the diner, the top cop stepped around the counter and looked at the young woman's face, gently touching it to hear her hiss at the pain. "Yeah, that's not a baseball strike, Eileen. Try again," Eli ordered.

The chief saw the tears in her eyes, which made his stomach turn. "I had an accident. If it's anything other than an accident, my husband goes to jail. While I have no problem with that particular outcome because he's a mean bastard, what do I tell my boys?" Eileen asked.

"How about you tell them nobody deserves to be a punching bag? How about love and kindness is worth everything? How about we look after our own in Haven's Point?" Eli pressed, feeling the anger flood his body.

Eileen wrapped the apron around her waist and smiled at him. "How about that's a lovely dream? How about the disability checks that Dirk receives help to put food on the table, and the fact that I was out of work for two months and couldn't find another job put pressure on my husband, and he snapped. There's not a lot of opportunities in this town, Chief," the woman offered before she went to work that morning.

Later that afternoon, Eli went to the Inn and found Mrs. Wickersham in her garden, sitting on a bench while Jex was weeding a raised bed of gorgeous pink, white, and fuchsia bushes.

"Those are really nice. I don't think I've ever seen plants like those before," Eli told the old woman as he sat down next to her.

"They're oleander bushes. They're beautiful, aren't they?" Mrs. Wickersham remarked.

"Yes, ma'am, they are. Anyway, Jex, Lena said hi. Her new busboy is working out well, and things are mostly back to normal now that the diner is opened again...well, except for the fact Dirk Stewart decided it was a good idea to beat the crap out of Eileen again."

"Of course, I can't do anything about it because the woman refuses to even admit he hit her, much less file charges against him. Her story is she got hit by a baseball when she walked between her kids while they were playing. Of course, that's bullshit, pardon my French. I've seen enough domestic disputes to recognize the shape of a fist on a cheek or an eye when I see it," Eli complained.

He watched as Jex gathered the weeds from the garden and shoved them in the trash bag before he removed the gardening gloves and walked over to Eli, taking his hand. "How about we go for a swim? The guests are off for dinner and then the fireworks in town. Oh, wait, you need to go to that, don't you?" Jex asked.

"Yeah, but I'll be back by ten, and we could take a dip then. You can't come to town for the fireworks?" Eli asked. Jex offered a gentle kiss to his lips and took his hand to lead him out of the garden while Mrs. Wickersham sat on the bench alone.

"I need to do a few things around here. How about we stay at your house tonight instead of here? I have a feeling Mrs. Wickersham will fall asleep before the guests get here, so I'll wait for them and then meet you at your house after I lock up."

"I find myself not wanting to sleep in clothes tonight, and I don't want you to sleep in clothes either. I don't think either of us would feel comfortable doing that in Mrs. Wickersham's home," Jex suggested with a sexy smile. It was the best thing Eli had seen or heard recently. He'd get to hold Jex Ivers in his arms all night once again, and that sounded like the best idea, ever.

Life was filled with simple pleasures, and Eli was going to embrace every one of them. He would always be grateful for Jex Ivers coming into his life. It was exactly what the chief needed.

XII

Certain truths were hard to hear, but Jex had heard, and *felt*, his share of awful realities over his lifetime. When his mother was killed, and he was all alone in the world, the news rang through his brain and wouldn't stop.

When a foster family didn't want to have him stay with them because he was too weird or too queer, they said it loud enough the whole neighborhood heard it. When Bernie Overman was unhappy with his behavior, not only did Jex listen to it, he felt it over and over again.

He had the scars on his body and his heart to prove he'd been taught many lessons the hard way. It seemed, however, his luck might be changing.

Meeting Mrs. Wickersham turned out to be a wish granted by a fairy godmother Jex never knew existed. The old woman had come along at the perfect time, or so Jex believed, and he didn't want to ever upset her or feel her disapproval for something he did.

He remembered back to a discussion the two of them had the Tuesday after Mr. and Mrs. Manning left the Inn. At the time, he wasn't sure exactly what she was going to tell him, but Mrs. Wickersham made things quite clear before the discussion was over.

"Sit down, dear," the old woman ordered as Jex folded the bed linens he'd brought from the clothesline behind the garage where they'd dried in the warm, summer sun.

"I was just trying to..." he began before she tamped her cane on the kitchen floor and pointed to the table.

Jex sat down and looked at the sweet, old woman, unsure of the reason for her pissy demeanor. "I'm sorry, Mrs. Wickersham. Did I do something..."

"You stop right there, young man. You've never done anything to anyone that should have brought the hell I'm sure you've survived, and I want you to stop those awful thoughts right now, Jex. You're a beautiful, kind person, and you did nothing to make that awful man cause you pain."

"You need to expect more for yourself from the people around you. I realize you aren't used to expecting anything, based on your experiences growing up in foster care, but those days are over, Jex," the old woman insisted.

He wished he could learn to do as she'd said, expect better treatment from others, but his mind kept reminding him he didn't deserve to be treated like others. He'd come to accept how worthless he was over the years after his mother was killed when he was fifteen. Mrs. Wickersham trying to make him believe anything else was wasted breath.

"More what, Mrs. Wickersham? I know my place in the world, and I have no intention of trying to rise above it," Jex responded without thinking.

"Enough of that, now. We have things for you to learn, dear boy. I need someone to keep the Inn going, and I have no one other than you, Michael," Mrs. Wickersham said.

Jex took a deep breath. "Mrs. Wickersham, you know I'm not really your son, right? I wish I were because I'd be the luckiest guy in the world if it were true, but we both know it's not. I'm sorry if I've somehow let you believe it because I didn't want to remind you of the devastating loss you suffered. You've been so very kind to me, and I don't want to hurt you, but I'm not your Michael."

He watched as her face softened. "I think that's where you're wrong, Jex. I realize it sounds sort of insane, but I think there's a chance your mother might have given birth to Michael's reincarnated spirit. You are so much like him, I can't help but believe you might *be him, and honestly? What's the harm if I play make-believe that you're my little boy occasionally?"*

"His father, that unholy bastard, shot him because he liked to dress up in my clothes and shoes, and the two of us loved to have tea parties. He liked to paint my nails, because back then it wasn't acceptable for men to wear nail polish, and sometimes when his father was away on business, I'd give him makeup lessons. He so loved to look pretty."

"When he was older, he confided he didn't find himself attracted to the girls at school, and I understood it because I wasn't attracted to boys when I was in school either. We played pretend, Michael and me, but we weren't hurting anything or anyone."

"I guess it made both of our lives easier to live with our little fantasies since we knew we could count on each other to keep the secret. We only had each other, but we were fine with it."

"My mother and I used to fight when I was in school because she would introduce me to the sons of her friends, but I refused to date them. My favorite aunt took me aside one day, and she told me she understood how I felt about dating boys because she felt the same, but the only option for us was to marry anyway. It was what was expected of us. It was what she'd done, after all."

"Hers wasn't a happy marriage, and no children came from it. She reminded me I could never survive without a man, which was far too typical back in the sixties when I was finishing high school and going to college. Unfortunately, Aunt Louise couldn't live with a man, and she ended up hanging herself after no one would take it seriously that her husband brutally raped her every night of their three-year marriage."

"I met Neil when we were in college, me a freshman studying elementary education and him just starting law school. I was a pretty girl with good parents and better manners, and Neil Wickersham came with the right pedigree to suit my father."

"Our parents were much more in love with the idea of a marriage between the families than either of us, if the truth be told. Unfortunately, they held all the cards, so we married in a huge wedding in Dover."

"I endured the physical expectations of our relationship because it was necessary, but when I had Michael? I felt like I'd been reborn. My son was perfect," Mrs. Wickersham explained.

"Unfortunately, Mother Wickersham believed one male heir was enough in a family, and when I had a boy first, she and Neil decided that would be the end of expanding the Wickersham line. When I got pregnant with our second child, the two of them conspired to take that baby from me without my knowledge or consent."

"Neil's mother learned herbal medicine from her family, and she made a witches brew that caused me to miscarry my second baby. After that, I moved into Michael's room to watch over him, and when I decided Mother Wickersham was more of a hindrance than a help, I eased her into the afterlife with her own recipe I found in a box in the cupboard."

"Of course, Neil was too self-centered to even care that his mother was dead. All of his energy was focused on the reputation of the family and how he could benefit from it. He was the town lawyer, just like his father, and he believed everyone owed him the utmost respect because his mother gave him a very inflated sense of self. When our son was born, Neil tried to push the same agenda with my son, but I wasn't having it."

"Thankfully, my sweet little boy was nothing like his father, and over the years, I believe it became apparent to Neil as well. He would complain about Michael not being interested in sports or 'boy' things. When Michael didn't want to learn to play baseball or soccer, Neil became angry with me, blaming me for making our son a sissy."

"Over the years after his mother's death, Neil continued to become more and more cruel and heartless to both of us. One night he came home from a business trip to find the two of us dancing and laughing together, Michael in a red velvet evening gown I'd worn to a party the previous Christmas while I wore one of Neil's tuxedoes."

"We weren't expecting him early, and after he saw the two of us, Michael in full makeup with his hair in finger waves and me with a drawn-on mustache, Neil immediately went to his home office and slammed the door. We began cleaning up the mess we'd made before either of us changed, but I'll never forget the look of disgust on Neil's face when he looked at our son after returning to the room. I tried to send Michael from the room because I was sure Neil was going to punish me, and it wasn't something I wanted my son to witness."

"Neil was calm, which was unusual. When he'd beaten me in the past, I'd make Michael put on headphones because Neil would scream at me while beating me with a willow switch to break the skin or a large strap to leave horrible bruises. My back is scarred, not unlike yours. I've felt that pain as well," Mrs. Wickersham explained, drying a tear that slid down her face. Jex had been crying since she'd begun telling the story.

The old woman looked down at her clenched hands before sitting up straighter as if she felt she owed the rest of the story more respect. "Neil was calmer than I'd ever seen him, glancing between the two of us with a smug grin as I tried to push Michael out into the hallway."

"I saw the pistol in his hand and froze for a moment before I ran to get between them, but I was a beat too late. He shot my baby in the chest without even blinking, though later after I was sedated, he was questioned and claimed our son shot himself. I was too devastated to even comprehend what had happened for days to dispute his accounting of the events. That demon killed the most precious person in my life, and at the time, I wished he would have killed me as well."

"I should back up a bit. That night, Neil called the town doctor, who was a friend of his father's, before he called Chief Moore...not Eli, but his father. He told the doctor to knock me out because I was hysterical. He told the Police Chief our son killed himself because he was being abused by me and no longer wanted to live."

"Of course, before anyone arrived at our home, Neil insisted I change Michael out of the gown and makeup and into his pajamas while he staged the scene such that Chief Moore believed it to be exactly as Neil told him, so there was no shame on the family name. Then I was sent to take a shower and get into bed," Mrs. Wickersham detailed, which had Jex speechless.

Jex swallowed the tea he'd been drinking and held his breath for a few seconds before he asked a question he wasn't sure he wanted to be answered. "Do you...did Eli's father sweep it under the rug? Did he not investigate the shooting death of your child because he believed your husband?"

An odd smile crept up on Mrs. Wickersham's face. "No, he didn't sweep it under the rug because he wasn't...isn't that type of man. Unfortunately, after the doctor stopped sedating me, Neil disappeared just a week later, so there wasn't much of an investigation. Chief Moore saw the wisdom in allowing me to bury my son and leave Neil's disappearance behind, and that was the end of it."

Jex couldn't begin to comprehend what she meant. "You mean, he knew your husband shot..."

"Well, I'm not exactly sure if he knew Neil shot Michael, but he didn't pester me with questions and drag a bunch of outsiders into my grief. He respected my privacy, and for that, I'll be forever grateful. I think he suspected I exacted the justice necessary to lay my son to rest."

"Life isn't always what we expect, as you well know, Jex. Sometimes, it's better to handle situations quietly, without fanfare.

It was never discussed again, so let's just keep it between you, me, and the bees, shall we?"

"Now, on another note, I want you to call Dewey Zellner and ask him to haul away the old freezer in the garden shed. It's secured so no one can get inside and come to harm, but I don't think I need it anymore. It's time to let some things go," Mrs. Wickersham told him.

"What did you mean by saying I should keep it between you, me, and the bees?" Jex asked, finding the comment peculiar.

Mrs. Wickersham smiled. "It's an old European custom when one cares for bees. When I adopted the bees after Mother Wickersham passed away, I promised to keep them safe and up-to-date regarding the events at the Inn and things happening to people I know."

"If there's a birth in town, I happily share it with the bees, and they rejoice with me. If there's a death in the town, I whisper the grief to them so we can mourn together. The bees know all of the secrets, and they never tell a soul."

The answer was odd but fit with Mrs. Wickersham's personality. It was a bit quaint for her to speak of honeybees as members of her family, which was what he'd always remember when he thought of the old woman.

Over the next few weeks, Jex recalled the conversations many times, but he had no clear answers regarding the events that had occurred when Michael Wickersham was killed. He followed through on Mrs. Wickersham's request and phoned Dewey Zellner, the town's mechanic, who showed up with a large truck and trailer to haul away the old freezer.

They enjoyed the summer, meeting many new people who stayed at the Inn and more memories of wonderful times were ingrained in Jex's heart, most of them with the chief by his side. Eventually, the darkness of the events Mrs. Wickersham had explained faded.

To Jex, they just weren't relevant any longer because he'd finally found his place in the world.

Jex loved Eli Moore, and he could see himself staying in Haven's Point for as long as he was welcome. Based on Mrs. Wickersham's confession, Chief Moore, Senior, might have turned a blind eye to a murder, but the man wasn't responsible for the way the events had taken place.

It seemed the former Chief did what he thought would bring the woman the least amount of grief. Maybe it was all for the best the events of that night should remain a secret? Jex swore he would be like the bees. He'd never tell a soul.

The Fourth of July had been a fantastic day, or so Jex would always remember it as such. They'd held a volleyball tournament for the guests on the beach that morning, and Jex had made special picnic lunches complete with New England lobster rolls, potato wedges, homemade pickles, and deviled eggs, along with chocolate chip ice cream sandwiches.

After the cocktail hour, which featured Mrs. Wickersham's bourbon sours made with egg whites and fresh lemon and lime juice, the guests went off to dinner in town, and they all planned to attend the fireworks celebration that evening.

Eli was on patrol, but he'd promised he would be back at the beach after the fireworks, so Jex and Mrs. Wickersham worked to clean up the *hors d' oeuvres* they'd served that evening...fresh shrimp cocktail and bacon-wrapped scallops.

They'd received a large order of fresh seafood that morning, and they'd done the order justice in his opinion. Mrs. Wickersham had taken the time to teach Jex how to perfectly boil the lobsters for lunch and clean the shrimp and scallops for happy hour that evening.

Jex and Mrs. Wickersham had a quick dinner of the leftover lobster salad in lettuce cups instead of soft rolls, along with pickles and a sparkling-wine-soaked fruit salad before moving to the beach so they could observe the fireworks in town from the shoreline of the Inn.

They reclined in the bamboo green loungers with the green-palm cushions, each with a glass of sherry. The music from the boardwalk in town could be heard from their slice of beach, and Jex noticed a soft smile on Mrs. Wickersham's face.

"Did Michael like fireworks?" he asked, sure she was enjoying a memory of her son.

"Oh, yes, he loved things that were shiny, sparkly, glittery. He and I used to sit on a blanket and watch the fireworks after we cooked hot dogs over a fire on the beach. After the fireworks, we made s'mores. Those were lovely evenings for the two of us," Mrs. Wickersham reminisced.

Jex turned to look at her. "Didn't your husband join you? Sounds like a fun family outing."

She sat up and turned to look at the moon, an angry scowl on her face. "Neil never liked to spend that evening with us. He always said it was a frivolous waste of time, but Michael and I loved all the holidays and celebrated as much as we were allowed. I'll treasure those memories always, and I'm actually glad he didn't try to horn in," she whispered.

She was quiet for a moment before she took a sip of her sherry and turned to look at him again. "Tell me, Jex, that young lady, Eileen Stewart who the chief spoke of earlier? Is she an acquaintance of yours?" Mrs. Wickersham asked.

"Yes, she is. She's a really nice woman, but she's one of those people who always seems scattered. She was late for work every day when I worked for Lena Becker, but Eileen's a very sweet person who the customers all seemed to like. I enjoyed working with her when I was at the diner. Her husband, however, is a worthless piece of crap," Jex responded.

Mrs. Wickersham seemed to contemplate something before she offered a gentle smile. "You got to know him?"

"Not really, but Eileen came in with bruises more often than she didn't, and she has two little boys who she worries about constantly. I've seen them a few times when they've come into the diner toward the end of the day, and they're adorable little boys. They're both terrified of their father, from what Eileen mentioned a few times."

"I heard Eileen tell Lena her husband was a frustrated painter. Dirk used to paint houses, but he's always wanted to do custom murals. Unfortunately, not many people commission murals for their homes anymore, so he started working for a builder as a painter. He fell off a ladder and sustained a back injury that left him disabled."

"He receives a check from an insurance company, but it's not really enough to support his family very well. She says he gets frustrated because he has no creative outlet, and it seems like he takes it out on his family. Like I said, I think he's a piece of crap," Jex explained as the first bursts of light lit up the sky.

As the fireworks continued, Mrs. Wickersham tapped on her small sherry glass in time to the music they heard on the breeze. Finally, when there was a lull, Mrs. Wickersham asked, "Do you think maybe we should ask him to come by so we could offer him a job painting the third-floor apartment? I'm sure we can agree on a theme for him to sketch out for us so we can ascertain his level of expertise. The apartment could be fancied up a bit, don't you think?"

Jex decided not to ask why she had a sudden interest in the Stewart family because he knew her to be a kind person, but there was that sparkle in her eye that worried him. If her motives had anything to do with the life experiences she'd hinted at, he was sure he didn't want to know her intentions.

He kept telling himself ignorance was bliss, but he still knew there was the possibility the old woman had vengeance on her mind. He was sure when it came to those who couldn't defend themselves, Mrs. Wickersham's wrath could be deadly.

There was mounting evidence Jex couldn't dismiss regarding Mrs. Wickersham having nefarious motives regarding her invitation to have Dirk Stewart visit the Inn. It could be said if one were to live by the *Code of Hammurabi*, an eye for an eye, certain acts were justified.

For example, one might say any man who would beat his wife for things out of her control simply because he was frustrated with his own lot should be tied to a tree and receive thirty lashes with a bullwhip, but retribution rarely came in a tit-for-tat form. Jex didn't know for sure what Mrs. Wickersham had up her sleeve for Dirk Stewart, but he decided he didn't want the details. It was better to butt out.

"Sure, Mrs. Wickersham. I can tell Eileen to have him call the Inn so you can invite him over if that's what you want. Again, why would he want to come?" Jex asked, knowing he was bordering on becoming an accomplice to something more than likely illegal. If his assumptions were correct, Eli would have every reason to lock him away forever.

"Let's invite him over just to get to know him and see if he's a good painter. If he's not, maybe we can do the Christian thing and help him find a different vocation to better his family's circumstance?"

"Perhaps we can talk some sense into him regarding the fact using his wife as to relieve the pressure he feels by hitting her isn't good for the children. I've also been thinking about the Inn sponsoring some children's baseball teams. Those little boys play baseball, don't they?" Mrs. Wickersham inquired.

"Uh, yeah, I think so. I still don't know why you think Dirk would come out here looking for work. He doesn't know you, does he?" Jex asked.

Jex saw Mrs. Wickersham smile. "No. You're right, dear. Never mind about that business. You should get ready to go to Eli's house for the night. I'll handle things here at the Inn, I promise," she assured.

Jex went into the house and packed a small bag, still in a fog over the overload of information. He definitely needed to feel Eli hold him in his arms, but he didn't need the chief to become suspicious of the events coming together in Jex's mind. He didn't want to mislead Eli, but sometimes secrets were necessary to protect the innocent. Eli was definitely one of the innocent.

Jex strolled down the beach later that night, the sound of the water lapping at the shore calming his nerves, especially with the beautiful glow of the moon on the wet sand. Jex walked up the back stairs of the small beach house and knocked on the door. When Eli didn't answer, Jex turned the handle on the back door and found it to be open. He walked inside and turned on the kitchen light.

What he didn't expect was a bouquet of roses and bluebells with baby's breath in a frosted vase on the kitchen table. There was a card taped to the vessel with his name on it, so Jex gently removed it and opened the envelope to see a note written in all caps.

MY SWEET MAN,

I'M NOT TOO GOOD AT ROMANCE, BUT I'M TRYING, SO BEAR WITH ME, PLEASE?

WHEN I GET HOME, I WOULDN'T MIND FINDING YOU WAITING IN MY BED WITH CANDLELIGHT (ON THE DRESSER) AND SOFT MUSIC (ON MY NIGHTSTAND).

I THINK IT'S TIME FOR US TO EXPLORE SOME MORE, DON'T YOU?

I LOVE YOU

ELI

Jex buried his nose in the flowers and smiled. Never in his life had anyone done anything of the sort for him. The gesture and the note touched his soul.

The same old words rolled through his head without his bidding...*You're a worthless piece of shit...If I didn't take you in, you'd be dead by now...You owe me your worthless life, and if you don't do as I say, I'll take it.*

"No!" Jex shouted at himself in Eli's kitchen. Learning to accept Eli's love wasn't easy, but Jex was trying. If he died at any minute, knowing he was loved for even one day by a man as wonderful as Eli Moore, it would be enough.

Jex heard a vehicle on the driveway, sure it was Eli's SUV, so he hurried to the bedroom to find the candle and matches. He quickly lit it before he turned on the music Eli mentioned, hearing a soft tune over the speaker.

Jex didn't know much about music, but he liked what he heard, so he quickly stripped off his clothes and turned down Eli's bed.

He had every intention of the two of them doing something that would feel good that night, even if he had to battle his nerves. Jex was determined to move their physical relationship forward, regardless of how anxious it made him.

Jex slid under the sheet and sat up against the headboard, listening to the sounds of Elijah coming home from work. He heard the chief lock the front door, unload his pockets on the kitchen counter, and lock his gun in the safe in his front closet. "*Jex?*" he heard called out.

"*In bed, just as instructed!*" Jex called in response.

Eli showed up in the doorway, a worried look on his face. "No, no, I didn't mean to order it or instruct it. I shouldn't have said it like that. You didn't have to..."

"Shut up, Eli," Jex teased as he stood from the bed, trying not to be embarrassed because of his nakedness. He saw the hunger in the chief's eyes, and it made his cock hard, which was a new thing that surprised Jex every time it happened.

When Jex wrapped his arms around Eli's neck, the man didn't hesitate to pull him close and kiss him, tangling tongues and wrapping his right hand in Jex's long hair. When Eli broke the kiss, he was panting. "God, I'm so glad you're here. Let me..." Eli began before Jex pulled away and began unbuttoning the navy-blue uniform shirt the Chief of Police wore.

There were patches sewn onto it to let everyone know Elijah Moore was someone who would uphold the law. Jex worried the man might condemn him for keeping Mrs. Wickersham's alleged secrets.

Someone who had Eli's integrity would have a hard time not investigating something he believed to be a crime. Jex, in turn, never planned to tell the man what he knew or assumed, but maybe it didn't need to be said because Eli wouldn't suspect anything? That was Jex's hope, anyway.

When the two men slipped into bed, Jex savored the weight of the cop on top of him. It wasn't threatening at all, and he was grateful to feel the touch of a gentle soul. Knowing the man looking into his eyes wasn't a threat brought a sense of peace to Jex he'd never imagined he'd feel in his life.

When Bernie Overman demanded sex from Jex during his captivity, he never looked into Jex's eyes. It was always from behind and never with any romantic intentions. The fact there was a knife blade pressed against his skin, sometimes a little too hard which drew blood. It kept Jex on edge to the point he never enjoyed sex. The knife was there to remind him if he didn't do precisely as Bernie demanded or if he ever tried to leave, Jex would die a painful death.

As Jex looked into Elijah's gorgeous blue eyes, he felt his breath leave his chest for a moment before he remembered what he wanted to say. "I love you, Elijah."

Eli grinned and ducked down to gently kiss Jex's lips before he pulled away and studied him as well. "I love you, Jex. I'm so lucky you came along."

Jex flipped Eli onto his back, chuckling when he heard the man gasp in surprise. He could tell he'd caught the chief off guard, and it made him laugh as he scrambled down the man's sexy body. Jex didn't waste time before sucking Eli's hard rod into his mouth, and when the man moaned, Jex felt the rush of knowing he had pleased his master.

Suddenly, Jex was flipped on his back, and Eli was hovering over him. "No, baby, no. I want to give you pleasure. Trust me, I'm sure you can rock my world, but not until you allow me to try first," the sexy man whispered.

Jex didn't have it in him to deny the pleasure he was sure Eli would give, so he nodded. When his flaccid cock was sucked into

Eli's warm mouth, Jex closed his eyes to try to block out how wrong it was for him to be feeling the sensation.

In a moment, his cock was hard, and he almost lost his mind. It wasn't anything he'd ever felt in his life, and the fact Eli continued to suck and slurp his dick had Jex nearly breathless.

"Oh, God, Eli," Jex gasped as the man licked his balls and jacked his cock a few times before he sucked it into his mouth again.

"I want to...please?" Jex whispered.

"Come for me, baby. Don't ever hold back, Jex," Eli offered as he took his cock to the back of his throat and swallowed. It was over before Jex could catch a breath. For the first time in his life, Jex felt the pleasure of feeling the ultimate kiss on his dick from someone he loved.

Hell, it was the first time he knew what it felt like not to feel guilty about coming, but when he saw the glowing smile on Eli's face, he knew every encounter before that night had been wrong. When Eli moved up his body and wrapped him in his arms, Jex was stunned silent for a few minutes.

"You okay?" Eli whispered as he always did when they were naked together. Many nights they just held each other, which was great. That night, Jex appreciated the man's concern more than anything.

"I am. Are you? Can I...?" Jex asked.

Eli kissed his forehead and pulled him closer. "Another time, babe. I'm glad you were okay with what I did. I want to do it again, you know, but how about for tonight, we get some sleep? I rarely get to hold you in my arms for the night," Eli whispered as he blew out the candle on the bedside table.

The two men fell asleep with the moon shining into the bedroom window of the beach house. Jex didn't think about the new secrets he was keeping. They had their place...with the bees.

XIII

"Moore," Eli answered.

"Hey, Rookie. Just checking in. How's everything going? There's a trial coming up soon. Do you think you could come to Newark for it?" Denny asked.

Eli was ready for the question, but he had some of his own to be answered before he allowed Jex to be put in danger...again. "First, do you know who's dirty in your little world?" Eli asked. He wasn't entirely convinced Cather wasn't on the take, so before he ever made a commitment regarding the trial in Newark, he wanted more information.

He heard the older cop's laugh. "You're still a little asshole, aren't you? How's Molly?" Cather asked.

"I don't know anyone named Molly, but I'm sure she's just fine," Eli answered, hoping he wasn't making a mistake. Keeping Jex safe was his foremost mission. If he was wrong and Cather was on the take, Eli would blow the man's brains to kingdom come before he ever let anything happen to his love.

"Good. Can we meet in Ocean City, Maryland, in August? To catch up, ya know? My girls are down there at a camp for those last few weeks, so I thought maybe you could drive down for a day or two. Betsy would love to see you," Cather suggested.

Eli had met Betsy Cather a few times, and he actually liked the woman, though she was a bit flaky. She had a very upbeat personality, even if she didn't seem to have a lot of common sense. Eli doubted the detective would lie about having his wife along, so he agreed. "Sounds great. When and where?"

The two men agreed to meet at a restaurant on the boardwalk on the twentieth of August, and Eli ended the call after. He hoped to fuck he was protecting the man he loved, not setting him up for an attack of some kind, but Eli couldn't be entirely sure he had it covered. He really didn't know how to proceed because he'd never been in a situation of the sort.

Eli was counting on his gut to guide him because it hadn't let him down in the past. If it failed him, the consequences were too dire to consider.

"Chief, what's your location?" Eli heard Yolanda West ask over the radio. It was Tuesday, the fifth of August, and Eli was standing in his bedroom, tucking his shirt into his jeans when he saw Jex's eyes open.

"Hi, babe. Sorry to wake you," Eli whispered before he kissed his lover good morning. He picked up the radio from the nightstand to respond. "I'm at home, Yolanda. What's up?"

Eli sat down on the side of the bed and took Jex's hand, kissing it. Jex sat up and smiled. "Can you come out to the Inn for lunch? Mrs. Wickersham ordered racks of ribs from the butcher, and we're going to grill. I'm making a special slaw with a honey dressing. Oh, and a macaroni salad the old gal says is the best ever," Jex whispered as he kissed along Eli's neck as they waited for a response from the police officer.

The two men had been steadily progressing in their exploration of each other's body, though Jex was more hesitant to allow Eli to do the exploration he craved. His love was still leery of allowing Eli to show him how good making love could be, but Eli was patient. They had a lifetime to decide what they enjoyed with each other, and every little step was a victory. That was the best thing about the love they shared...there was no rush to do things they were yet to experience.

"I'd love to," Eli told Jex as he kissed his lips, seeing the man's face was red from the whisker burn due to the previous night's ravaging Eli had done to him. He wasn't sorry, but he did reach for the Arnica gel from the nightstand and hand it to his lover to apply to his face.

"It's Dirk Stewart, Chief. Got a call earlier from some of the guys who works for DDOT out on Route One. They found his truck crashed into a tree about a mile from his house," Yolanda told him.

"Shit. Okay, Yolanda. I'll be there in ten. You call an ambulance?" Eli asked.

"Yeah, but not as an emergency, Eli. He's gone," his friend told him.

"Got it. Was Dirk alone?" Eli asked.

"Yeah. I saw Eileen at the diner this morning when I got the call from County. You want me to go talk to her?" Yolanda asked.

Eli sighed. It was the part of the job he hated the most, but he wouldn't saddle his friend with giving the bad news. "No, I'll do it after I check out the scene. Thanks for the head's up," Eli responded.

Once the conversation was finished, Eli looked at his lover for comfort. "I hate this part," he whispered as Jex pulled him closer and kissed his temple. Eli much appreciated the affection.

"I'm sure it's not easy to tell someone they've lost a loved one. Did your father ever give you any advice about it? He's probably had to do it before," Jex asked, which caught Eli by surprise.

Eli pulled away and kissed Jex softly on his lips, looking into his gorgeous green eyes. "You know, that's not anything I've ever asked him about, but I probably should someday. He'll be here next week, so if the opportunity presents itself, I might ask him. Thank you, babe, for suggesting it."

"So, uh, what time for lunch?" Eli asked before he stood to finish getting ready.

"I'd say about one. I'll make sure you have a full plate, Chief," Jex offered with a smile.

The two men bid their goodbyes, and Eli grinned as he left the beach house. Jex was still in his bed, and it gave the chief a sense of peace to concentrate on something that made him so happy. It was ridiculous to be so giddy about something so simple as knowing the beautiful redhead was content to spend time at the beach house. It was an unexpected, but profoundly appreciated, gift Eli would never forget.

Chief Moore drove to the scene of the accident to see it wasn't the awful mess he expected, based on the fact someone was dead. The gold, 1998 Chevy pickup was against a large elm tree on the front, driver's side and Dirk Stewart was in a body bag on a gurney by the side of the road. The ambulance was nearby, the EMT's waiting for Eli to sign off so they could transport the body to the morgue.

Eli scrawled his signature on the paperwork after taking a look at the deceased to see there were no noticeable marks to hint at anything other than the fact man fell asleep behind the wheel of his truck. It appeared, however, that he'd aspirated on himself at some point.

Where he'd been before the accident wasn't known, but it seemed as if he was heading home, though what happened to him on the way was a mystery. Fortunately, it didn't appear as if foul play was involved.

Eli walked over to where his officers were waiting for him, speaking quietly among themselves. "Ladies, Bellows. What do we know so far? Where was he? I suppose he was going home, right?"

Yolanda spoke up. "He's been dead for hours, Chief. Those two over there were headed to the DDOT yard in Georgetown when they came across the accident. He must have been headed home from having dinner out because he puked all over the front seat of the truck," she pointed out.

Eli nodded and headed to where two men were leaning against a caution-orange pickup with ugly, yellow strobe lights on top. "Gentlemen, thank you for hanging around," Eli offered as he pulled out a pad, though he didn't know why. Yolanda and Irina would have already questioned them and taken notes for the report.

"Sure. Pay's the same," the taller one offered.

"Excuse me?" Eli asked.

The shorter one laughed. "We called our boss and told him what happened, and he told us to stay here until we were released. We're getting paid to stand here and wait for you to say we're not needed anymore, so like he said, the pay's the same whether we're standing here or shoveling hot tar to patch a road. Poor bastard bit it bad, didn't he?" the man offered.

Eli shoved his little notebook into his pocket and stared at the two men for a moment. "Yeah, he did. What time did you find him?"

"We were coming through about seven. When we saw the accident, we checked to see if the driver was alive, but he wasn't. We called nine-one-one to report it, and we were asked to wait here," the shorter man explained.

"Was he bleeding or anything? I didn't check the body before they removed him from the truck," Eli asked.

The two men looked at each other and shrugged. "Nope. He looked like he fell asleep behind the wheel, and the truck just veered off the road. He was strapped in, and there ain't much damage to the truck, so I don't expect he was going very fast when the vehicle went off the road. It was like he just gave up. Oh, he puked all over the place, too," the short one said, and when the tall one agreed, Eli decided they didn't need to hang around any longer.

"Thanks, guys. My officers have your information if we have any questions?" he asked. Both men nodded, and Eli shook their hands before they left.

He walked over to the pickup and around to the front to see the front bumper was bent and the headlight was broken, but that was it. Dirk Stewart couldn't have been traveling very fast when his vehicle went off the road.

It wasn't out of the realm of possibilities that Stewart lost control of the vehicle because he was vomiting. He might have slowed down in an attempt to pull over before he let go, but something happened that caused him to crash. Nevertheless, the man died, and Eli was puzzled as to why.

"It's almost like he just rolled off the road and the tree stopped him," the chief stated to Irina Ford, who nodded.

"His foot wasn't on the accelerator or the brake when we arrived on the scene. His left hand wasn't on the steering wheel, but his right hand was resting in the five o'clock position, and his left hand had vomit on it."

"I'm guessing Stewart tried to cover his mouth to keep from puking in the truck, but he didn't make it," Irina replied as she pulled out her cell phone to show the chief a picture she'd taken before she allowed the paramedics to disturb the scene.

"The paramedics said it seemed like he turned the truck toward the ditch to get off the road. If he was suffering a heart attack, it makes sense. I'd guess the coroner could make a final determination if he does an autopsy. You sure you don't want us to go talk to Mrs. Stewart?" Irina asked.

Eli smiled at his officers. "Thanks, but I'll take care of it. I appreciate you all came out to handle this while I was gone. I'll be in later," he explained before he went back to his SUV and hopped inside. He pulled his phone from the console and called the diner.

Kade Ford answered. "*Lena's Home Cooking,* Kade speaking."

"Hey, Kade. It's Chief Moore. Is Lena available?" Eli asked.

"Sure, Chief. Hang on," he heard before the line went silent. No way was he going to attempt to tell Eileen Stewart her husband was dead without Lena being there for backup.

A minute later, the line clicked. "Chief, what can I do for you?" It was Lena, and Eli was relieved.

"Eileen's still working, yeah?" he asked.

"Yeah, she's here until we close at three. Everything okay?"

"No. I'll be there in ten," Eli told her before he hung up and drove back to town. The idea of Dirk Stewart having a heart attack at his young age stuck in Eli's brain. The guy was claiming disability from something job related, though Eli wasn't sure about the injury.

In the chief's opinion, Dirk was the type to screwing over his former boss by claiming he was disabled, but without evidence, it was just speculation. After seeing a bruised and battered Eileen more than once when Eli went into the diner for breakfast, it would never surprise him if there was nothing wrong with Dirk except being a lazy son-of-a-bitch who liked to take out his frustration on his wife.

The idea the man had a heart attack and eased his truck off the road and into a tree such that only about a hundred dollar's damage was done to the front end didn't really make sense. Something wasn't right, but Eli just couldn't put his finger on it.

The chief climbed into his vehicle to head back to town, pulling into the parking lot of the station before he walked over to the diner. Eileen was waiting on the late morning crowd, so Eli walked back to the kitchen to find Lena finishing up an order of pancakes.

"Eli, do you want something to eat?" the woman asked.

"Dirk Stewart was killed in a car crash sometime this morning. Did Eileen mention he hadn't come home or that he went out early this morning for any reason? It's not clear why he was out so early." The woman's silence was unnerving.

"Lena, how the fuck do I tell her he's dead?" Eli whispered as he looked out the pass-through window to see the young woman talking to the few customers who were finishing up their breakfasts. Eli saw Eileen laugh when some of the old men flirted like they always did. It was harmless, but what Eli had to tell the woman wasn't.

Lena walked over to him and touched his arm. "Wait for a little while, and before you accuse me of being selfish to get her to finish her shift, listen to me."

"That girl told me she suspected he was having an affair. She said he's been very secretive about what he'd been doing lately, so it probably didn't surprise her he hadn't come home last night. He was an asshole, so I'm sure nothing surprised her."

"Eileen's responsible for dropping off her boys at the day camp they hold at the school, and after you tell her he's dead, she's still gonna have to go get them."

"Let me call her mom to pick them up first, Eli. She's going to want Riley and Rooney when she gets home, so let me call Mrs. Hendricks to be prepared. It's the kindest thing to do," Lena suggested, and Eli couldn't disagree.

At three-thirty that afternoon, Eli sat across from Eileen Stewart in a booth at the diner and told her about the death of her husband. The woman cried for a few minutes before she nodded, seeming to accept the news without asking any questions. It seemed she wasn't even surprised.

After the short discussion, Eileen gathered her things so Eli could take her home. He hung around at her place while she explained the situation to her boys, who cried as well.

Once Eli was satisfied the widow and her sons were in good hands with family, he got ready to go home. Eileen walked him out to the SUV and offered an appreciative smile, which surprised him. "Thank you for telling me, Chief. I think the boys and I will be just fine. It was just a surprise, but maybe it was for the best," the woman told him with a light about her that surprised him.

"Uh, do you need anything?" Eli asked, not exactly sure what to say.

The woman looked at him for a minute before she chuckled. "Tell Jex I miss him at the diner. Thank Mrs. Wickersham for calling to check on me yesterday and offering to sponsor the boys' baseball teams. She's a very kind woman," Eileen offered. Eli nodded before he left.

The funeral was a few days later, and when Jex and Mrs. Wickersham arrived with Trudy Somerset, Eli was thankful the man he loved was fitting in so seamlessly with the residents of Haven's Point.

He quickly observed the only person who seemed sad to watch Dirk Stewart's coffin lower into the ground of Green Lawn Cemetery was the groundskeeper. He would have to put in another few hours to clean up the graveside.

Eli walked over to Jex and Mrs. Wickersham to check in with them. "New guests arrive in the morning, right? Can I steal this one for the night?" Eli asked as he touched the small of Jex's back.

The beautiful redhead was wearing a suit that seemed very old fashioned, but it looked incredible on him. The grey, chalk-stripe jacket and trousers fit his gorgeous frame perfectly, and with his red hair and beautiful features, Jex Ivers cut quite a striking appearance.

"Of course, Chief. I think it's a good idea the two of you take some time for yourselves." Mrs. Wickersham then turned to Jex. "I invited Trudy and Lottie over for dinner this evening. I'll see you in the morning, dear," the old woman explained before she walked away to stand next to Mrs. Somerset.

"How'd you get here, by the way?" Eli asked, having forgotten Jex didn't know how to drive.

He pointed to Trudy Somerset. "That crazy little woman drove us. Thank you for not making me ride home with the two of them. I was scared to death. Trudy doesn't know the gas from the brake," Jex complained as he unbuttoned his jacket. It brought a chuckle from Eli.

The two of them walked hand-in-hand to Eli's SUV, and he opened the door for Jex to get inside. When he walked around to the driver's side and got in, the chief looked at the man sitting next to him. "When you were a little boy, what did you dream about?" he asked, staring into Jex's beautiful green eyes.

He watched as his love looked down at his long fingers and picked at his cuticles for a minute before he looked up at Eli with a tender smile. "I dreamed that one day I'd wake up to be a princess. I know it sounds ridiculous, but I used to love fairy tales. I loved the idea that there was a happily ever after for everybody, even after I found out that was just bullshit."

Eli pressed the button to start the SUV, but before he reached for the gear shift, he reached for Jex's hand. "Did you ever see yourself with a permanent partner in your life? Did you think a prince might come along to give you a happily ever after?"

Jex looked out the window before he turned to Eli. "I'm not a princess, Eli. I'm the scullery maid who doesn't deserve the prince, even if there was such a thing."

"I plan to prove you wrong, Jex Ivers," Eli stated as he shifted the SUV into drive.

It seemed as if they'd gone three steps back, but Eli wasn't giving up. There were a lot of questions haunting him, but he wasn't a stranger to searching for answers, even if they weren't the ones he wanted to hear.

Karen and Glenn Moore had taught Elijah the truth might be hard to understand or even accept, but when one knew the truth, they had all the tools they'd need to handle any situation, and they could search for the silver lining. Eli was coming to believe it more than ever. Jex was his silver lining, and he'd make sure the man understood it as well.

XIV

"I think you should let me go alone, babe. I don't want to put you in unnecessary danger by having you there in case this is a setup. My officers can keep you safe here in town while I'm gone, and they don't have to know why they're doing extra patrols by the Inn."

"I'll really miss you, Jex, but I wanna go check this out on my own. I want to be sure it's not a trap, okay? Please don't get upset about this. I'm not trying to boss you around, I swear. It's just that your safety is more important than anything, and after the trial, I'll take you anywhere you want to go for as long as you want to stay. I have a lot of vacation time accrued, and I can't think of anything better than the two of us going on a trip together," Eli fast-talked, which made Jex smile.

"Okay, okay! Don't sprain your tongue. I happen to love it very much. You'll be back when?" Jex asked as the two of them sat under the stars on the beach that Sunday night.

The next morning, Eli was driving to Ocean City, Maryland, to meet with Detective Cather regarding the new trial for Bernard Overman. Jex could feel the nerves coming off of Eli about leaving him alone in Haven's Point, and as he considered it, there was a lot to worry about.

The cold, hard fact of the matter was...if Bernie Overman was going to find Jex and kill him, there wasn't anything he could do about it except try to save the people he loved. With Eli out of town, he had one less worry.

Jex had the happy fortune to meet Glenn Moore the previous week when Eli's father arrived in Haven's Point to spend a month with his son, and he brought a guest. Olive Rhodes seemed to be a lovely woman as far as Jex could tell, but he understood why Eli was leery of a stranger his father brought home without any warning.

Glenn made the mistake of surprising his son with a new romantic interest instead of talking it out with Eli like an adult before arriving at the beach house in Haven's Point. Jex thought he understood why Glenn chose to make his guest a surprise, though he believed maybe another approach would have been better. Eli wasn't really warming up to the woman at all.

After the trip to Ocean City, Jex planned to sit him down and remind him how his father needed someone to keep him company in South Carolina, just like everyone else on the planet. Maybe that was a discussion they could have to keep Eli's mind off the trial when they went back to Newark?

As it stood, the chief refused to even consider allowing Jex to go back for the trial alone, which was what Jex had wanted. He wanted Eli as far away from Bernie Overman as possible, but Mrs. Wickersham had taken Eli's side in that discussion, which was frustrating as hell.

"I'll call Detective Cather and have him find me a place to stay under protective custody. I'll be fine." The couple was having dinner at the Inn with Eli's father, his girlfriend, and the old woman. Glenn Moore and his companion had just arrived in town that afternoon, and Mrs. Wickersham had insisted they come for dinner. The former Police Chief and the innkeeper had seemed happy to see each other once again, and Jex was pleased to meet Eli's father, observing that the man loved his son above all else.

The table fell silent, so Jex looked up to see Eli and his father staring at each other before the chief spoke. "No, Jex. I'm going with you, and we're not going to depend on Cather to keep you hidden. I'm going to meet him in Ocean City alone to get a feel for what the hell is going on, because I don't trust him with your safety. He told me there are a lot of problems at his precinct, and I won't allow some greedy ass…jackass to jeopardize your well-being. I'll check it out first, and then we'll make plans. You're not going without me," Eli commanded.

Jex glanced at Mrs. Wickersham, who had a distressed look on her face. "Jex, I want you nowhere near that awful man, but if you have to go, I'd feel much better if Eli goes with you. We have so many plans, dear, and I can't accomplish anything without you."

Glenn Moore cleared his throat. "What's going on? Is Jex in trouble or something? I'll go along with you if you need help, Eli. Olive won't mind staying here, will you Olive?"

"I don't mind at all, Glenn. I'd be available to help Mrs. Wickersham with things while you're gone. Here, let me start by doing the dishes," Olive stated as she rose from the table and began clearing. Jex rose to help but suddenly had a different idea.

When Jex arrived in the kitchen with the dishes, he was a little nervous about what he was going to request. "I, uh, I usually do this myself, Ms. Rhodes. If you wouldn't mind, I'd like to speak to Mr. Moore alone. I hope to spend time with you, of course, but he's Eli's father, and I think you can see…"

"Say no more, Jex. I'll send him in, and yes, I'd love to spend time with you. Dinner was amazing, by the way," the woman praised, which made him smile. He'd made Mrs. Wickersham's glazed salmon with lime risotto, and he was quite pleased everyone seemed to enjoy it.

When Glenn Moore came into the kitchen, Jex was a bit tongue-tied, but he had things he needed to know that actually didn't involve Eli, so he showed the man out to the front porch. "I wondered if we could have a discussion without the others nearby. Mrs. Wickersham told me you were the Chief of Police here in Haven's Point when her son passed away. You knew her husband?"

Jex saw the man's look of repugnance, and he second-guessed himself for asking the question. "I'm sorry. It's not…"

"That son-of-a-bitch deserved to die a horrible death for what he did. Michael Wickersham was a great kid, and when I got the call from Neil that the kid shot himself? I knew for damn sure that was a lie. I would see Michael around town running errands for Hilda, and he was the kindest young man I ever met, always with a big smile and a friendly wave."

"When I arrived at this house that day, I knew in my gut it was a contrived scene. Blood was smeared everywhere, but not much of it was on Michael. There also wasn't a bullet hole in his pajamas like there should have been if he was already dressed for bed like Neil said."

"The angle of entry wasn't possible if the kid shot himself. Hell, the kid shooting himself that way didn't make sense either. Suicide statistics show us men go for a headshot if they're going to kill themselves. Women usually shoot themselves in the chest because they don't want to mess up their faces. The only conclusion I could reach was someone else shot Michael."

"Oh, there were a lot of other red flags pointing to Neil's story not lining up with the evidence I found on the scene. The fact the doctor arrived before me and knocked her out before I got to talk to her was a huge red flag."

"Hilda had been sedated, heavily, by the town quack who would have been a better veterinarian than he was a doctor. Neil answered my questions with what he thought I'd believe, but nothing he said added up to what I was seeing. Problem was, his family was well-respected in town, and if I was going to blame him for doing something so damn heinous as killing his own son, I had to have my facts straight. Given that the scene had already been contaminated by Neil trying to clean it up, plus the fact Neil was a damn good lawyer, I knew I didn't stand a chance."

"Putting Hilda through more hell didn't seem worth it because nothing was going to bring Michael back. When Neil took off on her? It was best to let things go, or so I told myself."

"Trust me, son, I wanted to make that man pay, but I was worried about Hilda's well-being. When I finally got the chance to talk with her once she wasn't whacked out on whatever that doctor was giving her, she said, 'Chief, does it really matter now? Michael isn't coming back, is he? I want to bury my son.'"

"Neil had held off on the funeral until Hilda was able to attend, though I'm sure he did it to remind her who was really in control of things. Anyway, I did what I thought was for the best. No one deserves to die because they love people others believe they shouldn't. Sadly, not everyone is of the same mind. Now, let's talk about you and my son..." Glenn Moore demanded.

At the end of the conversation, Jex knew Eli's father was a good man who loved his son for the man he was and wasn't trying to make him into anyone else. All he wanted for Eli was the very best life had to offer. Jex was more than sure he wasn't the best, but he vowed if he lived through the trial in Newark, Jex would do everything he could to show Glenn Moore how much his son was loved.

"I'll be back in three days at the latest. There's a reason I'm going, and it's not to party, Jex. I need to get information from Cather, and if I pick up on something not quite right, then you and I are getting the hell out of Haven's Point. I won't allow anything to happen to you," Eli insisted.

Jex reclined and pulled Eli down on top of him on the blanket they were sharing that night. "I want you to stay here with me tonight, please?"

Eli gave him a soft kiss and pulled away. "I'll be more than happy to stay, and not just because I don't want to hear Pop nailing Olive again. I'm really trying to give her a chance, but it's not easy to imagine him with anyone other than my mom. I still remember how much my parents used to kiss and hug, and to see Pop kissing someone else bothers me," Eli explained.

Jex didn't doubt it, but change was inevitable, and Eli was going to have to accept it. Instead of pushing the issue, he decided to promote one he'd rather focus on. They'd been enjoying each other's bodies in a pretty PG-14 rated fashion, but Jex was ready to ratchet things up to at least an R-rating.

He climbed on the top cop and balanced on his fists as they were placed on each side of the handsome man's head. "I want something from you, Eli," he whispered as he rubbed his hard-on against Eli's quickly stiffening cock.

The low moan that escaped from Eli's throat made Jex smile. "Anything, babe."

"I want us to do more physical stuff. I promise I'm ready," Jex announced with confidence. He had a feeling the chief would shy away from doing more than the touching and frotting they'd been doing up to that point, though there was the one blowjob Eli had given him, and it was sublime. Jex wanted more. He wanted to feel like he was just another gay man with a boyfriend, not someone who was so broken and damaged he couldn't enjoy physical pleasure.

It was time to stop running from the horrific memories of his life with Bernie Overman. If he continued to allow those horrible recollections to rule him, he gave the man a power he didn't deserve. Jex needed to replace the awful memories with the beautiful ones he was sure he could create with Elijah Moore.

Eli's face morphed into a huge grin. "I'm definitely ready for more, Jex. I was going to ask you if you'd fuck me."

His love was taken aback at the comment. "No, Eli. That's not..."

Eli sat up and pulled Jex closer, gently cradling his face. "You've never asked me what I enjoyed when it came to sex, but I used to like bottoming back when I was dating regularly. I topped too, but I got a lot of pleasure from bottoming," the man explained, stopping Jex in his tracks.

"You? You bottomed? You submitted to another..."

"Whoa, no, babe. Bottoming isn't even close to submitting. There's no transfer of power when you bottom. It's more about trust, Jex."

"That sick fucking shit Overman forced on you when he took you against your will? That's not a normal relationship by any stretch of the imagination. It's not a bad thing to want to take your lover into your body, okay? Will you consider it?" Eli asked, shocking Jex.

When he was younger, Jex didn't really know anything about having sex with a man, though he knew he paid a lot more attention to the guys he met in his everyday world than the women. Hell, he knew even less about having sex with a woman, having never done it. He didn't date when he was in the foster system because it was hard enough trying to assimilate into a family who didn't know him and usually didn't want him, much less try to find people who were like-minded when it came to sexual identity.

He mostly tried to keep from having the hell beaten out of him, which he wasn't usually successful at achieving. Trying to come to terms with his position on sex back then wasn't anything that really crossed Jex's mind until he was kicked out of his last foster home and became homeless. Life became real in a matter of hours that day and sleeping on a bench in a park near his previous address was a rude awakening. He only had himself from that day forward.

When Bernard Overman found him three days later, hungry and homeless, the man seemed to know he had a weakling he could control, and he took advantage of it. The next five years were a fucking nightmare, but Jex survived, somehow, and when he was released from his spot in hell, he vowed to himself to figure out how to make a good life, or he'd take his own.

Meeting Eli Moore, and then Mrs. Wickersham, had given him an entirely new perspective on his future. "If you really want me to make love to you, I'd like to try sometime, Eli. I'm not ready yet, but maybe we can work up to it?" Jex whispered as he kissed the person who probably saved him from himself.

Jex knew one thing for sure. He couldn't continue to depend on Eli to continually build him up. He had to find his own power and learn to be an equal partner to Elijah Moore if he wanted to spend the rest of his life with the man. Eli deserved someone who could not only love him but stand up to him if necessary. Equality was something Jex had never been taught to expect from anyone, but he knew it was essential for him to aspire to it if a relationship between Eli and him would ever have a chance.

Jex saw a smirk on Eli's face. It was sexy as hell, so he placed his hand on the man's bearded jaw. "What's going through that dirty mind of yours?"

Eli chuckled. "If you're not ready to fuck me, that's fine. We'll get there, but right now, I want to suck your cock. I know it wasn't exactly comfortable for you when I did it that other time, but if you let me try again, maybe we can move onto even more fun? Only if you want to, babe."

Jex considered Eli's position of being the one without sexual hang-ups trying to figure out the best way to show physical love to someone who has never experienced it. If Jex truly wanted a partner to share his life, he had to allow reciprocation. He so wanted to go down on Eli, but the man refused to allow him to offer pleasure until Jex was willing to take his turn in the hot seat again, and it was damn well beyond time.

"Okay," Jex responded nervously.

They were on a thick blanket on the sand, the moon and the stars seeming to give their blessing to the union. When Jex's shorts were unbuttoned, and his briefs pulled down with them, Jex fought the panic that swelled in his chest as horrible memories began to fill his mind.

Jex knew for a fact Eli wasn't going to hurt him. The man loved him, and he wanted to show his love physically by taking Jex into his mouth again. Jex needed to allow it if they were going to have a future together. Besides, Jex had only ever had one blow job in his life, and he was so nervous he barely remembered coming.

The heat of a warm, wet mouth was so much better than Jex remembered from the last time Eli had gone down on him, but when Eli sucked him inside that glorious cavern and applied a little pressure with his tongue, Jex's body went from one to ten in about point-three seconds. He tried to pull away because he was about to come too quickly, but Eli refused to let go.

Jex embarrassed himself by climaxing in under a minute. If he were still under Bernie's control, that would have been a colossal infraction that would have led to a punishment Jex didn't want to consider.

"I'm so sorry," he whispered as he turned away from Eli, offering his back in the event Eli wanted to punish him. It was what he'd grown accustomed to when he was with Overman. It was why his back was scarred and mostly numb from so many lashes with whatever Bernie had handy.

Of course, the top cop wasn't having it. Eli slid in front of Jex and turned his face to look into his eyes. "Why would you be sorry, and why the hell did you turn away from me? It's all still new to you, babe. Hell, if you could have lasted much longer, I'd have worried I wasn't doing it right."

Jex froze. "What? Oh, God, you did everything right, Eli. I'm sorry I couldn't hold it longer."

He watched as Eli flipped onto his back and looked up at the stars, or so Jex assumed. "Jex, you don't need to hold it longer. That's not the way love is made. Love is made when we enjoy the way we make each other feel. It's not a timed event, babe. You come when the feelings become overwhelming. That's the way it's supposed to be."

Jex considered the explanation, and he sat up, resting on the blanket. "Can I return the favor this time?"

Eli had refused to allow him to show his skills the last time, and Jex was eager to take his turn because he was sure of himself while he was performing sex acts. It was the rest of the time he felt uncomfortable in his own ugly skin. Besides, if they were going to love each other completely, Jex needed to show the man what he had to offer, right?

"Only if you want to do it," Eli replied.

Jex didn't waste time taking off the man's pants and sucking his ample cock into his mouth. He took his time showing Eli how much he loved him, edging the man to the point Eli pulled his hair a little and groaned, "God, it's so good, baby. I need it."

Jex sucked Eli's cock into his throat and swallowed around the head while he gently tugged Eli's balls, easing off his cock to nibble at Eli's taint. He went on to suck one, then the other, testicle into his mouth to show love to those parts of Eli's body.

The loud gasp and the release were enough to make Jex smile. He'd finally shown the man he had value. He could do many things to make Eli's life better, and they'd only touched the tip of the iceberg regarding what Jex wanted to do for the chief sexually.

"Come on," Eli insisted as he handed Jex his shorts and underwear. The two of them dressed quickly and hurried up the stairs to the deck. They hung the blanket over the railing and quietly slipped into the Inn.

They showered and crawled into Jex's bed together, wrapping their bodies around each other. It was the best night Jex had ever experienced in his life. He prayed there were many more because he could get used to being with Elijah Moore.

Jex stood on the driveway of the Inn, kissing Eli goodbye. The chief was driving an hour-and-a-half down to the Maryland shore to meet up with Detective Cather. "I wish you'd let me come with you," Jex whispered into Eli's ear.

Eli chuckled. "Right now, I need you here to look out for my dad because I don't want him to come with me. I don't know if I trust that woman yet, so keep an eye on her, okay? We're not rich, but I worry she might think we have money we don't, and she'll try to take what he has. You'll take care of him, right?"

"You're worrying about nothing, you know. Olive loves Glenn," Jex offered.

When Eli sighed heavily, Jex took his hand. "Yes, I'll look out for your father. Just be careful. If it feels wrong, get the hell out of there, okay? I'm counting on you coming back to me on Thursday, Eli. Don't leave me here alone, please?" Jex begged.

When the sexy cop wrapped him tightly in his arms, Jex felt as if he had the world on a string. "I'll bring you some saltwater taffy, I promise. I love you, babe," Eli whispered.

"I love you, too. I want you to know something before you go. My real name is..." Jex started before Eli put his finger over his lips.

"Don't tell me yet. I want this behind us before we begin making our future plans. We'll figure it out, okay?" Eli offered. Jex nodded and kissed him again, hoping more than anything the man kept his word and came back to him. Life was uncertain, but for the first time since he'd lost Molly, Jex had hope.

XV

In order to be less conspicuous, Eli swapped vehicles with Will West, his old friend who was also married to his officer, Yolanda West, to make the drive down to Ocean City, Maryland. He checked into a shitty motel on the beach and walked around until the meeting time at noon. Eli made his way to a dive bar called, "Froggy Bottom's," half expecting it to be a gay bar, but low and behold, it was just a shitty bar and grill with a frog theme.

He sat at the bar and checked his phone to see no messages. Jex didn't have a cell phone, so he didn't expect to hear from him, but he'd asked his father to keep him updated on the things happening around Haven's Point. Thus far, Glenn Moore hadn't reached out.

Eli was still reeling about the fact his father brought a stranger...a younger woman of forty...to the beach to visit him. Eli could help but compare that woman to his own mother, Karen, who was a kind, loving woman, always eager to do anything for anyone.

Karen Moore wasn't glamorous or flashy, but she possessed a natural beauty nobody would deny. She lived life to the fullest, and she loved Glenn more than anything such that when she died, Eli believed his father would shrivel up and die. His dad grieved her death hard, and it had worried the chief to the point he had to do something about it because he didn't want to lose his surviving parent.

It almost seemed as if Glenn went on autopilot and did anything he could to run from the memories of a wife he adored. He unexpectedly sold their ranch-style house on a small cul-de-sac in Haven's Point and moved out to a small beach house, which went entirely against the father Eli knew growing up.

After a year, Eli decided to move home to look out for his dad when he believed the man needed him the most, and it worked for a couple of years. His father perked up a bit and asked Eli to take a job at the police department under him.

Eli believed the two of them could navigate the aftermath of losing Karen together a lot better than separately, so he jumped at the job. His mother had been adamant they get along and take care of each other in the event anything ever happened to her, which would usually have both of them scolding her to stop such depressing talk.

The chief was sure his mother was doing her best to offer her support and love from heaven because she'd always been both of their biggest champions. Maybe it was a fairy tale to think she was looking down from somewhere on high, but the idea of it seemed to help both of them get through the initial heartbreak of the unexpected loss from an aneurysm so they could both begin to heal.

Eli was brought from his memories by a hand on his shoulder, so he turned to see his old mentor, Dennis Cather, with a big smile shadowed by a cheesy mustache that made him laugh. "Working in porn as a side hustle?" Eli joked.

"Ha-fucking-ha. I'm a man of a certain age, and the 'stache gives me authority when it comes to all the little assholes like you I have to endure. Show a little respect. I just got promoted to Lead Detective, and I'm takin' the fuckin' L-T's exam next month. How've you been?" Denny asked as he sat down next to Eli, and the two of them ordered a couple of beers.

"Where's your wife?" Eli asked.

"Where she is all the goddamn time, at a fuckin' outlet mall spendin' more money than we can afford. How's Molly?" Denny asked.

"I don't know anyone named Molly. Why'd you want me to go out of my way to meet you here?" Eli responded.

What Eli didn't expect was for Cather to grab his arm and pull him closer. "I'm not bullshitting you, okay? Bernie Overman is in the wind, and I've been trying to find the motherfucker for weeks. Where's Molly?"

Eli jerked away. "Again, I don't fucking know anyone named Molly. Like I told you, I had a cold case that was similar to the Overman case. You keep talking about a woman I've never met. What's your deal?"

The smell of desperation was filling Eli's nose, and he wasn't particularly thrilled about it. "Blackmail or on the take? Why?"

He saw the man seem to come apart right in front of him. "They have Betsy. They have my wife until I get them the kid. You've got to tell me where he is, Eli. My wife is my whole world, okay? This kid...he's not important to anyone except Overman. He's in Haven's Point, isn't he?"

"I wish I could help you, Denny, but you're seriously barking up the wrong tree. I was only looking for a connection to my cold case. I know nothing about anyone named Molly," Eli stated, deciding to stick to his guns and get the fuck out of Ocean City as soon as possible.

When Denny's phone buzzed, Eli saw the smirk on the man's face, and it pissed him off. "Too late. Worked out just like I planned. It's a shame, though, but you'll never get there in time."

He spun the phone around to see a picture of Mrs. Wickersham at the front door. Just as Eli was about to punch the fucker in the face and rush out the door, the place exploded with cops. "HANDS UP! DON'T MOVE!" Eli heard.

As he looked around, he could see they weren't police officers. They were Feds, and the shit was about to hit the fan. That wouldn't help him get to Jex any faster.

When they took his phone, he had no way to call his officers for backup at the Inn. It couldn't happen that way. He'd been lucky enough to meet the most amazing man in the world and was just starting to plan a life. It was too soon for it to fall apart.

It took five hours before Eli was released from the custody of the FBI at the Baltimore Field office. He grabbed a phone at one of the agent's desks and called the Inn, getting the answering machine. Guests wouldn't arrive until Wednesday morning, and there was the possibility Jex and Mrs. Wickersham were shopping or maybe even out to lunch, so they didn't answer the phone. They did the cleaning on Sunday afternoon and Monday, taking Tuesday for themselves, so Eli had a sliver of hope that the photo Cather had shown him was somehow a fake.

When he got no answer, he called the station, hearing the phone click over which meant it was forwarded to someone's cell. "Haven's Point Police Department, Officer Tibby speaking," he heard.

He hadn't called the emergency number because he didn't want to cause a panic if there was nothing to Cather's threat. "Joe? It's Eli," the chief responded.

"Oh, hey, Chief. How's your vacation?" Tibby asked. Eli had said he was taking a few days off for a mental health break. Now, he wished to hell he'd never left Jex back in Haven's Point. If he'd known the Feds were on Cather's trail, he'd have brought Jex along. The man would have been a hell of a lot safer.

"I'll be home tonight. Have you guys been checking out the Inn? Anything suspicious out there?" Eli asked, trying to tamp down his anxiety.

"Not that I know. Let me call…"

"Tibby, what's your location?" Eli heard over the radio. It was Irina Ford.

"Station. You need backup?" Tibby asked Ford while staying on the phone line with Eli.

"All hands. Four fatalities and one unconscious. One male in custody. Send multiple emergency units. Wickersham Inn. I'll call Bellows," Eli heard Irina's voice, and his heart nearly stopped.

"Is Jex all right?" Eli shouted over the phone.

Suddenly, the line disconnected. Eli fell to his knees and screamed. It couldn't end that way.

XVI

Hilda Wickersham had lived a full life, though not exactly an easy one. She had many regrets, but didn't everyone? Of course, they didn't have Hilda's sorrows, but then, how many people could say they'd met a kindred spirit who had suffered just as much devastation in his own life? Meeting Jex Ivers and hearing the parts of his life the young man was willing to share, whether intentionally or through a mindless comment, made Hilda feel she wasn't the only one with a broken heart. It wasn't exactly comforting, but their pain bound them together, and it was a relief not to be alone.

Jex Ivers wasn't anyone Hilda ever thought she'd meet, but the moment she saw him on the beach outside the Inn back in the early, chilly spring, she felt they had things in common. It was a bit confusing in the beginning, but when Eli Moore brought the young man to her home to ask if she wanted him thrown off the beach, Mrs. Wickersham knew in her heart the young man was sent for a reason. He would become her closest confidante, and he would remind her there were so many good things in life to appreciate, even after the tragic events of the past.

Hilda also knew people believed she didn't pay attention to many things around her, but they discounted her, which was a mistake a few people had made in the past and would never have the opportunity to do again. She's seen to it that they didn't get a second chance to disappoint or harm anyone.

For instance, Hardin Leland thought himself entitled to the property that had been in the Wickersham family for many years. He continued to badger Hilda about selling out to him, and the last time he called, he actually threatened to leave her penniless and without a home.

Yes, she'd allowed his threats go unanswered for too long, and of course, she was behind on her taxes, but the medical expenses not covered by Medicare, coupled with the additional physical therapy she needed so she could continue to live on her own, had ravaged her checking account.

If Hilda had remembered when the taxes were due, she could have taken a short-term loan to pay them. With Hardin Leland drawing attention to her predicament, Hilda was sure the taxman would be knocking on her door before she knew it.

With the advent of the summer season, Hilda would have made the payment as soon as the money from the first few weeks' bookings was deposited in the bank. Of course, Mayor Leland was a selfish crook and wanted to apply for his building permits before the Independence holiday. It would give him the fall and winter to turn her beautiful Inn into a crass, commercialized, overpriced, beachside convention hotel. Trudy Somerset's great-niece worked at the courthouse in Georgetown, and she'd told Auntie Trudy about the plans she'd seen filed in the county surveyor's office with Mayor Leland's name penned as the developer.

Mrs. Wickersham finally returned Hardin's call and invited him out for tea and dessert. She sent Jex off to Chief Moore's beach house for a romantic dinner date, and she went about preparing a small variety of snacks.

She pulled some fancy petit fours from the freezer and cubed some lovely Maytag blue and sharp cheddar cheeses ordered from a dairy farm in Wisconsin to put together something for the mayor to enjoy. Hardin Leland never turned down food, that much his girth told her.

Jex had been kind enough to set up the formal parlor for her, so she only had to carry in the tray of nibbles and the pot of tea. She remembered thinking what a good boy Jex Ivers had turned out to be, and she knew she finally had her reason to preserve the Inn for future generations.

After Hilda lost the love of her life...her Michael...she searched for the next caretaker of the magnificent residence. She wanted to leave it to someone who would treasure it as much as she'd loved it, once she rid it of the evil spirits...her husband, Neil, and his mother. She'd even contacted a Native American healer to come through and do a sage cleansing before she opened it to guests.

As she prepared everything for her guest, Hilda thought about the man's height and weight as she filled the small dish with honey. If he only took a teaspoon, it wouldn't be nearly enough, so she added a teaspoon of roots to the tea brew, scurrying to make a quick cup of Earl Grey for herself.

Sitting in the Queen Anne chairs while listening to a blowhard like Hardin Leland was tedious, but Mrs. Wickersham paid attention and nodded, as was polite. She added a full teaspoon of the honey to each cup she made for him, sipping her own plain tea, and when the second hour of their polite conversation passed, she sent him on his way with the promise of considering his monetary offer for the Inn and the adjacent garden lot.

The next day when Lottie phoned to tell her the man had been found dead not far from his home, Hilda actually... morbidly... congratulated herself for being so precise with her calculations. She wouldn't have to worry about her home getting into the wrong hands any longer. She had the proper caretaker who would cherish the property where her son had grown up and eventually lost his life, his grave in the back corner of the garden near a large Oleander bush.

The next Tuesday, Hilda had convinced Trudy Somerset to take her to Dover, skipping the needed appointment with an eye doctor. She'd make her old eyeglasses work for the time being and consider a new pair in the future. Her reason for the trip was to see the

Wickersham family attorney, Delbert Cox, III, to amend her *Last Will and Testament*.

The man wasn't a favorite person of Hilda's, but he didn't argue and did as she ordered. When she left his office that afternoon with a new *Will* witnessed by her dear friend, Trudy, she finally had peace in her heart.

The next problem Mrs. Wickersham had to address was Deputy Sheriff Terry Blake. He meant to cause trouble because he was interested in Chief Moore, but Hilda had already decided Eli and Jex were the couple she wanted to take over the Inn, so when the deputy asserted himself into their business, she concluded she had no choice but to take action to stop him.

His questions about Jex had unnerved, and frankly, pissed off Mrs. Wickersham. The man was clearly after any information that might indict Jex as some sort of a criminal, and she refused to allow it.

"So, Mrs. Wickersham, how did you come to meet the suspect?" the deputy asked.

"Suspect? What is Jex Ivers suspected of doing?" she replied, trying to keep her voice even in tone.

"I believe he's going to attempt to embezzle money from you. Jex Ivers didn't exist until two years ago, Mrs. Wickersham. He's lied to you about his reason for being here," Terry Blake explained.

Hilda contemplated things for a moment before the kettle went off. She had previously been reserving judgment (and punishment) to allow the man to prove her wrong, but when the man accused Jex of something the young man would never do, it was time to dig a little deeper into Terry Blake's motives.

"So, you and Chief Moore have been dating how long?" Hilda asked, finally settling on what she believed to be the crux of the matter.

The man chuckled. "We're not really dating, but we're interested in each other. He's just a little shy about anyone knowing about us. So, what do you know about Jex Ivers, Mrs. W?" the man asked, using a nickname she wasn't exactly pleased to hear, and her mind was made up...as was a pot of special tea and honey-shortbread cookies.

When she heard the news he'd been found in Love Creek, she said a silent prayer for his family. At some point in his lifetime, she was certain Terry Blake had been a decent young man. Somewhere along the way, he'd become a self-important narcissist who believed he was meant for Eli, which wasn't true at all.

Hilda had to take matters into her own hands, and she timed it out perfectly. Trudy called to tell her the tragic news, and as anyone with a kind heart would do, she sympathized with his family and friends. She was sure he had people who would miss him, but his interference into things that didn't concern him had ceased, and everyone could move onto happier times.

As she considered her reasons for approaching Dirk Stewart, Hilda felt a little guilty at first, so she'd backed off her original plan. She'd taken the man to the third-floor apartment, which wasn't easy for her, and she asked him to sketch a mural he'd paint on the wall to liven up the surroundings.

"This place is really a dump," Dirk Stewart offered as he glanced around the room.

The third floor of the Inn was filled with many memories of the early years in her marriage to Neil Wickersham. Hearing the obnoxious man characterize the space where she'd actually been happy at the beginning of her marriage as a dump? It did not sit well.

"Oh, and are you in real estate that you can make such an assessment? I was considering paying you cash to paint a beach

scene up here, but I think I made a mistake," Mrs. Wickersham dangled. 'Cash' was the magic word, and Dirk Stewart took the bait.

He sat down at the kitchen table, clearly not accustomed to the formality of tea service, and he ate the sandwiches and tea cakes as if he was a hungry lion with a fresh kill. He happily poured most of the bowl of honey into his cup. "Not a fan of tea, but it's fine. I'll make do if I sweeten it up."

Mrs. Wickersham had phoned his wife, Eileen, that morning to ask after sponsoring her sons' baseball teams, and the woman had given her the names of the coaches, graciously thanking her for her interest. Losing Dirk Stewart, who hadn't even mentioned his family during their conversation, wouldn't hold Eileen back in any way. Hilda knew Jex would ensure Eileen and her children were well cared for, come what may.

Overhearing Eli making plans with his officers to leave town for a few days made her worry about what could happen to him. She knew the trial of Bernard Overman was approaching in early September. While Hilda wasn't tech-savvy, Lottie Powel was actually quite proficient at computer research and would look things up if Hilda just asked.

Lottie, Trudy, and Hilda didn't play Bridge as they made everyone believe. They were amateur sleuths, and when Jex had come clean about his situation, the three women began researching the facts of the case, finding that investigative abnormalities had been the basis for a new trial for Bernard Overman. That was unfortunate, but Trudy offered an off-handed comment that caught Hilda by surprise.

"You don't think the man will be able to track Jex here, do you? Have you considered any safety measures in the event he tries to find the young man to kill him? It reads as if the only person who's left to put him behind bars is Jex, well, if he's the prime witness as you suspect. Should he leave town?"

After that, Hilda went into planning mode and put measures in place to ensure Jex Ivers wouldn't become a victim once again. He had such a bright future ahead of him, she wouldn't allow anyone to come in and wreck it.

When there was a knock on the door of the Inn that Tuesday afternoon as she was folding her laundry, Mrs. Wickersham looked out her bedroom window to see a large black SUV with tinted windows on the driveway. Hilda saw a large man on her front porch she was sure she recognized. Mrs. Wickersham knew, once again, the need to take things in hand. She had a hard time getting a good look at the man, but in her gut, she knew who was at the door, so she quickly walked out of her room and knocked on Jex's door.

When he opened it, she held her finger up to her lips for him to remain quiet. "Slip out the back door and down the beach to Eli's house and wait for me to call you. That awful man is here, and I don't think he'll harm me. I'm just an old woman. When he comes in and looks around, he won't find you, and then he'll leave."

"Make sure Chief Moore has a loaded pistol in the event it gets out of hand, but don't come back to the house until I call you after they leave."

"I've left a letter for you between my mattress and box springs if something happens to me. I don't mean now, I mean ever. I'll be fine dealing with this, but you need to go, now," Hilda Wickersham ordered.

"I won't run away from it, Mrs. Wickersham," Jex protested.

She couldn't help but offer him a tender smile and an affectionate touch of his cheek. "Dear, look at it this way. Why would that awful man want to hurt me if you're not here? He doesn't know me from anyone, so he has no reason to do harm to me. I suspect he's just grasping at straws, anyway. Now, go! I'll call you at Eli's house when they leave."

Hilda could see the hesitation in Jex's eyes, so she hugged him, remembering how much he reminded her of Michael, and she decided to use the only gun left in her arsenal. "I lost my little boy because I hesitated to act soon enough. I can't let it happen again, Jex. Please go. I can't lose you as well."

It did the trick, and after Jex snuck out the back of the three-seasons room and into the dunes, she went to the front door and opened it. "Good afternoon. What can I do for you? I'm afraid we're not open for business today, but if you come back tomorrow, I'll see what I can do to work you in," Hilda offered. As she began to close the door, the large, bald man with the two thugs behind him put his fist up to block her.

"You're Mrs. Wickersham, right?"

The old woman pulled up her fake smile and looked the man square in the eye. He had a scar on his right temple she recognized from a news clipping, and he seemed to be very full of himself. He didn't actually have manners, but he was one of those people who believed others should cower under his glare. He'd never met Neil Wickersham, nor did he know what the hell she'd suffered at that demon's hands. She wasn't one to flinch from anyone, not any longer.

"I am. Have we met before?" Hilda asked graciously.

"No, ma'am, but I heard my boyfriend is staying here. Is Madison around?" the man asked.

Mrs. Wickersham assumed he was referring to Jex, but she wasn't that easy. "I'm sorry, what's your name, young man?"

"I'm Bernard, ma'am. He and I had a little fight, and he took off because he didn't get his way. It was a misunderstanding between us, and he overreacted. I had to hire a private detective to find him, but I'm here now. I heard he's working here for you?" the slime asked.

"I'm sorry for forgetting my manners, Bernard. Please come in and introduce your friends," she insisted, not sure how she'd handle three men.

"Mrs. Wickersham, this is Bart and Clint. They're...they're my brothers," the man lied easily.

Hilda stared at the two men for a moment before she smiled at Bernard Overman. "You must have quite a colorful family tree," she offered, staring at the African American man whom he'd referred to as Clint and the Hispanic man he'd called Bart.

"Yeah, uh, we grew up together in foster care, which is where I met Madison. So, uh, when will he be back?" the horrible man asked.

Hilda Mahern Wickersham had endured her fair share of awful men. She was well versed in all of the ways they attempted to manipulate and assert their will against her own desires. She'd allowed many of them to take the upper hand, but there came a time when she realized they didn't know what was best.

They didn't love her, really, and all they wanted was control. It was control she wasn't willing to give them, but they still sought it. Unfortunately for the three men standing in front of her, they hadn't done enough research to know what a woman was capable of doing when she was protecting those she loved. In her mind, she was about to teach them the ultimate lesson of control. Unfortunately, they wouldn't realize it until it was too late.

"If you're referring to Jex Ivers, he'll be back in an hour or so. May I offer the three of you some sandwiches and maybe tea?" Hilda asked as she glanced at the clock over the fireplace. It wasn't nearly time for high tea, but one thing every lady knew was how to be flexible.

When the three of them smiled and took seats on her sofa and chairs, she knew she needed to take control of the situation, just as she'd done many times in the past. She had a feeling it might be her last time to deal with evil men, but she was going to protect her *found* son in the way she'd been unable to defend her biological one.

Do unto them before they do unto you. The motto was one Hilda had heard in a movie once, and while it wasn't exactly a religious prophecy, it made sense. If she was determined to keep Jex Ivers from harm, she needed to take care of the three men in her parlor who were waiting to kill him.

"Could I get one of you to help me carry in the tray?" She asked before she stood and exaggerated the limp she'd gotten over months ago.

Bernard Overman looked at the African American man named Clint and nodded, so the large man with the flashy earrings followed Mrs. Wickersham into the kitchen. She grabbed the kettle and filled it, placing it on the large gas stove and turning up the flame under it.

"So, uh, Clint, do you live in the area?" she asked, making small talk with the hope of finding any redeeming quality in the man.

"No, ma'am. I'm originally from Georgia, but I moved to New Jersey when I was in my early twenties after I lost my grandmother. She raised me," he stated, which ran contrary to Mr. Overman's declaration a few minutes earlier.

"Oh, that's a shame. I lost my son years ago, so I know how it feels to lose someone you love. I won't be presumptuous to say I know how your grandmother perceived things, but I'm sure she'd tell you herself she was happier to have passed before you. It's a pain that never goes away, losing a child," she offered as she quickly pulled ingredients out of the fridge to make sandwiches.

"Yes, ma'am, I'm sure you're right. Uh, you can just give me water, ma'am. I'm not one for hot tea," Clint responded.

Hilda stopped in her tracks and thought for a moment before she turned to him and smiled. "I'll gladly make iced tea. You being from the south, you'd probably prefer sweet tea, am I right?"

The man smiled uncomfortably before he nodded, seeming a bit embarrassed. That gave Hilda the necessary boost to continue her preparations. She quickly put together three roast beef and cheddar cheese sandwiches with her special aioli of mayonnaise into which she grated oleander root, garlic salt, crushed pepper flakes, and fresh cracked pepper. She then made three turkey club sandwiches, using the leftover aioli after she added a few additional herbs to taste, and she made a point of tasting the aioli where Clint could see her, so he didn't suspect anything was wrong with the food. One little nibble wouldn't hurt her.

Hilda went to the cupboard and pulled out the *special* honey and a large pitcher. "I sweeten my tea with my own honey. I have a few hives in my garden, and my bees make lots of honey. Have you ever seen a beehive up close?" Mrs. Wickersham asked as she put tea bags into the pitcher and added boiling water to steep.

"I've seen beehives before, ma'am, and I'm not in a hurry to see them again. Got stung eight times tryin' to knock one off the eaves of my grandma's house when I was a kid. Hurts like a mother...uh, those stingers aren't easy to get out," the man explained.

"Are you allergic to bees then?" she asked, knowing that sometimes allergies could develop after bee stings. If Clint were allergic, the man probably wouldn't want honey in the tea, and that would put a wrench in her plans.

"Naw, I'm okay. Can I help you do anything?" the man asked kindly. Hilda tried not to dwell on the outcome of her actions. She was sure the man had done something in his past for which he deserved punishment. Otherwise, why would he be working for that horrible man in her parlor?

Hilda glanced at the clock over the kitchen sink to see it was just after two in the afternoon. She hoped Jex followed her orders and stayed away. Eventually, someone would become curious and stop by, or Jex would come back because she hadn't called him for hours. If everything went perfectly, it would be too late.

XVII

Jex paced Eli's beach house, unable to think about what to do. He could call the police...he should call the police. Technically, Overman had left New Jersey and was in Delaware, and there had to be some rule about crossing state lines when one was out on bail or on house arrest as Jex remembered being mentioned in an article he'd found on Mrs. Wickersham's laptop computer on the front desk in the entryway of the Inn.

As far as Jex knew, Eli was the only one at the police department who knew about the restraining order Jex had against Bernie Overman, and with him out of town, nothing could be done to enforce it, not that it mattered because if he was anywhere near Overman, Jex knew his life was over.

Jex heard a car on the driveway of the beach house and prayed it was Eli, but it wasn't. He hadn't heard from the man he loved since the chief left earlier that morning, which already had him jumpy. With the news Bernie Overman was up the beach at the Inn, perhaps harming Mrs. Wickersham, he was about to jump out of his skin.

The front door opened, laughter filling the empty house. It was Eli's father, Glenn, and his girlfriend, Olive. "Oh, hello, Jex. Is Eli home?" Glenn asked.

"Not, uh, not yet, but Mrs. Wickersham is entertaining friends, so I thought I'd come down here and hang out. I'm sorry if I'm intruding. I can make myself scarce," Jex suggested.

"Nonsense. I'd love to get to know you better. Maybe you can help me figure out how I can win over Eli. He doesn't seem to like me very much," Olive assessed as she and Glenn began unloading groceries onto the kitchen table.

"Oh, let me help," Jex offered as he began emptying another bag.

"It's okay. I've got it. I was going to make some lunch if you'd like to join us," Olive suggested as she began hunting through the cabinets.

"No, really, let me. I'm the one who stocks the kitchen for us, so I know where it all goes. I'm sorry if you were short on things. I did the shopping before you came, but I guess..." Jex trailed off, seeing the woman had bought most of the same things he'd already stocked.

"Oh, I guess I didn't realize things were as well stocked as they are. We've had dinner around town every night since we arrived, so I haven't snooped around. Do, uh, do you spend a lot of time here?" Olive asked. She was a lovely woman with bright blond hair cut into a stylish bob. It made her bright amber eyes pop. She was definitely a head-turner.

Jex felt his cheeks flush, which brought a giggle from Olive. "Oh, you're so adorable. I apologize if I've stepped on your toes, Jex. Clearly, you and Eli are much more serious than Glenn knows," Olive assessed.

"Glenn knows what?" they both heard as Eli's father came in with more bags.

"We didn't need to go to the store, Glenn. Jex stocked the kitchen before we arrived. You didn't tell me he and Eli were so serious," Olive rebuked gently.

"Well, he didn't tell Eli about you at all, so I'm guessing our men are communicationally challenged," Jex remarked, this time seeing Glenn Moore's face flush a little.

"You didn't tell him *anything* about me?" Olive bristled. Jex suddenly felt guilty about opening his mouth, but knowing how bristly Eli was about the woman, maybe it was good to get it out in the open.

Glenn sighed as he pulled out a chair from the table and took a seat, grabbing a beer from the six-pack on the table and twisting off the lid. "In my defense, Eli and Karen were very close, and I thought the element of surprise would be best for him. If I gave him a chance to make a list of why he wouldn't like you, I was afraid he wouldn't give you a chance. I thought it best for the two of you to meet and get to know each other in person," Glenn surmised.

Glenn then turned to Jex, gesturing toward the carton of beer. Jex took one, opened it, and handed it to Olive before choosing one for himself. "Eli told me he met someone. It was around the time Lena's place caught on fire, and Deputy Blake was trying to blame it on you. Eli said the guy had a thing for him, but his advances weren't welcome. How'd that get resolved? Eli and I didn't talk about it again," Glenn mentioned.

It occurred to Jex at that moment, Mrs. Wickersham might have been one of the last people to see Deputy Blake alive. Did Eli ask her about it? What about Dirk Stewart? Eli mentioned Eileen said she'd spoken to Mrs. Wickersham recently. What was that conversation about, and had Mrs. Wickersham actually invited the man to her home to give an estimate for a mural in the top floor apartment? At the end of the day, Mrs. Wickersham looked as if she might have more to do with those deaths than Jex first thought.

"Can I use your phone?" Jex requested.

"Sure, son. Help yourself," Glenn offered, handing him the device. Jex quickly looked up the number for Dewey's Garage and called it from Mr. Moore's cell. He smiled at his two companions and walked out onto the back deck, staying out of sight of the Victorian.

"Dewey here," he heard answered.

"Hi, Dewey. It's Jex Ivers. You fixed my bike, remember?" he asked.

"Yeah, sure. The redheaded kid. What can I do for ya? Mrs. Wickersham's car on the fritz again?" the mechanic asked.

"No. I wondered what you did with the old box freezer you hauled away a few weeks ago. Mrs. Wickersham thinks maybe there were some tools inside she wants to get back. Did you open it?" Jex asked, feeling the nerves.

"No. I put it back in the junkyard to ship off with the other scrap metal. Good thing you called. You want me to bust the lock and check on it?" Dewey asked.

"Uh, no, that's okay. Can I come out and check? I don't want to bother you. I'm sure you've got enough going on," he offered, sure he didn't want the man to find what Jex suspected was inside that box.

"Yeah, I'm here all day. See ya later," Jex heard before he hung up.

Problem was, his bike was at the Inn, and there was no way to sneak over there and get it without being caught. It was time to ask for help, and since Eli wasn't around, Jex decided to enlist the other Moore man he believed he could trust.

He went inside and looked at Glenn. "I have a favor, and you can say no," Jex began.

"Whatever you need," Glenn answered without hesitation.

On the drive out to Dewey Zellner's place of business, Jex took a leap of faith and told Glenn the things about himself he was sure Eli had left out. Glenn knew Jex was a witness in a case in Newark, but Eli hadn't filled his father in on the details of it, which was another reason he told his father not to come with him to Ocean City.

After he explained his shame of being Overman's sex slave, he changed the subject because the real reason they were going to the junkyard wasn't related to Jex's case. It dealt with Mrs. Wickersham.

When they arrived at the large garage, Glenn turned off his SUV and turned to Jex. "I'm sure I know what's in that freezer, Jex. If we don't open it, we can forget all about it. You said Dewey is sending it off with the scrap metal next week. Nobody needs to know," Glenn offered.

Jex looked at him for a moment. "You mean you don't want Eli to know you turned the other way when Neil Wickersham disappeared? Give me a good reason why he shouldn't know, Glenn. I love the woman, but I believe she might be responsible for not just Neil's death around here."

Glenn banged his hand on the steering wheel and cursed. "Fucking hell! I thought things would be fine. Hell, Neil Wickersham deserved to die for killing his own son. I didn't help her kill him, but I didn't look for him when he disappeared. I thought if I ignored the implications, things would die down and everything would go back to normal."

"I'd contributed to Hilda having such a shitty life because I turned my back on the rumors and the bruises, the broken bones, the reports of shouting coming from the house. Trudy Somerset came to see me more than once and said Neil was abusing her, but I was as ignorant as anyone else in this town and believed what happened between a husband and a wife wasn't anyone's business. Hell, Karen and I had a few shouting matches of our own I'm sure the neighbors could hear, but nobody reported them because everyone believed it was best to stay on their own side of the fence. For the record, I never laid a hand on my wife."

"I should have come to Hilda's rescue, so honestly, all of it, even down to Michael's death, is my fault. Let's go look in that freezer, and if we're right, I'll take responsibility for Neil's death. Now, who else do you think she's killed, and how in the hell could a woman her age kill anyone?" Glenn asked.

Jex thought about his question and what it would do to Eli if Mrs. Wickersham had somehow been involved in those murders. Maybe Glenn should have investigated Neil Wickersham's disappearance, but it was too late to do anything about his death some twenty years later.

"I'll be right back," Jex remarked before hopping out of the SUV. He went into the garage and found Dewey under an old Buick.

"It's just me, Jex Ivers. I wanted to let you know to go ahead and send that old freezer for scrap. We found the tools," he told the man who rolled out from under the car.

Dewey smiled. "Sure thing. Tell Mrs. Wickersham that I said hello. Ask her if she needs me to come over to service her car. It's been almost a year, and if you ain't drivin' it much, it needs a full flush. Call me. I'll come out and get it for her."

Jex nodded, thanked the man for his time, and walked back to the SUV, seeing a look of concern on Glenn's face. "You're right. It won't change anything, and it will make things worse for Eli. This shouldn't fall on him. Do you have a gun?"

"Yeah," Glenn responded as he reached into the console of his SUV and pulled out a portable gun safe. He rolled the combination on the front and opened the metal lid.

"You gonna shoot me?" Glenn asked, not seeming to be joking at all. "I deserve it if you want to. I'll take us out to the cove, and you can shoot me and throw me off the dock. Wipe down the SUV, dump the gun, and leave the car. When they find my body, it'll look like I shot myself, so there should be no trouble for you. Just make sure Olive's..."

"God, no! I wasn't thinking anything of the sort. Take us to the Inn. I think we need to call the cops to meet us there. It's been a few hours, and if Bernie and his thugs are still there waiting for me, we need to get Mrs. Wickersham out of there," Jex explained.

Glenn peeled out of the parking lot and headed back toward the Inn at a high rate of speed. When the blue and red lights came on behind them, both men began cursing. Glenn pulled over to the side of the road and shifted into park.

"What do we say?" Jex whispered as if the police officer could hear them in the closed vehicle with the air conditioning running.

"Don't say anything. Looks like a woman, but it's not Yolanda," Glenn observed as he looked in the rearview mirror.

"It's probably Irina Ford. She's new in town. Her son, Luke, has my old job at *Lena's*," Jex responded.

"Okay. Fuck, this gun's not licensed in Delaware. My old gun is at the beach house. Don't make a move. I'll handle it," Glenn stated. He rolled down the window and tossed the unloaded gun out of it, keeping his hands where the police officer could see them.

Irina walked up to the rear of the vehicle and stopped. "BOTH OCCUPANTS, STEP OUT OF THE VEHICLE AND LAY FACE DOWN ON THE ROAD WITH YOUR FINGERS LOCKED BEHIND YOUR HEAD. DO NOT MAKE ANY SUDDEN MOVES," Irina yelled.

"Do what she says. Nobody needs to die here," Glenn instructed, so Jex slowly got out of the SUV, walked around to the front of the massive Ford, and lie down on the asphalt, fingers locked behind his head. Glenn did the same.

"Say nothing. I'll do the talking," Glenn whispered.

Irina walked over and picked up the revolver Glenn had thrown out the window. Jex saw her from his view beneath the SUV, so he wasn't shocked when she walked around it. "Glenn Moore are you related to the Chief of Police, Eli Moore," she asked, obviously having run his license plate.

"Yes, he's my son, but that's no excuse for me to bring an unregistered firearm into the State. You should cuff me and put us in your cruiser. Take us to the police station, but first, we need to go by the Wickersham Inn because we've been calling Hilda, and she's not answering. You can arrest me after. Jex has nothing to do with this," Glenn answered her.

"Jex? I thought you went with Eli to Ocean City for a few days," Irina responded.

He glanced up and smiled at her. "He was going to meet an old friend, so I backed out. It wasn't anyone I knew, and I didn't want to be a third wheel, so I stayed here with his father and girlfriend. Mrs. Wickersham is at the Inn, and I'm worried about her. Can we go?" Jex urged.

"Get up. Mr. Moore, I'm afraid I will have to take you in, and I'm going to have to cuff you, sir. We'll sort it out, but let's get to the Inn to make sure Mrs. Wickersham's okay," the woman urged.

The two men jumped up, and after Glenn was cuffed, he and Jex got into the back seat of the police cruiser. After she secured Glenn's SUV and brought the keys, Irina Ford hopped in the front seat. "Is she in danger?" the woman asked as she picked up the radio to call it in.

"I don't know. Can you wait to call it in until we get there? If Mrs. Wickersham's okay, she'll be pretty pissed at me," Jex decided. They were on a collision course with a hell of a lot of trouble, or so Jex feared.

If the men were still there and were somehow dead, Mrs. Wickersham would be in hot water. If they'd left after Jex hadn't returned in an hour as Mrs. Wickersham mentioned she was going to tell them and she was okay? Maybe Jex could explain away his concerns for her safety as overprotective paranoia, and no one would ever find out what had actually happened that day or to those residents who had recently died in the town. It was a possibility.

They pulled into the circle drive, seeing the large black SUV was still in the driveway. "You know that vehicle? It has New Jersey plates," Irina observed.

"I don't know the vehicle, but I think I know the people who are in the house. They're dangerous," Jex stated.

"Look, Officer, Mrs. Wickersham's in there alone with possibly three killers. Give me my gun and let's go inside. Take off my cuffs. I promise you, I'll only provide backup. I used to be the chief of police in town, but we can discuss that later. That man in there is a fugitive from New Jersey, and he's got cops on the take everywhere. Hell, you might be one," Glenn accused.

Jex saw the look on her face immediately. "I was a cop with the Atlantic City police force for twenty years before I decided to move my son somewhere he wouldn't get shot when he was hanging out with his friends."

"I have commendations for meritorious service working with the gang unit, and I have a scar on my belly where I got shot during an arrest. Some little asshole didn't think I could run as fast as he could, and when I showed him I could, the little fucker shot me. Now, anything else?" Irina demanded as she drove passed the Inn and stopped in front of the neighbor's house instead of turning into the driveway.

She unlocked the apparatus holding the shotgun that was fastened into the front seat of the cruiser and opened the back door. Once Glenn was out, she released him from his handcuffs and handed him the gun.

"I guess you know how to shoot this, yes?" she asked. Glenn nodded.

"Stay here and stay down," Glenn ordered Jex. He closed the back door, but it didn't latch, so when Irina and Glenn began rushing toward the house doing that crouching cop run Jex had seen so often on television, he hopped out to follow.

Once they were nearer the house, Jex caught up and watched as Glenn Moore kicked in the front door. The two of them entered the Inn just as the phone rang at the front desk. Jex rushed up the stairs and into the Inn, stopping immediately at the door to the parlor when the coppery smell of blood hit his nose.

In front of him were three men on the floor in a pool of blood, each with a bullet hole in their foreheads. There was a gun on the floor next to where Mrs. Wickersham was sitting in her favorite chair, broken glass on the floor with a lemon lying in a puddle of liquid. She'd thrown up on her blue, cotton dress, and her face was contorted into a grimace.

That was the last thing Jex saw before everything went black.

XVIII

It took Eli an hour and a half to get to Haven's Point from Baltimore after he was finally able to convince the Feds that he was the chief of police in the small hamlet of Haven's Point, and he wasn't involved in Cather's illegal activities. He hadn't told them what he heard over the phone before Tibby disconnected the call, because the last thing he needed at that moment was for them to interfere. He'd heard Irina tell Tibby there were four casualties, one person was unconscious, and one person was in custody, but no names had been given.

Eli had no idea what happened or who was dead, but if it was Jex, his life was over. When he got closer to Haven's Point, he called Bellows' cell, grateful the FBI Agent-in-Charge had returned his own phone when they finally decided Eli wasn't involved in the afternoon's clusterfuck.

It seemed Cather was on the take, though he initially claimed his wife had been kidnapped. One of the agent's told Eli that Betsy Cather was found alive and well at the community pool in their New Jersey neighborhood, daughters in tow. She said her husband was at a work retreat for the week.

Cather's story to Betsy was that he was investing in a new business venture and money would be tight for a while, so their family vacation to North Carolina would have to be postponed for a month, but after he returned from the work retreat he was attending, they could start looking for a new home outside New Jersey. He was going to retire from the police department, and they would start a new life anywhere she or the girls wanted to move. Betsy Cather bought the story, but as Eli had been told, she was about to find out what a real snake her husband had become.

The real story was, Cather had a huge gambling problem and was into a bookie and fight promoter from Atlantic City named

Doctor Jones for a million dollars. The man threatened Cather's daughters, so Cather was against a wall because he didn't have the money to pay the debt.

After Overman's conviction was overturned and he was released on bail, Cather contacted him through one of Overman's henchmen and offered to make a deal. If Overman paid off Cather's debt to Doctor Jones, Cather would find Jex Ivers for him.

After that, it was Overman's choice regarding what to do with Jex because Cather refused to kill him. Overman had been searching for him for years, but Jex had simply vanished into thin air, and the slimy bastard was frustrated. Overman jumped at the deal and promptly paid the money owed to Doctor Jones.

In the process of the transaction, Overman mentioned to Jones about the deal he'd struck with Cather, so when Jones got picked up for attempted match-fixing of an upcoming welterweight fight in Vegas, he gave up Cather and Overman's arrangement to get his charges reduced so he wouldn't lose his promoter's license. *It only takes one weak link in the chain before the trap snaps*, Eli told himself.

Cather told the Feds he'd passed on word to Overman of Jex's whereabouts, so Eli had to get to the Inn to find out what the hell had happened. His heart had stopped beating when he heard Irina over the radio, and it wouldn't start again until he looked into the beautiful green eyes of the man he loved.

The driveway of the Inn was full of first responders from neighboring jurisdictions. Eli parked Will West's truck and ran up the driveway, having attached his badge to his t-shirt. "Where are my officers?" Eli asked one of Sussex County's deputies he vaguely remembered seeing at the winter carnival the previous year.

The guy pointed toward an ambulance where Eli saw Yolanda and Irina, along with his father. He pushed his way through the crowd to get to them so he could find Jex. Suddenly, Eli's heart stuttered to life again, or so it felt as he approached to see Jex sitting inside the large red vehicle with a bandage on his head. A paramedic was taking his blood pressure, and Eli could see his love's eyes were very red.

He pushed everyone aside to get to Jex. "Oh, god, I've been so fucking scared. What happened?"

When Jex wrapped his arms around Eli's neck, the world righted itself. The sobbing came quickly, so Eli backed away a few inches to just look at him. He could tell Jex was in no shape to speak, so the chief glanced around and fixed his glare on Irina until she finally spoke up. "Mrs. Wickersham is dead. Seems she shot three men believed to be Bernie Overman and his accomplices before she had a heart attack. She saved Jex's life by getting him out of there before they found him inside."

"Sheriff Cummings took over the investigation since you were out of town. Since it involves Jex, we thought it was a good idea. Anyway, do you want to come inside? I think it's pretty cut and dried what happened, but another set of eyes wouldn't hurt," Irina suggested.

Eli looked at Jex, who nodded and grabbed more tissues from the box next to him to dry his eyes. "Why are you in the ambulance? What happened to your head?"

He saw his beautiful lover flush his favorite pink. "I passed out and hit my head. The smell of blood got to me, plus seeing Mrs. Wickersham in her chair like that was too much," Jex whispered.

Eli glanced at his father, who nodded. "Go take over for Gerry. This is your jurisdiction and responsibility, Eli. You should be in control of the investigation. We gave our statements already, and Officer Ford is going to take me to the county jail. I screwed up, but it's nothing to do with this situation," Glenn offered.

The chief did a double take before he looked at his officer. "It's not anything he really needs to go to jail for, but he's insisting on it." She grabbed Eli by the arm and pulled him aside. "He had an unregistered pistol in his SUV. I didn't know who he was when I stopped him for speeding, but now I know why he was in such a hurry, and I get it. It's really not that egregious a charge, Chief. I'd be willing to let it go if you'd like. Please talk to him. I feel guilty about this, especially the way he helped me out when we rolled up on the scene," Irina finished.

Given the current state of shit Eli had on his plate, he decided it was time to compromise. "Pop, will you take Jex home to the beach house? I'll have Irina write you a speeding ticket, and you surrender your firearm until you're ready to leave town. Why the hell did you bring it with you? You have your registered gun at the house," Eli complained.

When his father didn't answer, he decided to press on. "I'll be there after I deal with this and lock up the Inn. I haven't gone inside, but I want a look, even though it sounds pretty clear cut. You know what happened?" Eli asked.

His father nodded. "Looks like Mrs. Wickersham picked up that something wasn't right, so she shot those three and then had a heart attack, poor old girl. Back in the day, the family had a lawyer in Dover...uh, Delbert Cox, I think. I guess you need to contact him since Jex isn't related to her. There's likely a Will, somewhere," Glenn explained.

Eli touched his shoulder. "I'll handle it, Pop. Love you, and thanks for looking out for Jex. I want to hear the whole story later, okay?"

"Yeah, son. We'll see you later," Glenn offered. He gave Eli a hug and headed over to where Jex was still sitting in the ambulance. With Jex in his father's care, Eli felt an enormous sense of relief. If one of the dead was Bernard Overman, they were about to embark on making a life together without the fear of the bastard who had abused the man he loved for too many years. Eli was cautiously optimistic.

Eli walked into the formal parlor to see three bodies on the floor with .38 caliber bullet holes in their foreheads with no exit wounds. The caliber fit the Smith & Wesson revolver on the floor next to Mrs. Wickersham's hand.

"So, what do you think?" Eli asked Gerry Cummings, who was standing with the county crime scene investigator pointing out the spent shells under the chair for the man to collect.

"Clearly, Mrs. Wickersham was a crack shot. Three dead bodies, three spent shell casings. There were two cartridges left in the revolver. She didn't waste a shot," Cummings told him as he turned to Eli.

"What do you make of *her*? Did she have a heart attack, or did she choke?" Eli asked as he pointed to the evidence of her aspirating on her dress. The peculiar thing was, there was no food in the room.

The sheriff shrugged, and to Eli, it seemed as if the man didn't really give a good goddamn about what had happened on the scene. "I'd say maybe the heart attack caused her to choke and then aspirate. What about the kitchen?" Eli asked.

"Clean as an operating room. Even the trash was taken out. You want us to go through it or do you want your people to handle it?" Cummings asked, seemingly acquiescing to Eli taking charge of the investigation of the crime scene.

As he stood taking in the sights in front of him, something was nagging at the back of his mind again, but he couldn't hone in. One thing was sure, Eli wanted to go home, but he wanted to show respect to Hilda Wickersham, if for no other reason than she'd become Jex's surrogate mother. "No. I don't think this is anything we need to waste taxpayer money on. They must have threatened her, so Hilda killed them, and in all of the excitement, she had a heart attack. I believe when we get back their prints, we'll find one of them is Bernard Overman."

"He was looking for Jex Ivers, and I think she was willing to make sure they didn't find him. If you think I'm conflicted, speak up, Sheriff, and we can talk about it, but Jex was with my father and his lady friend, Olive, when all of this happened."

"Actually, one of my officers stopped my dad for speeding as he was coming through town. Talk to Irina Ford about it," Eli offered, feeling that familiar gnawing in his gut that something wasn't exactly right, but nothing was glaringly wrong.

"No, no. There's no evidence that this isn't as it appears to be. We'll clear out and get you a report. Sorry about Mrs. Wickersham. I know she meant a lot to the town," Sheriff Cummings offered.

An hour later, Eli had put in a call to a cleaning crew who dealt with crime scenes, and he locked the front door. He drove to the West's home to drop off Will's SUV and retrieve his police SUV, thanking Yolanda for her work that day.

By the time he got home that night at eleven, the beach house was dark except for a light coming off the beach. He walked through the house and down the stairs to see Jex had made a small fire in the firepit he'd obviously carried down from the Inn. "Babe?" Eli greeted.

The fire was blazing in the copper bowl, but Jex was nowhere in sight. Eli glanced up to see the moon shining brightly over the water, and it was then he noticed a shadow. Jex was standing in the water, chest deep.

Eli quickly stripped down to his boxers and waded out, happy to feel the relief of the cooling water on his body. Being inside the

Inn had been stifling, by both the smell of blood and gunpowder and the gruesome scene. It was such a fucking relief to find Jex alive and well, and Eli might even consider making a donation to a local church because someone kept Jex safe while he was gone. He also had his father to thank for his part in it, though he wanted to know where the two of them were going when they got stopped for speeding.

"Babe," Eli called out as he slowly waded out to where Jex was standing. He wrapped his arms around his love and kissed his neck. "I'm so sorry," Eli offered as he felt Jex sobbing in his arms.

"They knocked on the door, and she told me to leave, Eli. She told me they wouldn't hurt an old lady. She said not to worry about her, she'd be fine," Jex whispered.

Eli stepped around him and held him in his arms. "Cather was the mole, and his ass is going away for a long time. He got greedy, from what one of the FBI agents told me. We've got plenty of time to discuss all of this. I just want to be sure you'll be okay," he whispered.

Jex pulled away. "How could that be? He was the one who tried to keep me safe back then? He was the one who told me to leave town!"

Eli withheld the shrug because how did anyone really know what happened to fuck up decent people. "Something happened to him between the time he was helping you when he still had a conscience and the guy I ran into today. I think the bottom line is Cather simply let his greed get the best of him. He started gambling, which his wife knew nothing about, and when someone is trying to maintain a double life, they become desperate and fuck up. One of the agents told me he had a gambling problem, and it led him to do something he'd have probably never done otherwise. Unfortunately for him, he just kept getting in deeper."

"I'm sorry I wasn't here for you today, Jex. I need to really think about what I missed when I talked to Cather that I should have caught because none of this should have happened. I guess it's reasonable to assume that Cather found you because of me contacting him in the first place. I'm sorry about that."

"They came to the Inn looking for you because Cather told them that's where they'd find you. Hell, maybe I need to step down because I don't see everything as clearly as I should," Eli suggested, not feeling very secure in his skills at the moment. The fact he wasn't there to keep Jex from harm had definitely shaken his confidence.

"No, Eli. It was one of those situations where we couldn't have known how things would come together and how it would all turn out. We're alive. That's what's important. Can we make love?" Jex asked.

Eli took his hand, and the two of them walked out of the water and over to the fire Jex had built. They both tossed sand into the copper bowl to put out the fire before they walked up the stairs to the deck, rinsed off, and wrapped themselves in the towels Jex had left on the table.

They slipped into the house together, and after Eli locked up, the two of them quietly made their way down the hall to the master bedroom where Eli slept. After stripping off their wet underwear, they stepped into the shower and quickly washed off the sand and the salt. When Jex turned into Eli's chest and kissed up to his neck, Eli's cock made itself known.

"God, Jex, I want to feel you inside me," Eli whispered as he washed his love's slender body while Jex washed his long hair.

Jex stepped back under the spray to rinse for a few minutes before he slid conditioner through his long locks and turned Eli under the showerhead. "I want you to go first, Eli. It's weird but knowing Bernie's dead and can never hurt me again makes me feel incredibly free. I want you to be the first man who makes love to me. Please?"

Eli felt his knees buckle at the mere mention of making love to Jex Ivers. The chief actually thought it would never happen, and he hoped Jex wasn't premature with his desires because after the hell he went through at the hands of Bernie Overman, Eli never wanted to hurt him. His cock, however, was leaking and throbbing to remind him it was more than ready. "Are you sure, babe?"

Jex took Eli's hard cock in his fist and squeezed hard. "Slow down, Chief. I don't want things to end too quickly." It did the trick. Eli backed off the edge, and after the two men dried off and settled into bed, the chief went after Jex's ass, hungry for a taste.

"Oh, fuck, Eli," his love gasped as Eli circled his tongue around Jex's winking hole, slicking it up and taking in the taste of the man he craved.

Eli worked slowly to loosen up his lover. Once his tongue sunk inside easily and Jex was groaning with pleasure, the chief reached for the lube. He gently worked his fingers inside Jex's ass and waited until the man adjusted to his ministrations.

"Is this okay?" Eli whispered.

"You're trying to kill me, aren't you?" Jex complained, which Eli thought was awfully cute.

Eli removed his fingers and looked into Jex's gorgeous face, seeing a smirk. "What did I do?"

"You're taking for-fucking-ever. Let's get to the fucking, Chief," Jex demanded, which made Eli grin. He grabbed a condom from the nightstand and quickly slid it on and applied lube to his hard prick, adding a little more to Jex's hole.

"Oh, please, come on! I want to feel you inside me, Eli." *Well, who am I to hold things up?*

Eli took his time sliding against Jex's ass, waiting for the man to push back on him as Eli rested between his long legs. When Jex accepted him inside, Eli looked into his eyes to see the man wasn't wincing in pain.

"Can I move?" Eli asked as he gently sucked Jex's nipples while long legs were wrapped around Eli's waist.

"God, please do, Eli," Jex whispered.

After a sumptuous kiss, Eli began moving slowly, keeping his gaze on Jex's face in the event there was any pain. For the rest of his life, Eli knew he'd never be happy with anyone else. Jex Ivers was the man he'd love for the rest of his living days.

As their bodies rubbed together, Eli nearly lost his mind at feeling his cock inside the lithe body beneath him. When Jex pushed him over to his back and began riding him, Eli rolled through waves of bliss until Jex stopped moving altogether.

"What's wrong?" Eli asked, resisting the urge to thrust up into the gorgeous man on top of him.

"God, nothing's wrong. I love you, Eli. I want to spend the rest of my life with you. Do you think we can do that?" Jex asked, surprising Eli with his candid request.

Eli felt as if he was about to explode. "Yes, Jex, we can do that," he whispered as the tears made their way down his cheeks while Jex took control of the most incredible sex Eli had ever had in his life. When he released inside the man he loved, he felt as if his life was settled.

Jex let go, spewing all over Eli's chest before he bent over to rest on Eli, his gorgeous red hair providing a curtain for the two of them to stay in their own bubble. Eli looked up at Jex and smiled. "Not bad, right?" Eli asked, seeing the gorgeous smile on Jex's face.

"Yeah, Chief, that'll do." They both laughed as Eli slipped from Jex's body.

They wiped off with the damp towels and slid back into bed. Jex settled on Eli's chest, and the top cop couldn't keep his hand away from the man's beautiful hair. He thought about the best thing to say and finally settle on the most crucial sentiment he could think of. "I love you, Jex. I'm sorry this happened, but I'm even sorrier I wasn't here to stop him, myself."

Jex sat up and tossed his hair over his shoulder, offering a gentle kiss. "It's okay, Eli. You were trying to head off another threat, and I had the senior Chief Moore here to keep me out of the line of fire. I love you, too."

Eli couldn't sleep that night because something kept nagging at him. It was like an awful song that became an earworm one couldn't escape, but for the life of him, he couldn't figure out what the hell it was.

Jex was secure, which was the top cop's highest priority. The details, however, wouldn't let him fall asleep. Eli kept thinking about the crime scene...the Inn. The three dead men were easy enough to explain.

Clearly, Mrs. Wickersham had been an excellent shot to have killed those men without wasting one round. Eli had the gut feeling maybe Neil Wickersham hadn't taken off as it had been portrayed. Eli didn't suspect Mrs. Wickersham had shot her husband, but in light of the fact the woman was dead, and Neil had never turned up, the chief had to wonder what actually happened.

Then, suddenly, it occurred to him that Bernard Overman knew *precisely* where to find Jex. The chief knew for sure he hadn't given away his love's exact location, so how did Cather know he worked at Wickersham Inn?

Eli decided he wanted to talk to a few people in town to see if any of them had seen the three men around town over the last few days, maybe doing surveillance. They couldn't just drive into a strange town and know exactly where to go, could they? Nobody was that fucking lucky.

XIX

Jex stood on the front porch of the Wickersham Inn, looking up at the blue, shiplap ceiling to see it needed to be scraped and repainted. The scraping of the old paint could be done over the winter when the days were warmer, but the painting would have to wait until the spring when he planned to make some changes before he reopened the Inn for the summer.

The past two months had been a whirlwind of activity. Mrs. Wickersham was buried in the family plot on the property. It was at the back of the garden next to her son, and there was a lovely headstone placed next to Michael's.

Trudy Somerset was the executrix of Mrs. Wickersham's estate, and she'd carried out the instructions the old woman had given to the lawyer in painstaking detail.

The day Jex was allowed to gather his clothes before the Inn was locked up by the lawyer, Mr. Cox, he found the letter between the mattress and box springs of her bed, just as Mrs. Wickersham had mentioned the day Overman found him in Haven's Point. He went down to the beach the night after her funeral and read it by himself.

My dear Jex:

An old woman gets things in her head that beg to be written down, so I'm taking the time to leave you instructions I hope you'll appreciate. You will find out in a few weeks I've bequeathed everything to you as my sole heir. The only caveat, as is stated in my Will, is Trudy should get my jewelry, and Lottie always admired the tea table in the front parlor, so please see it's delivered to her.

I leave you with these details to do with them as you wish. I have no pride in what I've done in the past, but in my defense, I took specific actions to protect the people and things I cared about. I can't say there was no malicious intent on every occasion because some people just pissed me off, but that's what the fires of Hell are for, isn't it?

The following is a list of people I've judged and found guilty of acting in such a manner I could find no redeeming quality, nor had they made any contribution to the benefit of mankind. Let's call it a culling of the herd. I didn't take joy in my actions, but I suppose history will judge me for my behavior. I accept it without shame.

Mrs. Wickersham then went on to list seven people she'd dealt with…killed…a few of them Jex didn't know and a few he didn't suspect. The last person listed in the letter was Mrs. Wickersham, herself.

Counting the three crooks she'd shot, Hilda Wickersham had terminated the existence of eleven people, herself included. It was shocking to Jex because she'd been so kind to him, but he supposed she felt the need to confess her sins to someone, and since she'd basically adopted him as a pseudo-son, it was his burden to bear. The last few paragraphs of her letter touched him deeply, in spite of the things he'd learned.

I'm prepared to pay for my transgressions, but Jex, dear, always remember you did nothing to bring on the harsh treatment you suffered at the hands of people who didn't realize how lucky they were to know someone as precious as you. I believe, however, that you've finally found someone who knows how fortunate he is to have you in his life, and I pray you never take it for granted.

I hope when you open the Inn in the spring, you'll think fondly of me. I hope this home brings you as much joy as it brought me when I had Michael to love, and then after his death when I was able to lock away my heartache for those few years and see others enjoy this building as I did when my little boy was alive.

As for me, I'll beg the Creator for a moment's mercy to allow me to see my Michael once again before I'm delivered into the fires of damnation. I'll be spending my eternity with those on whom I brought vengeance, but don't feel sorry for me. I'll remind them of their sins just as they remind me of my own.

Love your Eli, Jex. Have a family. This house was meant for lots of children. The option was taken from me, but don't allow it to be taken from you. Live the best life you can, dear boy, because you deserve it.

All my love,

Hilda Wickersham

Jex dried his tears and folded the letter, putting it into the envelope and staring at it for a minute of indecision. His sentimental side wanted to hang onto her last words because he didn't get the chance to have any from his mother. Of course, there was a danger in keeping the confession of the woman who had taken him in because she'd have been classified as a serial killer in the eyes of law enforcement...in Eli's eyes.

Jex decided to keep her confession to himself, so he built a fire in the copper fire pit and burned the letter. Its contents didn't need to be disclosed to anyone, especially Eli. The man Jex loved would beat himself up for not knowing what was happening in his town, and the chief didn't deserve to feel guilty about things beyond his control. With Mrs. Wickersham gone, the disappearances and mysterious deaths would cease. Things could go back to normal.

Jex unlocked the front door of the Inn, anxious to unpack his things to settle into his real home. It felt quite odd to consider it because he'd never imagined he'd have a home of his own in his life. After Molly was killed, he'd never had a permanent home, and that was his frame of reference. Nobody ever wanted him to stay, ever.

Now, years later, there Jex stood in the entryway of a home he'd been given...a home he very much wanted to share with Eli. He considered the possibility of having children with the man he loved someday in the future, and while he knew it was a beautiful dream, Jex decided not to dwell on it because they'd never discussed the idea of a family. Hell, they'd barely talked about how permanent their relationship would be, which was something Jex wanted to clarify as soon as possible. If it were meant to be, the rest would come in time.

After he had his clothes in the dresser and closet of his old room, Jex walked into Hilda's bedroom to see it looked exactly the same as the last time he'd walked by it while she was still alive, except for the missing jewelry box that had a home on her art deco dresser. The lawyer had given it to Mrs. Somerset when he came to Haven's Point to read Hilda's Will.

Jex knew there would also be an empty space in the front parlor between the two Queen Anne chairs where the tea-table had rested, memories of the times there would be with him for the rest of his life. It was now at Mrs. Power's home as Mrs. Wickersham had requested, and he was happy her wishes had been respected.

The doorbell rang, so he hurried down the hallway to open it, smiling when he saw Mrs. Somerset and Mrs. Powers, each with a basket on her arm. "Ladies, how can I help you?" he asked.

Mrs. Somerset pushed her way inside without hesitation or apology. "It's Tuesday, dear. Bridge day," the woman told him as if he should know what she was meant.

Mrs. Powers followed her inside without hesitation. "How are you, dear? Settled yet? When is the chief moving in?"

Jex trailed behind them to the kitchen where Mrs. Somerset was already filling the kettle. "Well, no definite plans yet. I'm sorry, but did we make a date for Bridge? I, uh, I don't know how to play the game, and I don't remember setting up anything with you, ladies.

I haven't even been to the store to restock the kitchen yet," Jex offered in his defense for being a little hesitant to invite them to sit down.

Mrs. Powers continued to unpack everything from the baskets before she retrieved cups, saucers, and small bread plates from the breakfront in the dining room. The two women busily continued to pull out containers of finger sandwiches, cookies, tea biscuits, scones, and fresh preserves. There was a small plastic bowl of clotted cream Mrs. Powers put into a silver dish from the cupboard before she retrieved the teapot and loaded black tea inside.

"Thank you for bringing the tea table over to my house after the funeral, Jex. I've always admired it, and I'll take good care of it, I promise," Mrs. Powers assured.

"Sure, Mrs. Powers. Mrs. Wickersham wanted you to have it," Jex responded, feeling his head spin at the fact the two women had invaded the house when he was just trying to settle into it himself.

Mrs. Somerset went to the entryway and returned with the laptop from the front desk, placing it on the table. "Let's take a seat. Jex, dear, Lottie and I owe you an apology. I hope after we explain ourselves, you'll not hold it against us, but we are eternally sorry we didn't speak to Hilda before we acted on our own."

The woman then went to the pantry and returned with the jar of clover honey Jex had purchased from the grocery store. He smiled before heading to the pantry. "I think we can use the special honey, ladies. I know Mrs. Wickersham was very stingy with it, but she's gone now. I think she'd want us to use it," he offered before he stepped into the pantry and returned with the large jar Mrs. Wickersham kept inside.

Jex opened the jar and quickly added the golden sweetener to the honey pot Mrs. Wickersham had in a nearby cabinet, filling it with enough for the three of them to enjoy. He returned to the table with the jar, grinning proudly as he took his seat.

He noticed both women eyeing him suspiciously before Mrs. Powers spoke with a shaky voice. "I suppose you might want us to use the special honey, but please let us explain what happened before you kill us."

Jex was taken aback by the comment. "Kill you? Why on earth would I...?" he began his protestation.

"We're the ones who informed the police in Newark where you were," Mrs. Somerset blurted out nervously.

Mrs. Powers stood from the table and walked over to a drawer, pulling out the tea strainer before she brought it to the table. She placed it over each cup as she filled it before she set the strainer on a bread plate. She then began chattering at the speed of sound, which took Jex by surprise.

"Okay, you should know we don't play Bridge. None of us had the patience to learn, so we called our little armchair detective sessions 'playing Bridge' so people didn't try to strongarm their way into our group. Nobody wants to play Bridge around here. Besides, it's dull as hell."

Mrs. Somerset touched her arm. "Slow down, Lottie, before your blood pressure spikes." Trudy then turned to Jex and smiled. "So, The two of us read about Bernard Overman getting a new trial because of technicalities, and we started digging while Hilda was still recuperating from her surgery."

"It didn't sit well the two of us after we read about the first trial, so we began researching the reason it was being overturned. We'd missed the story completely, or we didn't remember it, so Lottie and I researched the first trial to figure out why Overman was even arrested in the first place, and when we found it was because of human trafficking and kidnapping, we were stunned."

"In our research, we found a picture of you when you were on the way into the courthouse to give your testimony during the first trial. For some reason, it stuck with me because you looked so sad and hurt in the photo, then one day in early spring I was at *Lena's* for breakfast, and I felt like I recognized you as I watched you bussing the table behind me. Of course, it took a few times of seeing you for me to understand why you were so familiar, but one day, it finally dawned on me. The hair was throwing me off."

"Anyway, when I pointed you out to Lottie, she disagreed with me at first, but as we continued to see you around, she finally came to the same conclusion as me…you were the young man we'd seen in the newspaper. A follow-up article mentioned the star witness had disappeared, and the district attorney wasn't sure when there could be a new trial because they had no one to testify."

"After I figured out it was you, I'd started to mention the whole thing to Hilda one Tuesday. I printed off a copy of the picture and showed it to her, but Hilda said you looked nothing like the man in the picture."

"Of course, your hair is a lot longer now than in the photo, but I was still sure it was you. Hilda didn't want to know anything more about it because she'd already determined she was going to hire you to help out around here, so I didn't pursue the conversation with her."

"I wrote it off that the picture wasn't very clear and Hilda's eyesight was awful. I talked about it again with Lottie, and the two of us agreed we wouldn't mention anything more to her about your identity."

"With everything she'd endured over her life, it seemed like explaining your situation to her ourselves would be overstepping. If you wanted her to know, you'd tell her," Mrs. Somerset explained as she inserted a thumb-drive into the USB port of Mrs. Wickersham's computer and pulled up a file on the laptop.

The woman then turned the screen toward Jex and pointed to a file. When it opened, she clicked on the article in question, and there was a picture of Jex walking into the courthouse during

Bernie's first trial. His hair had started growing out, though it was nothing like the length he was sporting as he sat at the table with it pulled back in a messy bun.

"So what did you do that makes you think I'd want to kill you?" he reminded, wondering what was really behind the comment.

"It was me, okay? Trudy had nothing to do with it, really. I was the one who called the Newark Police Department and spoke to Detective Cather, the lead investigator on the case. In our defense, we had no idea the man was a double agent until we read about his arrest in the paper after Hilda passed," Lottie Powers explained.

As Jex considered their confession, the way things went down with Overman finding him suddenly made sense. He couldn't really fault them, though. They seemed to think they were doing the right thing, and in the end, it all worked out...with a gruesome twist, but he was alive and well and out of danger.

"I get it, ladies. So, you didn't tell Mrs. Wickersham what you did because she'd already hired me, I suppose?" Mrs. Powers started to speak again, but Mrs. Somerset held up her wrinkled hand to stop her.

"We all loved to do research. Occasionally, we've been fortunate enough to find information for law enforcement to assist with other cases. You see, we never wanted the attention for ourselves, but we wanted to help the police where possible."

"With Hilda seeming so happy and back to her old self, we didn't want to bother her about anything we found out. We'd planned to explain it to her after you testified at the new trial. Of course, none of us knew things would end like this."

"We're so sorry, Jex, and we pledge to keep our noses out of your and everyone else's business going forward. If you'd like, we'll tell Chief Moore what we've done in the event there are any legal consequences," Trudy Somerset clarified.

"Ah, so you thought I'd want to kill you because you reported my whereabouts to that crooked cop? No, ladies, I'm convinced it's all just a horrible twist of fate. I'm certainly thankful they didn't find me, though I'm sorry Mrs. Wickersham died defending me," Jex tried to allay their concerns.

"Then why'd you get out the honey?" Mrs. Somerset asked, confusion forming on her wrinkled face.

"It's special, and Mrs. Wickersham wouldn't let me have any of it while she was alive. I thought, in honor of her passing, we could have some," Jex answered with a nervous grin.

"It's special all right. Use too much of it, and it'll kill you. It's Oleander honey, dear. It's poisonous. Hilda kept it around to use for rat and mice poisoning. Works better than anything I've ever seen in my life," Mrs. Powers told him.

"It's for rats...? No, surely..." Jex was too confused to make coherent sentences.

"Yes, dear. I got some of it one time to use in my garage, and one of the neighbor's cats ate a little of it and got sick. I was grateful the damn thing didn't die because my neighbors would probably have sued me. I looked it up and read about it. Hilda was right that it would make the cat sick. In humans, it mimicked the signs of a heart attack," Mrs. Somerset described.

It took a minute for Jex to put it all together before he remembered the letter he'd burned. Mrs. Wickersham had planned to kill herself all along, and she used the honey to do it...the honey she always told Jex to stay away from. "How can that be? Where'd she get poisoned honey?" he asked, not of anyone in particular.

"She's got that little voodoo garden out there, Jex," Trudy began before she suggested they go outside to the garden in question. The three of them walked down the path, and once they were in the far corner, Mrs. Somerset and Mrs. Powers pointed out all of the different herbs that were harmful if ingested or, in some instances, even touched.

The bright pink oleander bushes were in the back of the gardens, right next to the beehives. "The bees gather pollen from the oleander flowers, and when they make honey, the poison carries forward into the honey."

"I never got close enough to test the theory that a bee sting could be just as poisonous, but we've begged Hilda to get rid of the bees over the years. She used to come out here and work with the hives, talking to the bees the whole time. I suppose they got used to the sound of her voice and didn't harm her," Trudy Somerset pointed out.

"Did she harm anyone with it that you know?" Jex asked, not mentioning the list in the letter, nor that Lottie's own grandson was one of the names on the said list as a victim.

"Gosh, no. Hilda wasn't that way, really. I always wondered if she might have had something to do with Neil's mother's death, but I never asked her. I know about what his mother did to cause her to have that miscarriage, but I don't think she had it inside her to do harm to anyone."

"I think Hilda just loved the idea that she could kill someone if she wanted. Anyway, get rid of that honey and cut out those oleander bushes. In fact, clear out all of this stuff, so no one accidentally gets ahold of it by mistake," Mrs. Somerset urged as Mrs. Powers nodded behind her.

The three of them returned to the kitchen to finish their tea while they reminisced about Mrs. Wickersham and the fun they had together. The 'girls' told him stories about their friend and some of the things the three of them liked to do, driving into Dover once a month to go to all of their doctor's appointments and then they took turns choosing new places to try for lunch. It sounded very much as if the three of them enjoyed each other's company, and Jex was happy that Mrs. Wickersham had good friends.

"Who was Mary Ellen Charles?" Jex asked, curious about the only name on the list he didn't recognize.

Mrs. Powers rolled her eyes. "She was a thief. Hilda caught her going through her jewelry box, but we now know it was because she was planning to run away with her boyfriend. Luckily, the girl only got away with Hilda's gold wedding band," Lottie said.

"No, she didn't, actually. It was right there in the jewelry box with the engagement ring," Trudy corrected before she began gathering the tea dishes.

"Hilda never told me that. Anyway, I guess we better go, Lottie. Jex, dear, we're very sorry about causing you all of these problems, but we're thrilled you're going to stay in town. If you need anything, please don't hesitate to call us. I hope we can get together again soon," Trudy Somerset suggested.

Jex walked both of them to the front door along with their clean containers and baskets. "Yes, I'd like that. We'll set up something very soon," he promised as both women stopped in front of the door to the formal parlor.

"It looks so bare without the rug," Lottie lamented.

Trudy nodded before she spoke. "Oh, I believe there's an old rug in the basement. It was Neil's mother's favorite rug if I recall correctly. After she passed, Hilda replaced it with the other one the police took away. Are you keeping Hilda's chair?"

Jex walked over to the cornflower blue, orchid, and sage green flowered chair and remembered all the times Mrs. Wickersham and he sat in the parlor having tea, Hilda in her chair and Jex in one of the Queen Anne chairs.

"I am because I can't part with it. I'm sending it to be recovered and the pillows restuffed, but I want a very similar fabric because it fits this room. What color was the other rug?" Jex asked, not remembering ever seeing a rug in the basement, though he had only been down there a few times. It was creepy as hell, and there was only one lightbulb in the middle of the room. He didn't waste much time down there.

"I don't remember exactly," Trudy Somerset responded before they all bid each other goodbye. After the women left, Jex decided to trek downstairs with a flashlight he found in the pantry. He also grabbed the large jar of honey and the enamel tin with the painted flowers from the pantry. Mrs. Wickersham had explained they were a home remedy to make a drunk person sober up pretty quickly, but Jex wondered if there could be more to the story. He decided it was better to relegate them to the basement shelves until he decided what to do with them.

He roamed around the basement, seeing many shelves with empty jars on them standing in a row like soldiers. There were also odds and ends of furniture scattered around the space, including a wooden trunk he noticed in the corner.

Jex placed the honey and the flowered tin on a shelf in the corner and walked over to the chest. It wasn't locked, so Jex opened it, seeing lots of women's clothes dating back several decades earlier, he was sure. Jex illuminated the contents with the flashlight before gasping at the realization of what he was seeing.

There, inside the trunk, he saw red velvet gently folded and placed at the top of the chest, just as Mrs. Wickersham had described for him the night she told him about Michael's murder. He sorted through everything int the chest to see it appeared to be filled with many dresses, costume jewelry, feathered boas, and even a tiara.

Jex picked up the top garment, the red velvet dress, feeling the softness under his fingers until he felt the stiffness that reminded him why the velvet would be stiff. He propped up the flashlight on a nearby table and looked at the garment in his hands, seeing the fabric was stained all down the front.

There was a hole in the dress that would be near the wearer's heart, and it caught him by surprise. It was then he realized the trunk must have been Michael Wickersham's dress-up trunk. When Jex moved into the light to study the garment, he realized it was *the* dress. It was the dress Michael had been wearing when Neil shot him. Jex felt the tears come at how Mrs. Wickersham must have felt that night as she watched her son die. It shouldn't have happened at all, but it was too late to undo it.

After he gently placed the dress over the back of a nearby chair and removed the other dresses and accessories from the trunk, he delved further to find other contents. When he found picture frames, he moved the flashlight closer, but to no avail. Jex still couldn't make out the figures in the photos, so he picked up two of the frames, carrying them over to where the bare bulb was hanging.

Jex looked at the images to see two teenage boys, one tall and one short, though both quite handsome. They were standing arm in arm in one snapshot in the garden near the rose bushes. They were both in trousers and button-up shirts. One boy had a big grin on his face, and the other was looking down at him, appearing to be equally as happy.

The photo was from an instant camera, and on the bottom, white edge, there was a handwritten note. "Me and Dewey, Homecoming, 1995."

Jex held the photo closer and recognized Dewey Zellner as the taller boy. The shorter one had short red hair, and as he studied it, Jex saw Mrs. Wickersham in the boy's features.

It struck him that he was looking at a picture of Michael Wickersham, which stopped him cold because there were none of them anywhere in the Inn.

The boy did resemble Jex, though not enough they could be misconstrued for relatives. As he studied the photo, he decided it was no wonder Mrs. Wickersham called him Michael from time to time. There was a distinct resemblance.

Jex dug a little further and found more photos and the camera from where they likely came. He picked up another frame and saw it was the same day as the other photos, but instead of Dewey Zellner and Michael, it was Mrs. Wickersham and her son. Obviously, she knew about Dewey and Michael's friendship...or was there more to it?

He gathered up all of the photos before he repacked the trunk and closed it, rearranging the old blankets that had been resting on top. Jex took the photos upstairs and placed them on the kitchen table, wondering what to do with them. Finally, he came to a decision. There was someone who might value them more than Jex, and he wanted to ensure they found a home with someone who loved Michael as much as Mrs. Wickersham.

XX

Eli stopped at the beach house to change out of his uniform before he walked to the Inn to check on Jex. His love had been busy cleaning the grand building from top to bottom because he wanted to think about having some painting and redecorating done over the winter, so Eli took a step back to allow him to make his own decisions.

Things had been going well between the two of them, though Eli could tell Jex was still upset about losing the old woman. She left him the Inn and a small nest egg from the summer's season to help with expenses.

Jex had talked about finding a job over the winter to supplement his income because the taxes for the property were coming due late in the year. Eli had promised to help with the expenses, but he could see his offer would be the last resort for Jex.

Over the last few weeks, Eli had been investigating something he didn't want to contemplate...a mole in his police department. Someone had to leak to Cather where Jex was hiding, and the only conclusion he could reach wasn't one he wanted to consider...one of his own.

Eli had analyzed the facts many times, and the only conclusion he could reach was the one difference from when Jex first arrived in town until Bernie Overman showed up to do him harm. There was one variable Eli hadn't considered previously, and it was a new police officer...Irina Ford.

Irina had been hired early in the summer after Eli worked with the acting mayor, Tom Lahey, and the City Council to find another officer for Haven's Point Police Department. Irina had been a cop in Atlantic City for nearly twenty years and was a highly decorated officer. She'd been elevated to sergeant at ACPD, and she'd even been shot in the line of duty.

With Cather's gambling problems coming to light, it was entirely possible he'd met Irina during one of his trips to Atlantic City. Maybe the two were working together to find Jex?

After Eli called Cather to ask about the Overman case, Irina's resume landed on his desk within a few days. The chief couldn't eliminate the possibility the woman was a plant. He was doing his best to figure it out, but thus far, he had nothing concrete.

Eli arrived at the Inn and walked up to the three-seasons room, finding the door unlocked. When he went inside, he saw a decanter of gold liquor and two small, crystal glasses on a small table. There were cloth napkins on the wicker coffee table, and a platter with a wedge of Brie, white grapes, and water crackers. A small dish of what looked like honey was on a small silver tray, and there were two flannel blankets over the backs of the rocking chairs Jex had moved together to face the beach.

The back door of the house opened, and Jex walked out wearing a pair of grey lounge pants and a tight, black t-shirt Eli had never seen. His lithe body was hugged most exquisitely, and Eli's cock took notice immediately. "Good evening, sexy," Eli greeted as he stepped forward and wrapped Jex's long arms around his neck, reaching down to cup his tight ass.

"Welcome ho...welcome. I thought we could sit out here and have a glass of sherry and some snacks while the roast finishes. I have a few things to explain to you, and I thought it was such a nice evening, we could sit out here and look at the sunset," Jex offered.

"Okay, sure. How was your day?" Eli questioned between nibbles of Jex's neck to the spot behind his ear that drove him crazy. He felt the shudder of Jex's body against his and knew he had the sexy man's full attention.

Eli pulled away and smirked at the flushed cheeks and the hooded look of Jex's eyes. Then, the man snapped out of it. "Nice try, Chief. Seriously, I want to have an actual conversation before we spend the rest of the night in bed," he taunted, which was precisely what Eli wanted to hear. When Jex pushed him into the wicker rocker and climbed onto his lap, Eli laughed.

"Okay, what do you want to talk about? Seriously, how was your day?" Eli asked as he ran his hand under Jex's shirt, gently massaging the gnarled skin Eli loved more than anything.

"It was fine, but I missed you. Eli, I want you to move in. I want us to live here together. There are enough things in need of updating or repairing around here to keep us busy, and we could even think about extending the season through early October."

"We could decide if maybe we'd be up for opening in mid-April instead of waiting until the beginning of May, and we could think about hosting a New Year's party with fireworks and everything during the winter for returning guests," Jex suggested as he poured each of them a glass of sherry, handing one to Eli.

"Okay, that's quite a list, so let's go one-by-one. First, I'd love to move in with you. We can do all those things you suggested, but I'll have to work in that pesky job of mine as the Chief of Police while we do them. As a matter of fact, I'll have to start running for office again soon. I hope I'll get your vote," Eli teased as he touched his glass to Jex's, "To us and our beautiful future."

"To us. So, you're going to run again? You really like your job?" Jex asked, which gave Eli pause.

"Well, uh, yeah. I love my job. What's wrong? Don't *you* like my job?" the chief asked, hoping it wasn't going to become a thing between them. He couldn't live without Jex, but he'd hate to quit his job. He was good at being a cop, or so he believed.

"I just worry about you. I mean, you could get shot or stabbed. I don't like worrying about you when you leave to go to work," Jex offered, which touched Eli.

He pulled his love closer and released his long hair from the messy ponytail, running his fingers through the soft strands. "I swear I'll be extra careful, okay? I mean, the worst thing that happens around here are the summer with tourists and the shit they get up to, but I don't think I'm in danger regularly. I do think I figured out who snitched to Cather that you were here to help Overman find you," he offered as he took a sip of his drink. Dry sherry wasn't his favorite, but it wasn't bad. Eli was getting used to it.

Jex turned to him with concern. "Did they come to talk to you, too? What else did they say?"

Eli's eyebrow arched in curiosity. "Who? I'm investigating Irina Ford. I think she might have…"

"Let me stop you, Chief, before you make a big mistake. Trudy Somerset and Lottie Powers were amateur detectives in their own mind, and they gave a tip to Cather I was here in Haven's Point working for Mrs. Wickersham. They thought they were just being good citizens."

"They wanted me to testify against Overman, so he didn't get away with the horrible things he'd done. It's really not their fault because they didn't know Cather was on the take. They apologized to me when they came over for tea yesterday."

"As soon as the weather gets cold enough, I want to move the beehives over by the family plot. I'd like to clear out part of the garden and make a nice picnic area. What do you think?" Jex asked.

"Sure, babe. What are you taking out?" Eli asked as he reached for the platter of cheese and crackers, placing it on Jex's lap. He gave the man an imploring look and smiled when Jex put down his sherry glass and spread Brie and honey on a cracker, holding it up to Eli's mouth and shoving it inside, whole.

Jex chuckled while Eli chewed. "We're taking out the oleander bushes. I just found out they're poisonous. Seems it would be a liability to have them on the property, don't you think?"

Eli considered his words and nodded as he swallowed. "Oh, sure. That sounds like a good idea. Is this honey from our bees?" Eli asked, seeing a glowing smile on Jex's face before he gave him a soft kiss.

"No. The honey our bees make isn't really good enough to eat, but having them around makes the flowers so lush, I think we should keep them. Plus, I keep reading articles about how bees are disappearing in huge numbers, and they're supposed to be helpful to the environment. We'll just get someone to move them and leave them to themselves," Jex explained.

Two hours later, Jex was behind Eli, hammering away at his prostate, which was the best feeling in the world to the chief. It was the first time Jex was willing to top him, and it wasn't nearly going to be the last. Eli loved feeling Jex inside him, and the fact his cock was long and effortlessly hit his hot button was an unexpected plus.

"I'm about to come," Eli moaned. Jex slowed down, which wasn't what Eli wanted at all.

"Dammit! Don't stop," Eli groaned.

Jex chuckled behind him. "I want to have you ride me. I wanna see why you like it so much when I ride you," Jex explained.

Eli laughed and raised up on his knees while he waited for Jex to lie on his back and adjust the condom, which had slipped a bit. "I wanna get rid of these damn things," Eli stated as he moved over Jex's torso and held the man's cock until it was buried inside of Eli once again.

He braced his hands on either side of Jex's beautiful head and smiled down. "I'm so damn glad we got here, Jex."

With only a nod from his love, the two were off again, Jex's long fingers wrapped around Eli's hips as his long hair made a halo around his beautiful face on the white sheets. Eli came first, painting Jex's creamy skin with his essence. The beauty's eyes squeezed shut as he climaxed, "*Fuuuuckk!!*"

Eli couldn't hold the laugh. "You like that, Big Red?" he joked.

Jex was trying to catch his breath but still joined Eli in his laughter. "Big Red?"

"Well, that big sausage inside me is surrounded by short red hair. Seems fitting," Eli joked again before he reached around and held the condom on Jex's cock so he could rest next to his love on the bed.

Once they were resting next to each other, Jex rested his head on Eli's shoulder while the top cop remembered what he wanted to ask. "So, Trudy and Lottie were the ones who called Cather? Irina Ford has nothing to do with it?"

Jex smirked at him. "No, Inspector Gadget. It was the two little old busybodies in town. They didn't even tell Hilda about me, and they apologized for the way it turned out. What could I say? It wasn't really their fault, it was just a crazy twist of fate."

"I have something I want to tell you, Eli. My real name is Madison Jacob Oakes," Jex told him before he turned to face Eli, sitting up and twisting his long legs into the shape of a pretzel.

Eli sat up as well, knowing this was a precious piece of information Jex was giving him. He wanted to give it the respect it deserved. "Okay. Did you prefer Madison or Maddy or Jacob?" Eli asked, trying to ease into the conversation because he knew it would be painful.

"Only Molly called me Maddy. We were Molly and Maddy Oakes...together we were mighty as an oak, she used to say all the time. Turns out, not really," Jex whispered.

Eli took a deep breath and released it slowly, trying not to tear up at those words. "Oh, but that's where you're wrong, Jex. You could never have survived the shit you did if you weren't strong like an oak, babe. Your mom knew it too, I'd bet. How'd you decide on Jex Ivers for your new name?"

Jex wiped the tears from his cheeks and smiled. "My mom used to love this band, Bon Iver. She used to play their music all the time around the house while we cooked or cleaned together. My favorite song of theirs was _Skinny Love_. When I was running away from Newark, I was at the bus station and heard the song playing over the speakers, which seemed like a sign to me."

"I listened to the lyrics as I waited for my bus, and I realized I'd remembered the lyrics all wrong. It's actually a pretty sad song, but there were lyrics about patience and kindness, and I decided maybe that was the lesson Mom was trying to teach me with the song."

"Anyway, that night I decided to go by Jacob Iver, but then I read a story about a guy in a band who changed his name from Jacob to Jex, and I decided it might be the difference between someone finding me or not, so I grew my hair, changed my name to Jex Ivers. I kept signing it with the 's' since I was used to Oakes. Anyway, that's me," Jex explained.

Eli sat up and gently kissed Jex's full lips before pulling the man to sit on his lap. He grabbed his t-shirt and wiped his spunk from Jex's chest, kissing the harsh brand over his heart and wrapping his arms around Jex's back. "I don't know Madison Jacob Oakes. I know Jex Ivers, but if you'd prefer, I could get to know Madison Oakes and love him as well."

"The way I see it, Madison Oakes was the guy who went through hell and somehow escaped it. Jex Ivers is the man who emerged on the other side. He's the man I met and fell in love with when he started working at *Lena's*. You tell me who you want to be," Eli urged, kissing his neck to reassure him.

Jex moved his hair back behind his ears. "I think I'm going to cut this mop off. I worry about the drains here and at the beach house with the hair," he stated.

Eli couldn't help but chuckle. "I'll go to Toomey's tomorrow and pick up a drain snake. Leave your hair alone unless it's bugging you. I love the way you look right now, and I'll love the way you'll look if you decide to cut it. I think you're gorgeous, but I vote to leave the hair."

He saw Jex flush a little before he leaned forward and kissed Eli with enough passion for igniting an inferno, and Eli's cock noticed immediately. He pulled away, panting hard. "How about we try something new?"

Two minutes later, they were sixty-nining each other, both making enough noise Eli hoped the neighbors didn't hear them and call it in. It was incredible when he swallowed Jex's release before the man deep throated him and took him to heaven.

They both laid down on their backs, Jex's head on Eli's thigh while Eli was in the same position. "I like what you said about Jex being the person you fell in love with, so I'll go by Jex. Let's let poor Madison Jacob Oakes rest with his mother, Molly."

"Okay. So, when am I moving in, or should we move to the beach house for the winter while we have the work done? Would it be easier?" Eli asked.

Jex stood and pulled him up so they could shower before they changed the sheets to settle in for the night. "What do you think about kids?" Jex asked.

Eli looked at him with a smirk. "I'd appreciate a ring before you knock me up," he teased as they climbed into the tub shower in the downstairs bathroom, both of them laughing at Eli's cheeky comment.

That night, their lives began moving forward. They discussed what they wanted in the future and agreed having children was on both of their bucket lists. The Wickersham Inn had enough rooms to accommodate a house full of kids. Eli wasn't sure of the details, but he was actually looking forward to the possibilities.

XXI

It was a crisp, autumn day, and Jex was standing outside the garage at the Inn waiting for Dewey Zellner. There was one more thing he wanted to clarify before he put the past behind him.

Michael Wickersham was a young man when he died, but it seemed to Jex that Mrs. Wickersham's son had left behind a person about whom he'd cared very deeply. Jex believed Dewey deserved to have any of Michael's things he wanted to help him remember the young man. It felt like something Mrs. Wickersham would have wanted Jex to do.

When Dewey pulled into the drive with the tow truck, Jex smiled as the awkward man stepped out. He was tall, maybe six-foot-four or -five? The man had short brown hair and sad brown eyes. He was about forty, Jex was guessing, and he looked like someone who had given up on life, which broke Jex's heart.

"Hi, Jex. How's your bike doing? Don't forget to check the air in your tires as the temperature drops. They'll be flat before you even know it," Dewey told him as he walked around the front of the tow truck.

"I'll remember that, Dewey. I'd like you to take Mrs. Wickersham's car in and service it. I think I'm going to sell it because I never learned how to drive, and I'm fine with my bike. Eli has his SUV anyway, so we're fine without a car. I think it's a decent car. The mileage thing only says thirty-three-thousand miles," Jex informed.

Dewey chuckled. "Yeah, and those are actual miles, I can attest to it. Mrs. Wickersham drove that car around town and to Dover a few times a year. The three widows took turns driving up for appointments, and I made sure all of their cars got them there and back without any problems."

"I always asked them when they were going, and I stayed at the shop until I knew they were back in town in case something happened to one of their cars. I owed it to *him*...well, they're sweet women, and I feel like it's my responsibility to make sure their cars are in top condition."

"This Ford probably hasn't been driven for almost two years, so I need to work her over, but I'll only charge you for parts, Jex. Anything else I can do for ya?" Dewey asked as he walked over to the garage door and pulled it open, making sure it caught so it didn't come down on his head.

There was no automatic garage door opener in the two-car garage, but when Jex was having work done at the Inn, he was going to have someone install an electronic garage door opener for the chief.

"You wanna come in and have some coffee cake? I made it this morning. I also have some things you might be interested in taking with you. You have time?" Jex asked Dewey. He saw the mechanic nod and pull a rag from the back pocket of his coveralls to wipe his hands.

"You can wash up inside, Dewey. It's not a formal affair," Jex offered, hoping he had a welcoming smile on his face. He could see Dewey Zellner was an introvert, and Jex believed he knew part of the reason why.

"Oh, uh, thanks, Jex," Dewey announced as he followed him into the three-seasons room and slipped off his boots and then his coveralls. He followed Jex into the kitchen in a t-shirt and jeans, and when Jex pointed to the hall bathroom, Dewey disappeared inside and closed the door.

Jex pulled the cinnamon-spiced coffee cake from the warm oven and placed it on the stove to cool a bit. He started the coffee pot because everyone didn't like tea, and he went into the front parlor and retrieved the trunk he'd carried up from the basement. It was filled with everything Jex found down there that might have been Michael's. He'd decided to allow Dewey to choose what he wanted if he even wanted any of it.

When the man came out of the bathroom, he had a worried grin, so Jex placed the coffee cake on the table and cut into it, having already set out plates and cups. "Tea or coffee?" he asked.

Dewey looked around and smiled when he saw the teapot. "I'd prefer tea if you don't mind. Mrs. Wickersham always served tea when I came by to see her. Oh, two sugars, please," he requested.

Jex made his drink and prepared a cup of coffee for himself. He sat down and looked at Dewey, who was digging into the cake. "Tell me about Michael Wickersham. You guys were friends, right?" Jex asked as he placed a picture of the two of them on the table for Dewey to see.

The mechanic put down his fork and picked up the instant photo, looking at it for a minute before he closed his eyes, and the tears began to fall. Jex felt horrible, maybe making a terrible mistake, but when he reached to take back the picture, Dewey grabbed his hand to stop him.

"No, please. I'm sorry for getting upset, but I have only one photo of the two of us. Mr. Wickersham threatened to kill me if I ever came around here again, and I was only able to grab one picture before he made me leave."

"I was sixteen and already driving, and I was actually teaching Mike how to drive because his father wouldn't. Mike didn't have the patience to learn from his mother because she was so protective of him, it drove him insane. I loved Mrs. Wickersham for how much she loved her son. She was a great mother, and she was supportive of us."

"Mike and I were in the same grade in high school, but I was a year older than him because I had to repeat the fourth grade. Family crap kept me from attending school enough to go on to fifth grade with my class, but then, I met Mike, and we became best friends that year. Hell, we grew up together."

"Of course, Mr. Wickersham called me white trash because my mom was a single parent, but Mrs. Wickersham supported our friendship. When we got older and figured out we both didn't like girls, we hung out together a lot more until we decided we wanted to be boyfriends."

"Mike decided he wanted to be an actor, which made a lot of sense because he loved to dress up in costumes. Hell, he could have been the world's best drag queen if he'd had the chance. He loved to dance and sing like there was no tomorrow, and he was good at it."

"When the Dark Lord...um, Mr. Wickersham...was out of town, I'd come over here, and the three of us would have parties. Mrs. Wickersham gave me my first taste of champagne, though it was a champagne cocktail which had more seltzer than champagne. It was Mike's fourteenth birthday, and we had a big celebration, the three of us.

"Mr. Wickersham came home and saw the three of us together. He got furious and threatened to kill me if he caught me there again, so I grabbed a picture like this before I left. I didn't see Mike again for a week, and when he came over to my house, he had fading bruises on his face."

"I knew what had happened to him, and I apologized to him for taking the beating his father wanted to give me. After that, I didn't go to their house unless I knew for certain that bastard wasn't anywhere in the vicinity."

"The night Mike...the night he shot himself, I'd been over to the house that afternoon. We were celebrating the new year, the three of us. Mr. Wickersham wouldn't allow Mike to come with me to a party at a friend's house, so when he went out of town on business the next week, Mrs. Wickersham planned a party for the three of us."

"See Mike and I were in the drama club, and one of our classmates was having a bash for the holidays. Mike wanted to go to the party in the worst way. It was a dress-up thing, and we were trying to work out our costumes until his dad said he couldn't go."

"Mrs. Wickersham let Mike call and invite me over that Saturday because his dad was out of town, and we decided on a *Great Gatsby* theme because we were supposed to read the book over the winter break. His mom and I dressed in tuxedoes, and Mike wore a pretty red velvet dress that really nice on him. His hair was short, but it was in a thirties style with waves like a starlet. He was so beautiful, he took my breath away."

"We danced and had a fancy dinner with all the knives, forks and plates on the dining room table. It more than made up for missing the other party until we heard the car on the driveway. Mrs. Wickersham ran to the window and saw who it was, so she sent me out through the back of the house and told me not to tell anyone I'd been there that night. This is the first time I've ever mentioned it to anyone."

"When I heard the next day that Michael committed suicide, I couldn't believe it was true. We'd been making plans to leave town as soon as he turned eighteen so he could get away from his father. I thought he loved me enough to hang on, but when I heard he killed himself, I was so mad at him," Dewey explained as he teared up again.

Jex felt as if he owed the man the truth, so he took Dewey's arm and led him into the parlor where the trunk was waiting. Jex opened the wooden box and pulled out the red dress, holding it up. When he heard the gasp from Dewey Zellner, he wondered if he'd done the right thing.

"I'm sorry if..." Jex began before Dewey walked over to him and gazed at the dress. Jex handed it to him and the man sunk to the floor with it, examining the front of the garment, especially the bullet hole.

"I knew it. I knew that son-of-a-bitch shot Mike. Mrs. Wickersham would never say anything about that night, but I knew in my heart that Mike loved me too much to take his own life."

"That was why I helped Mrs. Wickersham load that bastard into the freezer when she called me and said Neil had shot himself because he couldn't handle the fact Mike was dead. She said Neil didn't deserve to be buried next to Michael because of the way he'd treated him when Mike was alive, so I helped her get rid of the old man's body," Dewey whispered before he leaned forward over the dress and held it into his arms as if he was holding Michael.

Jex kneeled down next to the man and wrapped an arm around Dewey's back, trying to provide comfort. "You were right, Dewey. Michael didn't kill himself. Mrs. Wickersham told me Neil shot him. I guess it was after you slipped out."

"Hilda said Neil forced her to change him into pajamas before he called the police. Neil called a doctor and had her sedated so she couldn't tell anyone what happened. It sounds as if it was a huge mess. I found this stuff in the basement and wondered if you might want to have it."

"I have a question, and I won't share the answer with anyone, I swear. Was Neil Wickersham in that freezer you took away?" Jex asked.

"Yeah, he was. After Michael was buried, Mrs. Wickersham called my house one night and asked if I could come over and help her move some furniture. Mom said it was fine, so I came over. There he was, that son-of-a-bitch, dead on the floor with a hole in his head. I noticed the fancy rug was rolled up, so he didn't bleed on it."

"Of course, when Mrs. Wickersham asked me to, I didn't hesitate to carry him out to that freezer and drop him inside. I plugged it back in because it hadn't been used in years, and when the damn thing started running, I came back a few days later with the latch and padlock."

"That freezer was on for years, and when you called to tell me to take it away, I set up a pickup for scrap metal. Nobody will ever find him. That was why I didn't want you looking inside. I knew there weren't any tools in there," Dewey confirmed.

Jex didn't doubt it, but he had one more question. "Mary Ellen Charles?"

Dewey flinched a little. "She dropped dead in Mrs. Wickersham's home. Hilda told me she was a thief and had reaped her own reward, so I put the woman in the trunk of her car and towed it to the junkyard. Eventually, the car was sold for scrap. Are you going to have me arrested?"

Jex took his hand, and the two of them sat down on the floor in front of the open trunk. "Not at all. I just wanted clarification on a few things. Here are all of Michael's things that I could find. You can take them all or leave them here, Dewey, but you need to learn how to let him go. I doubt he'd want you to suffer any longer than you already have. You deserve a life filled with love, and if Michael were half the man I believe him to be, he'd insist on it for you."

It was easy to preach it, but if Jex had been in Dewey's shoes, he doubted he'd have been able to recover from the shock of being told the person he loved had killed himself. That wasn't an easy pill to swallow, but Dewey Zellner had lived with that lie for so many years, Jex wasn't sure what else to say to him.

Dewey hugged Jex without saying a word. He took the trunk with him to his tow truck and put it inside before he hooked up

Mrs. Wickersham's old car and towed it out of the garage. "I'll call you when it's ready, Jex. Thank you so much for everything." The man didn't wait for a response, but Jex knew what he meant.

Later that afternoon, Jex Ivers dressed in the beekeeper's costume he found in the machine shed and walked over to the hives in the gardens. It was a beautiful day for mid-October, and the bees were active.

Jex stood over the first hive and took off the cover to see the little workers were busy preparing for the winter. He pulled up one of the screens to see it was dripping with honey...poisonous honey.

"Hello, bees. I'm your new caretaker, Jex, and I'm going to move your hives once you go into hibernation. I came to tell you that Mrs. Wickersham passed away. She went to be with Michael, and she's finally at peace. I hope you'll mourn her loss with me. She told me you would, so while you're at it, could you mourn my mother's loss as well?" Jex whispered softly as he continued to check the hives.

Mrs. Wickersham had told him she whispered the bad news to the bees so they'd mourn with her. Jex decided it was best to confess the bad news about their former keeper so they didn't think she'd just abandoned them. He didn't believe asking for some sympathy for Molly Oakes was selfish. They probably had enough compassion to go around.

Losing loved ones was heartbreaking for most people. Feeling as if you were the only one suffering from the grief was painful. Having someone, even if it was only honeybees, to mourn along with you made it a little easier.

After all, the bees didn't share the secrets of love and loss confided to them. They mourned and rejoiced with you in equal measure. They tried to make life a little sweeter, but one couldn't forget, sometimes the sweet life was deadly...and, the bees still wouldn't tell a soul.

~THE END~

Epilogue

Eli stood a short distance away, watching Jex as he knelt next to the third grave in the Wickersham family cemetery at the back of the garden next to the Inn. His lover had been distraught when he'd learned the news, and Eli was worried about him.

Eli had seen a lot of crime scenes during his time at the Newark Police Department, which gave him nightmares for weeks after. None of them was more disturbing than seeing Dewey Zellner covered by a red velvet dress with his brains splattered on the wall behind his recliner.

Dewey was clutching a picture of himself with Michael Wickersham when they were teens in one hand, and the pistol he'd used to kill himself in the other. It was resting on his lap. The whole scene surprised Eli, but he quickly determined there were details he'd keep to himself to allow Dewey to have his privacy. There was no need to give the town gossips anything more than the fact Dewey had committed suicide.

Eli got a call from County Dispatch that they'd received three nine-one-one calls reporting the sound of a gunshot at Dewey Zellner's garage, so Eli went to check it out. Dewey lived in a single-wide trailer home parked behind the garage when he wasn't at his little cabin outside town. Eli noticed the garage seemed to be locked up twice, which was unusual for noon on a weekday.

The car Dewey had purchased from Jex, the old Buick Mrs. Wickersham used to drive, was sitting next to the trailer, and the tow truck was parked in front of the garage. Eli knew Dewey should be on the property with both vehicles present.

After checking around the cinder block building where Dewey's business was housed, Eli determined it was empty. He began knocking on the door of Dewey's home for ten minutes to no activity.

The chief could hear music coming from inside, but Dewey still didn't answer. Finally, Eli decided to break a window to let himself inside, which was where he found Dewey.

Dewey had left a letter addressed to Jex, but in the spirit of ensuring Dewey hadn't been a victim of foul play, Eli opened it.

Dear friend Jex:

I'm sorry to leave you like this· I'm sure we could have been best friends, but I've missed Michael for too long· When you confirmed my suspicions that Michael didn't take his own life, and on the slightest chance I might get to see him for even just a moment, I've decided I'd rather not suffer alone any longer· I've missed him too much·

I heard Eileen Stewart has offered to be a surrogate for you and Eli, and I'm so happy for you· I know you'll love your children the way a parent should· I wish Michael and I could have had friends like you and Eli when we were younger· Maybe things would have been different for us·

Contact Delbert Cox, Mrs· Wickersham's lawyer· Everything is already planned out· I was going to do this before you came to town, but Mrs· Wickersham always talked me out of it· When she passed, I postponed it to be sure you were okay, and now I know you are· You and the chief take care of each other·

With gratitude for your friendship,

Dewey Zellner

The chief decided not to give the letter to Jex. There was no need for his love to blame himself for another death. Mrs. Wickersham's passing had been hard enough for Jex to process since she had become his new family. Eli decided he wouldn't put him through it again.

He contacted Delbert Cox, Dewey's lawyer, and Eli was told Dewey had recently updated his Will to name Jex as his Executor. Everything was to be sold, and the money should be donated to a few LGBTQ+ charities that helped at-risk youth.

Jex had decided Dewey should be interred in the family plot with Mrs. Wickersham and Michael. "That way, he'll have family around to keep his new home tidy. Dewey can also talk to the bees," Jex had said which made Eli smile. He couldn't love the man more.

Dewey had been buried two months earlier, and the dirt had finally settled on the grave, so Jex was planting flowers for the bees to enjoy. Eli had wanted the bees moved, but Jex assured him they wouldn't hurt anyone who didn't deserve it. It seemed an odd thing when Jex said it, but Eli hoped he was right about the bees.

"Babe come on. We need to get moving if we're going to make the doctor's appointment on time," Eli called out to Jex who seemed to be speaking to himself. Eli smiled. Every time he found Jex in the garden, he was talking adamantly with himself. Eli prayed it wasn't a signal something might be wrong.

Jex gathered the gardening tools and the box where he'd been propagating some plants from cuttings he found when he went over to Dewey's place to clean out the man's personal things before a buyer came to pick it up.

Eli phoned a cleaning service to handle the organic matter inside, and then he hired Joe Tibbey's brother-in-law to put new carpet in the living room. The garage was proving to be a little harder to sell, but Jex wasn't giving up.

"You ready?" Eli asked as he took the tools from the man and wrapped an arm around his shoulders. "Everything okay?" Eli asked.

Jex sniffed. "Yes, it's fine. I'd like to have someone put a gate at the entry of the cemetery so we can be sure our children don't accidentally get inside. Can we do that?" Jex asked.

"Of course, we can. What kind of gate do you think you want?" Eli asked as they walked through the garden toward the house so they could get ready to go to the doctor's appointment with Eileen.

Eileen Stewart had been implanted with five embryos eight weeks ago...a month before Dewey Zellner took his life. She'd taken a pregnancy test that gave a positive reading, so they were going to see how many babies were waiting for them to love.

Eli was worried if all five of the embryos stuck how they'd manage it, but he knew if they were blessed with that many children, he'd be okay with it. He and Jex were actually going to help out with Rooney and Riley to take the pressure off of Eileen during her pregnancy, and Eli knew Jex was looking forward to getting to know the boys. He called it training for what they both hoped to come in the future, and Eli couldn't ignore the smile on his love's face.

"You've never asked me about Dewey and Michael," Jex reminded as they went back to the bedroom so he could change to go to the doctor's appointment.

"Well, I assume they were best friends or more. I guess if they were more, Michael was the reason Dewey never had a relationship with anyone that we knew about," Eli guessed, hoping he wasn't giving away anything contained in the letter Dewey had left behind that Eli hadn't shared with his love.

"That's what I think. That's why I thought the two of them should be buried together. Michael and Dewey couldn't be together in life, so they should be together in death. I want to be with you when I die, Eli," Jex offered.

Eli nodded. "How about in life?"

When Eli dropped to his left knee and retrieved a silk pouch from his pocket, Jex stopped tucking in his button-down. Eli emptied two gold rings into his palm and held them out, smiling at Jex when he heard the man gasp.

"If we're going to have babies, you're right. We need to make honest men of each other. Will you marry me and let me marry you?" the chief offered awkwardly. Eli never imagined he'd be asking anyone to make a life-long commitment that would actually be legal in all fifty states, but there he was on one knee and everything.

Jex kneeled down in front of him and kissed him, pulling away with a big grin on his face. "I would be honored to have you marry me and happy to marry you. You're right. We should make honest men of each other."

The two men kissed again and made plans the whole way to Dover, where a top-notch OB/GYN had agreed to help them create a family. The day was one of the best in Eli's life.

Two baby girls had come to bless the home of Elijah Moore and Jex Ivers. The two men had married at the Inn in late September before Karen and Molly Ivers-Moore came to join their family.

When they brought home their daughters from the hospital, they made the decision not to invite guests to stay at the Inn any longer. It was their home, and they had two daughters who demanded their attention. Their lives were full.

Eli was at work, and the girls were napping on an April morning when Jex walked out to the garden, checking the beautiful flowers he still attended in Mrs. Wickersham's memory.

He had the baby monitor with him, so he made his way to the family cemetery to attend to his bees. He had the beekeeper's costume on for safety, and as he approached the hives, he felt joyful.

Karen Ivers-Moore had a full head of red hair, just like Jex, while Molly Ivers-Moore had dark hair like Eli's. The men hadn't requested paternity tests because they were both the parents, but none of their friends in town could deny which child was which man's daughter. It didn't matter. They were a family.

"Hello, honeybees. It's me, your keeper. How are we doing this beautiful April morning? I see you've been busy," Jex remarked as he checked the screens, seeing the combs were full. He cleared the screens and filled one jar...the one Mrs. Wickersham had marked appropriately and kept in the pantry. Jex kept it in the basement on a far shelf.

Once he finished with his bees, he walked over to the graves of Hilda and Michael Wickersham and Dewey Zellner, seeing his bushes were flourishing.

"And, how are you, family? I see the oleanders are doing well. I truly miss all of you, and the bees and I think of you every day," Jex greeted before he walked over to the bees and sat down on the ground.

"Mrs. Powers passed away last evening. I went to see her yesterday afternoon at the nursing home she hated after she had her stroke. I took some honey with me, and we had tea together. She was grateful it was over," Jex whispered as he sat with his bees and cleared out the weeds from under the hives.

Life wasn't an easy proposition for anyone. It had taken time for Jex to understand Mrs. Wickersham's logic when it came to life and death, but he finally got it. There were many types of suffering, and to see it happen to those one loved was horrible to witness. That was why Jex planted the oleander near the hives in the cemetery.

The honey wasn't harvested with malicious intent, but if it ever became necessary to take things into his own hands to right a wrong or protect his family? Well, the bees had already proven they were trustworthy. Like his dear friend Hilda, he'd do whatever it took to protect the ones he loved.

A Note to My Readers

I hope you've enjoyed this story, and I'd like to thank you for spending your time reading it. I hope to provide you with more intriguing tales in the future.

I appreciate your support when I needed it; your honesty when I needed to hear it; and the fact you always come back for more. Thank you ever so much. I am humbled and grateful.

~ *Sam*

ABOUT THE AUTHOR

I grew up in the rural Midwest until I was fortunate enough to meet a dashing young man who swept me off my feet and to the East Coast where I now live with my family, one aging Yorkshire Terrier, and a tremendous amount of gratitude for the life with which I've been blessed.

I have a loving, supportive family who kindly overlooks my addiction to writing, reading, and the extensions of my hands...my computer to write, or my Kindle to read the stories others write. I'm old enough to know how to have fun but too old to care what others think about my definition of a good time. In my heart and soul, I believe I hit the cosmic jackpot with the life I have, and I try to remember to thank the Universe for it every day. Cheers!

If you enjoyed this book, I'd appreciate it if you'd leave a rating and/or a review at Amazon.com and maybe a kind word on Goodreads. If you have constructive criticism to help me evolve as a writer, please pass it along to me. You can find me at:

Website: www.samekraemer.com

Facebook: Sam E. Kraemer's Book List

Instagram: @samekraemer

Twitter: @samekraemer

Email: samekraemer@gmail.com

I'd love to hear from you!

Also by Sam E. Kraemer

The Cowboys of Katydid Farm
Loving the Bull Rider

Loving the Lawyer

Loving the Broken Man

The Valentine's Trilogy
A Valentine's Choice

A Valentine's Quest

A Valentine's Loves

The Lonely Heroes
Ranger Hank

Guardian Gabe

Cowboy Shep

Hacker Lawry

Positive Raleigh

Salesman Mateo

Weighting…

Weighting for Love

Weighting for Laughter

Weighting for a Lifetime

Single Novels

Sinners' Redemption

A Flaws and All Love Story

Forgiveness is a Virtue

Miles to Monroe

The Secrets We Whisper to the Bees

CPSIA information can be obtained
at www.ICGtesting.com
Printed in the USA
LVHW091032191119
637663LV00051B/349/P